Accolades for America's greatest hero Mack Bolan.

"Very, very action-oriented.... Highly successful, today's hottest books for men."
—*The New York Times*

"Anyone who stands against the civilized forces of truth and justice will sooner or later have to face the piercing blue eyes and cold Beretta steel of Mack Bolan, the lean, mean nightstalker, civilization's avenging angel."
—*San Francisco Examiner*

"Mack bolan is a star. The Executioner is a beacon of hope for people with a sense of American justice."
—*Las Vegas Review Journal*

"In the beginning there was the Executioner—a publishing phenomenon. Mack Bolan remains a spiritual godfather to those who have followed."
—*cury News*

D1115598

STRIKEOUT!

H. Boll Ltd. indiscriminately supplies arms, making it possible for terrorists and enemies of democracy around the globe to flourish. But not for long. With fire and thunder, Mack Bolan is waging an endless battle against international terrorism wherever he finds it. He is known and respected, misunderstood and feared worldwide. He is the Executioner.

"Mack Bolan stabs right through the heart of the frustration and hopelessness the average person feels about crime running rampant in the streets."

—*Dallas Times Herald*

DON PENDLETON's
MACK BOLAN.

Moving Target

A GOLD EAGLE BOOK FROM

WORLDWIDE.

TORONTO · NEW YORK · LONDON · PARIS
AMSTERDAM · STOCKHOLM · HAMBURG
ATHENS · MILAN · TOKYO · SYDNEY

First edition February 1989

ISBN 0-373-61414-4

Special thanks and acknowledgment to
Gayle Stone and Mark Sadler for their contribution to this work.

Copyright © 1989 by Worldwide Library.
Philippine copyright 1989. Australian copyright 1989.

All rights reserved. Except for use in any review, the
reproduction or utilization of this work in whole or in part
in any form by any electronic, mechanical or other means,
now known or hereafter invented, including xerography,
photocopying and recording, or in any information storage
or retrieval system, is forbidden without the permission
of the publisher, Worldwide Library, 225 Duncan Mill Road,
Don Mills, Ontario, Canada M3B 3K9.

All the characters in this book have no existence outside the
imagination of the author and have no relation whatsoever to
anyone bearing the same name or names. They are not even
distantly inspired by any individual known or unknown to the
author, and all the incidents are pure invention.

® are Trademarks registered in the United States Patent and Trademark
Office and in other countries.

Printed in U.S.A.

When the necessity for arms ceases, armaments will disappear. The basic causes of war are not armaments, but in human minds.

—Mahan, 1840-1914
Armaments and Arbitration

Anyone who indiscriminately deals in arms for profit, without a thought about whose hands they'll fall into, might as well be committing genocide. I will not stand by and let that happen.

—Mack Bolan

PROLOGUE

The elephant grass on Angola's central plateau flattened beneath the rotor wash as the old workhorse Huey descended through the badlands' shimmering heat. Dust and diesel fumes clogged the air.

A ragged band of Angolan freedom fighters from the National Liberation Front, the FNLA, squatted on the perimeter of the big, irregular disk of hard-packed soil that for a short time would be a landing field. Some were descendants of turn-of-the-century Portuguese settlers. Most were black villagers.

The forty-two guerrillas were dressed in mismatched pieces of combat uniforms, civilian clothing and worn-out boots. They carried the usual obsolete, patched and wired weapons. They had less than thirty rounds of homemade ammo among them, but they were smiling.

As the lumbering helicopter touched the ground, a half-dozen ran toward the open door, hunched low. In the chopper the veteran aircraft commander pulled off his helmet and popped his belts. The door gunner jumped out and the AC shoved a crate toward him. The rotors continued to roar. The copilot watched uneasily over his shoulder, his hands on the throttle, ready to take off.

The gunner passed the first crate to the FNLA and turned to receive the next one from the AC. They unloaded all six crates.

Then the RPG-7 exploded ten yards behind the Huey's tail.

Pulverized elephant grass and dirt clods spewed into the air. The AC leaped back into the chopper, and it started to rise as mortars pounded the area. The use of the big shells confirmed this was a planned ambush, not an accidental contact.

The Huey seemed to quiver, suspended. Sweat glistened on the crew's sunburned faces. The gunner let out a frustrated, unaimed blast from his M-60 at the hidden enemy.

Bullets from the ambushers' AKs beat into the dry earth. A dozen bleeding freedom fighters fell to the ground, dead or dying. Others humped with the crates toward the elephant grass. One man tried futilely to open a crate as he ran alongside it.

A few stood their ground and fired their old weapons, but most ran scared toward cover. Their firearms were unreliable, used for show—to reassure the worried villagers of this poor, sparsely populated land that they were safe from communism.

Its lone gun stuttering, the Huey began to rise to safety above the badlands. The second mortar barrage hit it dead center. The chopper exploded in a hot orange fireball.

The FNLA soldiers dropped the crates and tore into the elephant grass, followed by a fusillade of AK bullets.

The helicopter fell onto its nose, balanced for a moment on the tip of one skid. The fire blazed, radiating heat. The Huey collapsed, its three crewmen incinerated.

In the elephant grass more freedom fighters fell dead. RPGs pocked the ground. The FNLA had no chance. Their twisted corpses sprawled over the plain.

The six crates lay scattered, some flat, others upended. Two had broken open, their contents—new Uzi submachine guns—spilled out.

Except for the crackle and roar of the helicopter fire, silence fell on the Angolan plain.

Then two dozen Marxist Popular Movement soldiers, the MPLA, emerged over a low rise, their Kalashnikovs up and ready. They entered the kill zone, checking bodies. Their shots rang out as they searched the open ground and tall grass, confirming kills. At last they repacked the two open crates, carried all six toward trucks that would take them to Luanda, Angola's seaside capital. They were singing.

In Luanda the news of the pickup was relayed to Prague and then to East Berlin, where the private intel specialist pocketed fresh tourist papers and walked from the dismal dark of his city, through Checkpoint Charlie and into the glowing neon night of West Berlin.

He caught a taxi that delivered him to a tall steel-and-glass building on Budapester Street. There, in a deserted room on the fourteenth floor, he phoned the Hamburg offices of H. Boll, Ltd. They were waiting for his call.

"Ship the Luanda order for Uzi ammo and parts," he said.

"You'll receive it tomorrow," a woman with a cool voice assured him.

"Very good."

He hung up, felt his pocket for the wad of deutsche marks. He wouldn't return immediately to the East. Not tonight. First a few hours of pleasure in this decadent, imperialist hellhole. He left, his palms sweaty with excitement.

In the cubicle next door a gray-haired woman listened for his exit. As his footsteps echoed down the hall, she touched the buttons on her radio and began her report.

A longtime agent, she sensed more than heard her door crack open. As she said "Boll, Ltd." she turned, grabbing the small Colt from the desk. She was too late. The silenced Walther fired from the doorway. The impact of the bullets slammed her against the wall.

The door closed with a soft click.

The dead woman slid to the floor, leaving a wide swath of crimson dripping down the wall.

EARLIER THAT WEEK at the mouth of a valley at the edge of Italy's Alps, two shepherds and their dogs watched over a flock of sheep. The winter grasses were green and lush. Deep in the valley under a stand of fragrant pines stood their crude hut. A cool, light wind ruffled the clean clothes hung on a line to dry.

Two trucks lumbered along the narrow dirt road that ribboned the foothills. At the valley mouth the lead truck stopped, the driver apparently asking direction from one of the shepherds. After a pause, he backed his truck into the valley, got out and mopped his face. The other driver joined him under a tree, where they ate their lunch. In an hour they drove away.

Their trucks rode higher now on the rough road, although no one noticed.

That night, dark, shadowy figures crossed the mountains into the valley and left again, carrying loads on their backs. The Red Brigades commander was pleased. The new delivery was worth close to two million American dollars—nearly two hundred firearms, rockets and grenades, eleven bulletproof vests, machine gun barrels, weapons manuals and some seventy-one thousand rounds of ammunition.

Included were fifty new Heckler & Koch P7M13 9 mm handguns—compact, light and highly accurate. One had simply to grasp the handgrip, and the ambidextrous gun was cocked, ready to fire. Releasing the grip uncocked the gun. The gas-retarded inertia bolt system kept it on target between rounds, and the polygonal design of the barrel increased velocity and accuracy.

Two days later on Rome's busy Via Condotti, American businessman Loren Mines stood outside his rented stretch limousine, waiting for his wife to finish her shopping. He inhaled the crisp winter air. The sun was shining and he was feeling good. Very good. He smoothed the lapels of his white Italian silk jacket.

At home the Securities and Exchange Commission, SEC, was investigating him and his corporation for insider trading, but he knew how to beat that. A month, maybe two here in Italy and they'd be on some other poor bastard's tail. With closer fish to fry, they'd forget him. Besides, there was no way they could produce evidence to prove their case. No way at all.

He watched the Italian women swing by in their high heels, breasts bouncing, the sunlight revealing the long legs under their skirts.

As far as he was concerned, she could take all afternoon shopping; she could spend ten grand. He'd give her a couple more minutes, then he and his Italian chauffeur would go around the corner...

He grunted as sharp pains stabbed his sides.

Two wiry, swarthy men stood on either side of him, holding newspapers against him. No. Not just newspapers. And then he knew. His heart pounded with fear.

Guns. Pistols. They had pistols under those newspapers, jammed into his sides.

"W-wait..." he stammered.

The muzzles of the handguns locked against him. The chauffeur—the friendly Italian chauffeur who had promised heavenly delights in an apartment around the corner on the Via Due Macelli—vanished hatless into the crowd of well-dressed shoppers.

Mines swung his head, searching the throngs. The carabinieri. Where in hell were the carabinieri?

One of the terrorists opened the limo's back door.

"Help!" Mines bellowed, waving his arms. "Help! Kidnapping!"

The terrorist shoved him into the car. Mines lunged back up. The Italian thug whipped the stock of his new H&K P7M13 across Mines's face.

The American fell back, stunned. The hot pain penetrated his mind. He tasted blood. Shocked, he raised a hand and touched his face. He looked at his fingers. Bloody.

The terrorist kicked Mines across the seat. He sat where Mines had been, then slammed the door closed. The other terrorist walked around the limo as if he owned it.

Dazed, Mines looked out the window. The crowds passed unnoticing, undisturbed in the invigorating air.

The second terrorist climbed into the driver's seat and put on the chauffeur's cap. He started the motor, gunned it, and the limo shot out into the street.

Horns blared and drivers cursed.

The limo's new driver laughed.

Almost as if in a dream, Mines watched cosmopolitan Rome pass by.

The limo stopped, its engine idling. The terrorist in the back seat reached across Mines, opened the door and pushed the businessman out onto the oily dirt of a deserted warehouse complex.

Mines studied the empty buildings. He looked in the Italian killer's eyes and saw the crazed lust. This was no ordinary kidnapping of a rich foreign businessman. The guy was nuts!

"Red Brigades," Mines whispered hoarsely. He scrambled to his feet.

The terrorist chuckled. Slowly, carefully, he aimed his weapon.

Mines stumbled and ran toward the nearest building, his white silk jacket flapping.

The Red Brigades commander squeezed off a round, pleased. This new H&K P7M13 had a most pleasant feel.

The American arched into the air.

The commander fired again, the second shot catching Mines in the midsection, his feet off the ground.

The dead American crashed spread-eagled against the earth, his massive back wounds exposing torn red flesh and a shattered spine and rib cage.

The commander remained in the limo, his gun in his lap. He smoked a Soviet-made Marlboro.

The Red Brigades driver walked out to the road to a phone booth to begin the negotiations with Mines's corporation for his safe return.

Five days later the corporation's new president—once Mines's assistant—delivered the four-million-dollar ransom. In return the Brigades produced Mines's corpse, straight from a deep freeze.

News of the kidnapping and murder covered the front pages of newspapers around the world. Outrage, horror and sympathy spread. The SEC dropped its investigation of both Mines and the corporation.

The corporation's new president called his nameless contact in Paris. "A most remarkable arrangement," he told the power broker. "I'm grateful. Has your payment arrived?"

"Yesterday," the contact said pleasantly, "as you promised. You'll go far."

"Thanks to your help," the new top man said.

After the call, the Parisian instructed his secretary to forward the payment, together with their share from the Red Brigades' ransom, to H. Boll, Ltd., in Hamburg, with the report that all was satisfactory at the American end of the deal.

The secretary cabled both payments, then had lunch in bed with her new lover, who was also an American. She found Americans fascinating. They had a lot of money, and such sexual appetites!

As soon as they parted, her lover got into his car. He began his report on the radio, had just mentioned H. Boll, Ltd., when he turned on the ignition.

The car exploded.

The agent and twenty pedestrians were killed instantly. The blast left a hole five yards in diameter and knocked out window glass for four blocks.

IN THE RUGGED MOUNTAINS of Colombia two farmers led donkeys along switchbacks and down the forested slopes. The donkeys pulled carts piled with corn, cabbages, beets and young squash. The two animals were the envy of the farmers' village. They were nimble and good-natured, bought with the profits from past harvests.

As they came out of the mountains, the farmers saw dust clouds and jeeps in the distance. They looked at each other eagerly. The government jeeps pulled alongside, and the officers, their M-16s balanced over their arms, walked circles around the two carts. The farmers stripped off the muslin that protected the vegetables and then unloaded them until a row of black plastic sacks sat exposed on the carts.

One of the government officers whistled. "So much, eh?" he said with admiration.

They inspected the sacks of crystallized cocaine, then ground a few samples into powder.

While one man paid the farmers, the others loaded the jeeps, then climbed in and started the engines.

"Grow more for us, old men!" one shouted.

The jeeps sped away, trailing clouds of dust. The farmers closed their eyes and shielded their donkeys' faces from the flying dirt. When the opened their eyes again, they looked at each other and laughed. *¡Estupido!* The local government was *estupido*!

At their headquarters the officers turned in their coke. It would pay for an important shipment of the best and most modern arms, including the coveted hand-launched missiles and American personnel carriers that would bring victory over mobile Communist rebels and bring prestige to themselves and their region.

While the officers made plans, the two farmers arrived at a secret Communist camp. As the Communists watched, AK-47s at the ready, the two wily farmers again unloaded the vegetables. But this time they pried up the floorboards of the carts.

There, under the false bottom, were more plastic bags of the snowy white drug.

The rebels tested the coke and were pleased. While one paid the farmers, another radioed a contact in Cartagena. The contact placed an order with a local representative of H. Boll, Ltd., for five hundred Ruger automatic rifles and one hundred thousand rounds of ammunition.

In the basement of the Cartagena building, the American agent took off his earphones and sat thoughtfully. This was the second big weapons order today. Both from the same region, apparently financed by cocaine.

One order had been placed by the government, and the other by the Communist rebels. Yet both orders were relayed to Boll.

The young agent made sure the recording equipment was still on automatic. He stood, his face serious. He wanted to report this personally to his superior.

He put on his dark glasses, wishing for a moment that he was back in California where the sun was winter mild. He shoved his hands in his pockets, hunched his shoulders and walked down the hall and out the back door into the blistering tropical sunshine.

The man was hiding in the shadow of a freight doorway in the alley. He watched the agent walk briskly away, lost in thought.

The man slipped up behind the agent. He snapped the neck back and shoved the stiletto straight up under the rib cage and into the heart. An expert job.

A scream strangled in the youth's throat.

The man held him for the moment of useless struggle, then let him fall to the cobblestones. He pulled out the stiletto. Blood spread red and thick over the agent's shirt.

He wiped the stiletto on the shirt and walked away. He had his own report to make.

CHAPTER ONE

In a small basement office of the White House, colored pinpoints of light flickered on a global wall map. A computer hummed, registering rows of data on two screens. Stacks of documents were arranged neatly on a long, narrow metal desk. The aroma of fresh coffee filled the air.

"So you see the problem, **Mr.** Brognola," said USAF Brigadier General Arnold Capp, a member of the National Security Council. He was a burly man, thick-chested, with restless dark eyes that wandered the room. He and Hal Brognola were alone, the regular occupant of the office sent away on an errand.

They sat across from each other in padded metal chairs, drinking black coffee. Capp was impeccably dressed, the creases of his blue uniform knife-sharp, the stars on his shoulders shining. His hair was trimmed in perfect crescents over his ears, and he wore the maroon beret of the USAF Pararescue Service, one of the world's least-known elite forces. Capp was a man who was dedicated to doing things right.

"I think so." Brognola put his cup on the corner of the desk. "The NSC's discovered what looks like high-level double-dealings in arms and hijackings."

"That's right. Angola, Italy and Colombia."

Brognola nodded. Legs crossed, he sat relaxed, but there was an air of constant alertness about him. "And there's one particular corporation that seems to link them all," he continued, "a corporation nobody's heard of."

"H. Boll, Ltd."

"Operating out of Hamburg."

Capp studied Brognola. "No one seems to have a line on the strange deals . . . or on Boll," he said. "Not the CIA, the FBI, the DIA, Pentagon intelligence. Nobody. I've talked to the President, and he agrees. There could be a cover-up. Maybe collusion. Or now with all the congressional snooping around and hand tying, maybe it's a clever KGB plot that the Company and the others have missed."

"You want Sensitive Operations Group intel."

"Precisely. We need SOG input. The Communists are a disease, Brognola. Diseases need to be stamped out. It's our job to go the extra mile for the President in this war, and this may be part of it."

"I understand, General. We're already on it."

Brognola and the general stood and shook hands. The general's grip was firm. Brognola nodded and left.

The general paced the room, his blood racing. There was so much to be done, and so little time. Too few people, even inside the National Security Council, saw clearly what needed to be taken care of. Brognola was okay, though. A good man. The President had a lot of respect for him. But Brognola had to be watched, just like everyone else.

As the door opened, the general turned. A broad smile covered his square face. He walked forward.

"Janet."

She stepped in, smiling, too, and closed the door. She was a tiny woman, barely five foot four even in her high-heeled pumps. Her black jersey dress clung to her curves, its wide leather belt studded with rhinestones. Her long brown hair brushed her shoulders. Although she was thirty-one, she looked twenty-two, her skin smooth and glossy, her eyes dark and mysterious.

She wrapped her arms around his neck and lifted her face, her lips hungry. He kissed her deeply and felt the old, hot thrill rise. Once he had thought that part was over for him, dead with his lifeless marriage. And then he'd met Janet.

"Hello, darling," she said, her voice husky. "How did your meeting go?"

Always concerned for him. "A piece of cake. Brognola bought it."

"I knew you could make it happen." She smiled again. "He'll send his best man?"

"He'll do what we want," the general assured her.

THE NEXT DAY, not far from the Hotel D'Albe on Paris's Left Bank, Hal Brognola sat at a sidewalk café, chewing on a cigar and drinking bad French beer.

The sky was a wintry, gunmetal blue, but the sun was bright and warm. The streets were full of Parisians on the go, a moving rainbow of sweaters and light coats in the international fashion capital.

Brognola studied the pedestrians and glanced inside cars, aware that the sweaters or coats might be worn not for warmth but to hide a gun, a grenade or a bomb. Terrorism was turning Paris into an armed camp. Gen-

darmes and soldiers patrolled in pairs. Plainclothes-
men haunted airports, bus stations and train depots.

The American embassy on the Place de la Concorde
had grown into a fortress reminiscent of the embassies
in Beirut or Saigon. Concrete barriers protected the
building. French police and uniformed guards kept
watch. And, of course, alert U.S. Marines were sta-
tioned at all the entrances.

Brognola swallowed some beer. Paris was no longer
the pick of all posts for U.S. diplomats, soldiers and civilians. It was a beautiful city, an historic place, offer-
ing the epitome of European charm and opportunities
to rise high in international politics, but it was also le-
thally dangerous—for Americans in particular.

A car came screeching around the corner. Brognola's eyes flashed in the direction of the noise. He sat
forward in his chair, his watery beer forgotten.

The car was an old, beat-up Citroën. It sped down the
winding street.

Pedestrians stopped and stared, horrified. The front
passenger window was rolled down. The driver wore a
dark cap pulled low over his eyes.

As the car approached, the pedestrians stepped back
from the street and began to scatter into stores. Brognola waited only long enough to see the arm flash across
the passenger seat. He dropped the unlit cigar, leaped
to his feet and ran. From the corner of his eye he saw a
projectile hit the sidewalk. Smoke streamed from it.

He raced around the corner of the café and down a
narrow, bricked alley. Others followed, frantically
looking for safety.

"Hal."

His name was spoken in a rough whisper that was familiar. He stopped and looked around. There was a shadow in a recessed doorway, a figure darkly clothed, unmoving.

"Striker?"

"This way. Fast."

Hal Brognola turned again, this time to follow the tall, muscular figure of Mack Bolan. Bolan moved his six-foot-plus, two-hundred-pound-odd frame with speed and grace; he was a man who lived on the physical edge, always in readiness. He had dark hair, steel-blue eyes and craggy, determined features. He was wearing jeans and a loose windbreaker.

As they entered the low doorway and ran down a dim corridor, Brognola looked closely and saw the hint of a bulge that marked Bolan's 9 mm Beretta 93-R automatic holstered in a shoulder rig beneath his left arm.

They hurried up a narrow, dim staircase and along a maze of dirty hallways that led through two other buildings. The smell of Moroccan cigarettes and French fries filled the air.

Bolan slowed at last. Brognola breathed heavily, glad to see that Bolan's face was at least sweaty.

"Dammit, Striker."

"We're almost there."

"What's this all about?"

Bolan headed down another hall that seemed to be a dead end, but instead angled abruptly to the right. He stopped near the end, in front of an unmarked door, which he unlocked with an old-fashioned, oversize key. He gestured Brognola inside and locked the door after them.

"The bomb hasn't gone off," Brognola said suddenly, realizing there had been no explosion.

"Right," Bolan said, and smiled.

He walked to the dust-coated window. Brognola followed, and the two men looked down. They were now at a sixty-degree angle to the sidewalk café where Brognola had been drinking beer and waiting to meet Mack Bolan.

The two men had an unobstructed view of the area. Gray-brown smoke layered the air below them. A few people emerged from doorways, their curiosity greater than their common sense. Others leaned out of shuttered windows.

Brognola swore at Bolan. "Damn! A smoke bomb. One of your little tricks? Why?"

"They were onto you, Hal," Bolan said simply. "Over there. The skinny black. He tailed you from the airport."

"Who is he?"

"That's my question. No one I make."

Brognola studied the thin black man who was leaning against a pharmacy wall. He wore jeans, a patched bomber jacket and a beret. He was smoking a cigarette and appeared nervous, dancing a little as if from jitters—a familiar sight in the City of Light, where drugs were as much a part of the culture now as alcohol. As pedestrians ventured back onto the sidewalks, they avoided looking at him.

"Check the shoes," Bolan suggested.

Brognola looked. The guy must have been rushed into this tailing assignment, with no time to change out of his shiny new wing tips. "Looks like our man leads a double life," the big Fed said dryly.

"Looks like." Bolan allowed himself a slight smile. "I asked Atkins to watch him."

"Atkins threw the smoke bomb?"

"Yeah."

Brognola scanned the street. At last he spotted Andy Atkins's short, muscle-bound frame. The Justice man was sitting behind a full glass of beer at another café, apparently eyeing the sexy Parisian women hurrying by in their high-heeled boots and hip-swinging skirts.

"There he goes."

The black man was on the move. He wandered across the street, then back again, his eyes checking cars and pedestrians, storefronts and sidewalk tables.

He walked into the alleyway where Bolan had been waiting for Brognola, then wandered out again. He had seen other people emerge from the alley, and figured Brognola should have, too. The black had lost his man, and he knew it.

Meanwhile Andy Atkins chugged his beer, paid for it, tipped his cap to the pretty waitress and hit the sidewalk, too, meandering after the other guy.

The black made a decision and strode into the alley again, with a purposeful gait. He didn't look as if he were planning to come out again until he found what he wanted—Hal Brognola.

Atkins strolled after him.

"What can I do for you?" Bolan said as he and Brognola watched the alley.

"You read about Loren Mines?"

"Yeah. The American businessman the Red Brigades snatched, then returned dead, frozen."

"He's the one. There are two other incidents you should know about. That's why I wanted to meet."

Brognola detailed the three for Bolan: the arms sold, the killings committed, the drugs used as payment, the obvious double- and triple-dealing, and all of it linked to the name of H. Boll, Ltd., headquarters in Hamburg, West Germany.

"Mines's death was arranged through Boll, probably by the man who took his place in the corporation and some supporters," Brognola concluded. "The Red Brigades' payment was a big weapons shipment. In return Boll got half the ransom from the Brigades and a hefty chunk of cash from the corporation sent through a front in Paris."

"The SEC know?"

"You bet. They're investigating Mines's replacement on the old insider trading charges. Justice is looking into the link to Mines's murder and the Red Brigades."

"Yeah." Bolan nodded knowingly. "But like always, it'll be slow going, hard to prove. Witnesses disappear, others won't talk." Such a slowness led to inaction, and if allowed to follow its course would encourage more kidnappings, more deaths, often of innocents. It all added up to growing power for the Red Brigades and other terrorists.

"We know what happened to the Angola shipment," Brognola said. "A leak to the Luanda government told them time, date and place of delivery. They were waiting for the FNLA, and once the shipment was on the ground, they opened fire. Most of the freedom fighters didn't even have working weapons."

"A massacre," Bolan said grimly. "You catch the leak?"

"We took care of him," Brognola assured him. "He had a paycheck from H. Boll. In Colombia we found the farmers. They were fronting a big coca plantation. The central government went in and wiped it out while we located the Communists' camp." He paused. "It's gone now, too."

Bolan nodded. He watched the street below and said nothing for a while. Gendarmes were blocking traffic and questioning witnesses. A bomb squad had cordoned off the area and were cleaning up. As he watched their neat, precise work, the familiarity of it all raised the old questions: when would the violence end? When would decent people be able to live in peace?

"Your problem is Boll," Bolan said at last. "They're new, and in the arms business a new company almost never shows up, so you want to know who's really behind them. Where they actually get the weapons they're selling."

"That's it. Boll has popped up too suddenly. They have to be a front. From our information, they're getting to be the biggest broker of weapons in the world. But they have to be buying the actual hardware from some old-line manufacturer or supplier. We have to find who, Striker."

Again Bolan was silent. He seemed tired, weariness etched deep in his craggy, determined face.

Brognola watched him, quiet, too. They were old friends, soldiers who had fought a lot of battles.

Bolan was thinking about statistics he'd heard recently, that global weapons exports were worth more than thirty billion dollars a year, not including black and gray markets. In about two-thirds of the cases, governments sold to other governments and were pretty open about it. Private weapons manufacturers sold the rest. Where did H. Boll fit in?

In such a lucrative industry, enormous gray and black markets had grown up. Freedom fighters needed weapons even if they couldn't afford them. Terrorists kidnapped, stole or sold drugs to get what they needed. In the end, somebody made a handsome profit—an illegal one. International terrorism grew. More people died.

"H. Boll, Ltd., is merchandising death," Brognola said at last. "None of our sources could find out where Boll came from, who owns it, who's running it, even where it's located. The Hamburg office is an empty room and a telephone. Just a message clearinghouse, a drop."

"This is a routine job for the CIA," Bolan said, "or Interpol. You know that, Hal. I need to be doing other things, things I can take care of personally, where I can be more effective. You know that, too. So what haven't you told me yet?"

Brognola was silent for a time. "Three of my people are dead."

"Killed by Boll?"

"It's the best connection we have. They were the ones who put us onto what little we do know."

Bolan stared at him, grim-faced. "Who?"

"Doug Wilson, Dave Wueste and Mary Cheadle."

"Mary Cheadle?" Bolan repeated, thinking fondly of the gray-haired woman who used to work with Aaron Kurtzman at the Farm. His face went hard. "When? How?"

"She was killed in West Berlin. She's the one who gave us the intel on the Angola disaster. And there's more. Two days ago our safehouse in Algiers was bombed. Luckily no one was there, but the building and records were destroyed."

Bolan looked down at the street. The bomb crew was gone. All but one of the gendarmes was gone. Traffic had resumed its normal pace, and pedestrians walked the sidewalks as if nothing unusual had happened that afternoon.

"None of the agencies has made any real progress cracking Boll," Brognola continued. "I heard that intel yesterday from an Air Force general who should know. He's staff at NSC. What he told me dovetailed with my intel. Anyone could be behind the dummy companies—some multinational cartel, a consortium, the French, the Israelis, the Swedes, the Bulgarians, the Soviets." Brognola paused and grimaced. "Or even our own government!"

"The United States government?" Bolan asked.

"No one likes to think it, but people the President trusts could be betraying him," Brognola said. "You have to understand, this isn't official. But Boll—whoever or whatever it is—must be stopped!"

Bolan nodded, his steely-blue eyes suddenly icy. H. Boll, Ltd., indiscriminately supplied arms, making it possible for terrorists and enemies of democracy around the globe to flourish. Mack Bolan's number one priority was the suppression of international terrorism. It was a grueling, lonely fight to allow ordinary men, women and children to live the lives they chose outside the shadow of fear and destruction.

"Who knew what your plans were today?" Bolan asked Brognola as he walked quietly toward the door. He reached inside his windbreaker and pulled out the Beretta, modified for him with suppressor and specially machined springs to cycle subsonic cartridges, effectively silencing the weapon.

"I thought about that, too," Brognola said. "Only the people who had to know. My staff."

"You've got a leak, or you've been compromised."

Brognola couldn't deny the obvious. "You're going to run into major trouble on this one," he predicted, dropping his voice. "Maybe from all of them...the terrorist groups and the government agencies. Where will you start?"

And then he, too, heard the sounds in the hallway. Footsteps. The guy was trying to sneak in, but the hall floor was wooden, and the tap of his heels was distinct.

Mack Bolan glanced at Brognola and smiled slightly. He raised a finger to his lips, a silent warning. "You've been penetrated, Hal," he said simply. "I'll be in touch."

The Executioner unlocked the door.

CHAPTER TWO

Outside the Paris apartment cars hummed noisily along the street. An occasional horn blasted, accompanied by shouts and the usual French insults.

Inside, all was tense silence.

Bolan paused, his hand on the doorknob, as he heard the soft click of the lock.

The warrior and Brognola looked at each other. Quickly the big Fed moved behind Bolan, pulling a Colt Cobra from beneath his sport jacket.

Bolan hunkered down, nodded once to warn Brognola and yanked open the door.

A barrage of fire burst down the hall.

"Mack Bolan!" The guy spoke his challenge with a Puerto Rican accent. "Bolan, baby. Come and get me. I have a present for you!"

"The black guy?" Brognola wondered aloud.

Bolan didn't take the time to question, or to answer. He dipped his left shoulder, leaned his back against the left side of the doorframe and fired left-handed up the unseen corridor. The answering burst of fire raked the corridor at an angle, ceiling to floor.

"Cover me," the Executioner snapped. He crossed silently to the window of the small room.

Brognola took Bolan's position at the door and squeezed off two spaced shots from his Cobra. The automatic fire responded.

Bolan wasn't in the room to hear. This was his setup, his room, and no one caught Mack Bolan blind on his own battleground. He was already out the window and into the next, moving along a narrow rear corridor used in the last century by servants. He reached a locked door that opened into the main corridor again.

Bolan unlocked the door and stepped out.

The black heard him. Too late. As Bolan had figured, the smart guy had expected his boasting would smoke Bolan out into the far end of the corridor, to blast his Beretta at where he thought the black would be.

But the black was ready. Or thought he was ready.

He was waiting above an opened door, holding on to the overhead pipes of the old building, a lethal mini-Uzi in his hand, staring back along the corridor to where he expected Bolan to appear.

He heard Bolan behind him and turned in alarm. Surprise contorted the black's smooth features.

Bolan's Beretta spit twice.

The hitter's Uzi sputtered into the ceiling as he crashed like a rag doll to the floor, plaster dust and chips spraying the air.

From opposite ends of the corridor Bolan and Brognola ran to the fallen gunner. He was dead, his chest and throat ripped open. Blood poured onto the hardwood floor.

Brognola patted him down and found a stiletto in an ankle sheath. Otherwise the guy was clean. He carried

no ID. Only the shiny wing tips told them something—
his other life was prosperous, traditional.

Voices clamored in the distance. People had heard the
gunfire. They would call the gendarmes.

Bolan and Brognola ran along the dirty, smelly hallway, Bolan leading the way through the maze of corridors, past closed doors. A knot of people scattered
when they saw the two men bearing down on them.

And then Bolan stopped, and turned back. A trickle
of blood showed beneath a door. He opened it.

Inside, crumpled amid brooms and pails, was the
muscle-bound figure of Andy Atkins.

"Andy!"

Bolan knelt in front of him. Blood soaked Atkins's
shirt and jacket and had seeped onto the floor. It was a
knife wound, with massive bleeding. The black's attack on Atkins had been professional, silent.

Atkins took a ragged breath, then opened his eyes
slightly. "Boll," he whispered.

"Don't." Bolan's voice was husky. "We'll get you
out of here."

But Atkins wouldn't stop. "That guy . . . said he was
with Boll. . . ."

Then, with a sigh, he gave a final, involuntary shudder and died.

Bolan's face was grim as he closed Atkins's eyes. The
man had been a good soldier. "Come on," he said to
Brognola. "Let's get the hell out of here."

IN HIS CORNER PENTHOUSE office atop a giant, smoked-
glass skyscraper in Johannesburg, Philip Carlisle swiveled his chair to stare out the floor-to-ceiling window

behind his enormous walnut desk. Johannesburg spread
before him as far as the eye could see. The bustling
modern city was South Africa's biggest, and a nerve
center for engineering, manufacturing and communi-
cations. Philip's segment of the Carlisle family's global
business included the gold mines of Carlisle Mining
Corporation. The racial strife caused by South Africa's apartheid policy affected him very little. As long as
black bellies needed to be fed, his mines would have
workers.

He turned back to face the room and glared at his
staff, who were sitting in soft leather chairs on the other
side of the desk. They crossed and recrossed their legs
and looked at one another nervously, waiting for Carlisle to speak. Only Michael Jones, his personal assistant, didn't cringe. Jones yawned, bored by the waiting.

On the wall behind Philip Carlisle hung framed sets
of glittering gold Krugerrand coins, a fortune under
glass. His mines produced nearly half the gold of South
Africa's two-billion-dollar-a-year output, and the opulent furnishings of his penthouse reflected that afflu-
ence. There were hand-knotted Oriental rugs, sparkling
cut-glass chandeliers, rich silk wall coverings, and
priceless floor statues by famous sculptors. All were in
impeccably good taste—his decorators had guaranteed
it.

But Philip Carlisle's pride was invested elsewhere—in
the photographs that covered an entire wall of the office. They were photographs of Carlisle hunting in
South Africa's great wilderness areas and of the celeb-
rities who stood with him beside his game trophies.
From leading government officials to Hollywood movie

stars and international business tycoons like Adnan
Khashoggi, the important people who clamored to be
Philip Carlisle's friends were vital to him, more signif-
icant even than the wild animals he hunted and killed.

In his thirty-five years he had learned that having
such power over people was immensely pleasurable, yet
his desire for more power was never satisfied.

"So you've located him," Carlisle said at last. "What
took you so long?"

He had a boyish, oval face, the cheeks smooth. His
hair was styled in the "natural" windblown look that
was possible to maintain only with an on-staff barber.
His nails were neatly trimmed and covered with clear
polish, the cuticles clipped. Such a well-groomed exte-
rior was necessary in his sophisticated circles; it distracted people's attention from the cruelty in his eyes,
from the way his thin lips smiled when he ordered death
in the city, the mines or the veld.

"You're damn lucky we found him at all," Jones
said, his voice steady.

The hard, muscular roughneck stood alone, unin-
timidated, leaning against the office's closed door. He
was six feet tall, forty-one years old, a dark, handsome
man dressed in twill slacks and an open-necked shirt.
There was a restless air about Jones, as if the outdoors
were the only place he was comfortable in. Once a
professional soldier, now he was a professional con-
sultant, who worked for Carlisle because he was paid
generously. He had a certain respect for the insanity that
lurked behind Carlisle's expensive cosmopolitan mask.

"Well?" Carlisle asked impatiently.

"They were in Paris. Brognola's returning to D.C."

"Bolan?" Carlisle prompted.

Jones refused to be rushed. He crossed his arms and watched with interest as the delay caused a flush of anger to creep up Carlisle's cheeks.

"We're not sure about Bolan," Jones said.

"Not sure!"

"He's traveling northeast and could end up anywhere from Hanover to Vladivostok."

"Hamburg?" Carlisle asked worriedly. "Have you warned the Boll office in Hamburg?"

"Of course."

"I suppose there's no problem anyway. We've all dodged probes before."

"We've never had to dodge Mack Bolan," Jones said.

Carlisle shrugged. "He's just another killer for hire." He looked around the room to his four top staff people—management, finance, planning and records. Four pampered vice presidents with six-figure salaries. They avoided his gaze.

Even his lover was afraid of him, a beautiful blonde who spoke Afrikaans, the Dutch-based language of her heritage. She carried a small Walther for protection in this stricken nation with the world's most heavily armed population.

"Killers don't have much intelligence," the vice president for finance suggested. "Bolan's a killer."

"Besides, we've handled tough problems before," the vice president for management said. "Look at the Sudan deal. We had to fool Mr. Carlisle, Sr., himself to make that work, and that's the toughest damn thing in the world. If he ever found out . . ."

Philip Carlisle smiled at the mention of one of his proudest moments. He'd helped the hard-pressed Sudanese government out from under one of Khaddafi's whims—a military outpost on the White Nile. The madman Khaddafi had wanted air-conditioning, tanks and a battalion of small arms in one of the most remote jungle areas of the world. Nothing there to protect, and nothing nearby to invade.

The weapons order meant a big buy through Boll's predecessor, Daniel Garsky, Ltd., in London. But Philip Carlisle heard of it and intercepted the money before it reached Garsky. The weapons arrived on schedule in the Sudan. When the payment didn't turn up, Philip's father hit the roof. David Carlisle ordered no more arms shipments to Khaddafi and launched a major investigation that never discovered in whose pockets the money had landed.

Khaddafi couldn't find the payment either, and because of his general fickleness, and then the American air strike on Tripoli, he lost interest in the military post. The Sudanese turned over half the weapons to him and kept the rest. They never discovered who their benefactor was. Philip Carlisle, after paying off personnel and expenses, had pocketed a cool two and a half million dollars. A very sweet deal.

The planning VP laughed. "Philip can outsmart his father anytime he wants." He and the other vice presidents had made a tax-free hundred thousand each on the transaction.

"Even the old man can't live forever," the finance VP suggested.

"Philip should be the head of Carlisle International," the management VP announced.

The four vice presidents looked at one another from their chairs and smiled. The meeting was back on the right track.

For a brief moment Philip Carlisle's eyes were naked with greed, hungering for the power of his father. Only Michael Jones saw it, or would have admitted seeing it. Almost immediately Philip Carlisle hid the raw emotion. He had learned one major lesson from his famous father—never play your cards too soon.

"We were discussing Operation Strikeout," Philip said coldly. "We've got to stop Bolan before he compromises Boll. Boll is important to my father, and to the family." He gave a wry smile. "No one steals from Boll but us!"

The men laughed, even Jones. He, too, had cleared a hundred thousand on the Sudanese weapons deal.

"Call it a challenge, a rehearsal," Philip continued, his tone again serious. He paused to make sure he had their complete attention. His voice went wintry cold. "If we can't handle one two-bit killer, how are we going to take over the whole company?"

The vice presidents stared at Philip Carlisle, absorbing the enormity of his challenge. What if they lost? What if they tried to beat David Carlisle, the head of Carlisle International, and failed? Years of work would have brought them nothing. Where else could they go? Where else would they find jobs—incomes—like this?

At last one of them rallied. "Of course we can get Bolan!" he said.

The other three took up the chorus. A piece of cake.

Carlisle turned to the only one who remained silent. "Jones?"

"Like I said," the former soldier repeated stubbornly, "Mack Bolan's different."

"But you've got a fix on him," Carlisle prodded. "So get out there and finish him."

"We've got him under total surveillance. My men are good, they know their jobs, but he's already killed one of them—a savvy Puerto Rican who'd survived Nicaragua, Grenada and Cuba. Then Bolan gets him in Paris. Bolan's good. He isn't called the Executioner for nothing."

"A one-man army?" Carlisle scoffed, and looked at his vice presidents for confirmation. They smiled uneasily, wanting to believe their boss, and wanting to believe that a lone man could never penetrate a Carlisle enterprise.

"I've fought Bolan before," Jones continued. "A deal I was arranging through the KGB. Bolan found out about it and wiped out my contact and his unit."

"You scared?" Carlisle sneered.

Jones studied him, waiting until the younger man dropped his gaze.

"No, I guess you're not," Carlisle admitted.

He stood up, walked around his massive desk, athletic, graceful, a big man as all Carlisle men were. He stopped in front of his vice president for management and stared into his face only inches away. The man sweated, but his eyes remained steady.

"Bolan's just one man," Carlisle said. "And he's a fool. He lives like a monk—no fun, no money, no comforts. He owns nothing, a damn idiot who doesn't know enough to get his and live in luxury while the rest of the world slaves away."

Carlisle moved to his planning vice president and locked eyes. The VP swallowed hard.

"Yeah," Jones said dryly. "Bolan's a damned fool, a stupid patriot. He loves the little man and the rest of the slaving idiots. But remember, he's a deadly fool. He's incorruptible, honest. Hard as nails. He's not like anyone else you've had to deal with. You can't buy him off, or trick him for long. All you can do is try to kill him."

Carlisle stood facing his financial man. The sweat poured off the vice president. He tried to grin. Carlisle had his victim. He picked up the VP by the collar and back of his three-piece pin-striped suit.

The man's face was gray, glistening with sweat.

Carlisle dragged the limp, unresisting body across the office to a side window. He unlatched it and swung the glass out forty stories above the city.

Faint traffic sounds entered the opulent office.

He shoved the VP's head, shoulders and torso out the window, hanging on to his belt and the seat of his trousers.

"Then kill Bolan," Carlisle told Jones.

Paralyzed with fear, the vice president in the window vomited.

Carlisle hauled him in and dropped him on the carpet, then turned and stared at Jones.

"Or I'll kill you," he added.

Michael Jones nodded slowly.

AFTER THE MEETING in Philip Carlisle's office, the four vice presidents hurried out, pale and drained. The trembling financial vice president clutched the American thousand-dollar bill Philip Carlisle had tossed him. "Get your suit cleaned."

Michael Jones strolled out last, leaving Philip to lunch privately with his beautiful Afrikaner woman in their bedroom.

The vice president for finance was light-headed and still nauseated from his ordeal. He pocketed the thousand-dollar bill and rode down the executive elevator with his chin up and his eyes straight ahead. He willed his stomach to settle and kept repeating to himself that Philip Carlisle was a madman, that he was there only because his real boss had sent him.

He got into his Jaguar XKE and drove to an underground parking lot on Marshall Street. There, in a shadowy section where half the overhead lights were smashed, he met a tall, slim, cobralike man, who had eyes that seemed to pierce flesh. He detailed the information he'd heard at the meeting in Philip Carlisle's office, leaving out any mention of his humiliation.

When he had finished his report, he answered some questions and then drove back to the Carlisle Mining building.

He had no lunch that day. His stomach couldn't take it.

THE COBRALIKE MAN watched his informant's Jaguar exit the parking garage. He found a telephone booth, called Mexico City and repeated what he'd learned.

The contact relayed the intel to an elegant, austerely furnished office at the top of a Mexico City landmark skyscraper, where two men sat drinking aged brandy. They discussed the news.

"You knew about the Khaddafi theft?" the older of the two asked.

"Sooner or later I know everything. I want the boys to think for themselves, make their own mistakes, take risks."

"Even against you?"

"That's the only way the company will survive another three hundred years, Sam," David Carlisle told the older man.

"You think Philip can make it?"

"All we can do is wait and see."

They sat in companionable silence and watched the snowcapped volcanoes in the distance.

On the street below, Janet Lovelace sat in her sleek Rolls-Royce, thinking about the intel from Johannesburg. She listened to the short conversation between the two men in the office high above the city. She smiled. Events were unfolding on schedule.

CHAPTER THREE

The ferry rocked and dipped as it left the crowded seaport of Helsingör, Denmark, and headed out across the white-capped straits to picturesque Hälsingborg, Sweden.

Mack Bolan leaned against the forward railing, enjoying the biting wind, the roiling ocean and the hardy gulls that circled and dived. Saltwater sprayed up and filled the air with its sharp, pleasant smells.

Because of moderate-to-heavy seas, the crossing was rougher and slower than usual. There were fewer passengers, and most stayed inside where it was warm and sheltered. They drank, played cards and wandered the duty-free shop, while outside, Bolan and a half-dozen others rested against the railings.

Bolan watched the sea and thought about the events of the past twenty-four hours, including the meeting with Hal Brognola. He thought about people he'd known and liked who had died in the battle against mindless evil. But all the while he was thinking in the biting sea wind he was aware of the two men who had come out on deck. He'd heard the door's wind-prodded slam, the slow, careful footsteps. He didn't move, but watched them from the corners of his eyes.

Big and tough-looking, they wore long trench coats. As they walked, Bolan began to make out the faint outlines of bulges under their left armpits. Skorpions, maybe, a kind of machine pistol favored by terrorists.

They pretended to watch the gulls and the sea, but they focused on Bolan and kept track of each other. They were bracketing him.

Slowly they came. They didn't want to draw the attention of other passengers.

Again the ferry door opened and banged shut.

This time Bolan had better luck—a uniformed Danish policeman of medium height and a good, solid build. The cop spread his arms, breathed in the salt air with great gulps of pleasure and grinned. He banged his thick chest, and marched across the deck, his face growing pink in the wind.

The two tough guys glanced at each other, broke their strides and moved farther away from Bolan.

Bolan kept his shoulders hunched, his head dipped low, as if only the whitecaps had his attention. The two men were trying to look innocent. They would have little inclination to pull something with the cop around. And the last thing Bolan himself wanted was trouble with the police on a ferry, where he could be trapped and lose a lot of time.

Bolan stood up straight, yawned and stretched as if wakening. He turned and strode through the door and inside.

Startled, the men in trench coats followed.

Bolan smiled inwardly at their dismay at the turn of events. They'd probably planned on an easy, quiet kill at the railing, and then slipping his corpse overboard.

As they entered the ferry's cabin the warrior tensed, hesitated, looked nervously behind him. He pretended to spot the thugs and allowed fear to show on his face.

One of the men grinned, and the other gave a knowing glance at his partner. Their confidence was restored. They thought they had him.

Bolan moved past rows of seats where families smiled, chatted, held babies, past the cafeteria where passengers drank Danish beer and ate from platters of bread and cold herring, ham and cheese.

He ran down the narrow metal stairs, his footsteps clanging quietly. As he hurried along the corridor, he pulled the Beretta from beneath his windbreaker, its weight perfect, an old friend in his hand. Diesel fumes drifted in the hallway, and the muffled whoosh and clang of automated pistons and turbines could be heard.

As the thugs' footsteps sounded heavy on the stairs behind him, he rounded a corner and flattened against a wall. But there was a surprise waiting for him there.

The engine room seaman had entered the corridor from the opposite end, walking noiselessly in canvas shoes. He wore blue work denims, his sleeves rolled up to expose stringy, tattooed arms. Surprised to see Bolan, or indeed any passenger here, the sailor looked at the Executioner, and then he looked again.

His gaze locked onto Bolan's ice-cold eyes and for a moment he seemed to freeze. Then he tensed to run, opening his mouth to call for help.

The thugs were approaching, heavy footed, methodically exploring.

Bolan had no choice. Before the seaman could react, he slammed a rock-hard fist into the old guy's jaw. The man's head snapped back, and he staggered for an instant. Bolan caught him in midair.

Listening for footsteps and the low rumble of conversation, the warrior swept his gaze along the passageway. He was running out of time. Then he spotted a door with a lock.

He hefted the unconscious sailor, ran to the door and got lucky. The room contained only luggage and crates. Bolan dumped the limp body inside and spun the lock. The man would have a sore jaw and headache, but otherwise he'd wake up fine.

"There he is!" The shout was triumphant.

A hardman in a trench coat stood at the end of the passageway, aiming the rugged, reliable and efficient Skorpion machine pistol with sound suppressor. Overconfident, he fired too soon.

The bursts streaked harmlessly past Bolan's ears, ricocheted once from a steel door and penetrated a thin wall. But before the bullets had struck, the Executioner was moving.

In one smooth motion he hit the floor, rolled up, aimed his 93-R autoloader just above the middle of the man's trench coat and squeezed off a 9 mm parabellum round with deadly precision.

The guy was shocked. His eyes widened as he realized his mistake, recognized the simplicity of the trap. He pitched backward. His coat flapped open. Blood spread thick and fast across his chest as his heart pumped a few last seconds.

His partner rounded the corner, but Bolan was gone, slipping into the engine room with its dense oily smells.

The second gunman came after the Executioner, his feet hard on the metal floor.

In spite of the thudding automated machinery, Bolan heard the sounds, felt the reverberations of the pursuer's feet. He disappeared behind a pillar from where he could have an unobstructed view of the door. He chose his place carefully, made sure he was backed up tight against a corner, for protection from ricocheting bullets.

And then he waited. There was nothing. No footsteps, no reverberations.

Bolan refused to be lured out.

At last the door blasted open. The gunner barreled in low, Skorpion at eye level. Bolan was ready and squeezed off a 3-round burst. But his big, sloppy opponent could move amazingly fast, and Bolan's fire exited harmlessly through the doorway.

The hardman took cover behind one of the pounding turbine engines and returned fire. The bullets ricocheted through the gray room, pinging and screaming from wall to piston to turbine to wall.

Bolan crouched low to make a smaller target as ricochet rounds whizzed past a second time in their deadly flight, and a third. It was like being in a crazy shooting gallery with blind men firing in all directions. Eventually the spent rounds, battered and flattened, dropped to the steel floor among the pounding piston rods.

"Give up, Bolan," the man bellowed. "You're dead!"

"Yeah?"

"Yeah." The voice came somewhere from Bolan's right.

The new guy pointed his Skorpion straight at Bolan's heart as the door closed behind him. Bolan's unobstructed view had been used against him. There was another entrance to the engine room.

The newcomer hadn't been on deck outside earlier, so he must have been sitting with other passengers in the cabin or café, waiting, an unplayed card.

They had Bolan trapped between them in the engine room corner. The first man laughed and walked out from behind the turbine. Bolan was looking down the barrels of two Skorpions, and at two opponents eager to blast him away.

But they'd already made their first mistakes. The one behind hadn't shot him instantly from ambush. And the other one had come out into the open to laugh at his victim.

They enjoyed killing. It was always a mistake for someone to send killers who enjoyed killing. They didn't have their minds on the real job.

Bolan kept his Beretta trained on the first gunner.

They started to walk toward him, cutting down the range, daring him to fire. They enjoyed the risk, too, playing with death.

"You guys must like your work," Bolan said.

The two hitters kept their Skorpions at eye level, the stocks extended. Firing from the hip-assault position would pitch a handful of empty cases up into their faces because of the ejection port's location on the top of the upper receiver.

"Listen to him," the one nearer to Bolan said as they moved in closer.

"You think he's playing for time?" the other one said.

They laughed at their joke, toying with their victim, sure there was no way Bolan could get them now. Their next mistake. And their last.

Bolan dropped flat on his back to the steel floor. Suddenly facing each other, the gunmen hesitated a split second.

Bolan blasted the one behind him over his head, then shot the second before he could react.

The two hardmen crashed to the floor.

One let off a useless blast from his Skorpion as he fell, the bullets ricocheting. And then they both lay still, limbs sprawled awkwardly.

Bolan remained in his corner, crouched, as the ricochets sang from wall to engines and finally to the metal decking. He watched the dead men's blood pool on the floor.

When the last of the bullets had landed, Bolan put away his weapon and hauled the three corpses to the storage closet that held the old seaman.

Bolan wanted off this ferry before anyone asked any questions. He had work to do.

On deck, he again stood alone at the railing, enjoying the fresh air and the vast, sparkling sea. He watched as the ferry approached the quaint Swedish city of Hälsingborg, and he thought.

The three guys were Boll's men, all right. H. Boll, Ltd., Hamburg, West Germany. But who or what was Boll?

CHAPTER FOUR

White sandy beaches, fertile farmlands and medieval castles and churches lined the windswept Swedish coast. Mack Bolan drove a rented Saab along the coast on Highway E6 north from Hälsingborg, enjoying the quickness and maneuverability of the sturdy compact.

The winding highway followed the turquoise Kattegat, an arm of the North Sea between Sweden and Jutland. Winter was in the air. Silver birches trembled as biting gales gusted off the ocean. The sun shone low in the sky, but with little warmth on this resort coast just over six hundred miles south of the Arctic Circle.

As he drove, Bolan thought about the man he was going to see. Would Lars have answers?

Pulling off the highway onto a two-lane side road that led away from the sea, he saw a flock of swans winging overhead. He drove past ancient rune stones and Viking burial mounds and into a pine forest.

Darkness was falling. Clouds gathered overhead. The gray twilight spread, thickening in the forest as it closed around the car. In the last rays of the sun, Bolan found the right side road, turned down it and was soon in a meadow edged with birch and juniper.

In the center of the meadow stood a three-story half-timbered house he hadn't seen in years. He remembered magnificent views of the Kattegat from the house's second-floor living room. In the backyard stood children's swings and a slide. Good hiking and horse-back trails ribboned the mountainside.

"Who's there?" a woman called from the front door. She stepped onto the open porch, wiped her hands on her apron and peered at the Saab. Pale blond, statu-esque, beautiful still. Majvor Marlett.

Bolan turned off the engine and got out of the car. "It's me, Majvor. Mack Bolan."

"Mack?" She remained perfectly still, then turned to call into the house. "Lars! Lars, come here! It's Mack Bolan!"

She ran down the steps, laughing, shaking her head. "Mack! It's been a long time!"

LARS MARLETT WAS a tall redheaded man, with the small, strong hands for which Vikings are known. Bo-lan watched Lars's nimble fingers tamp tobacco into his pipe, flick tobacco leaf from his leather vest and scratch a kitchen match across the arm of his chair. The pipe lighted, Lars puffed solemnly, a twinkle in his eye as he gazed at his old friend.

"H. Boll, Ltd.," Lars said. "Sounds like you're going after mighty big game. You know what you're getting into?"

"Not totally," Bolan said.

"But that never stops you."

The pungent aroma of Lars's Swedish tobacco filled the birch-paneled living room. Dinner over, the two men sat comfortably in front of the massive stone fire-place where a fire blazed and crackled.

Lars Marlett was one of the world's top weapons experts. Bolan had first met him in Vietnam where Lars had been a volunteer with the ARVN. He had saved a lot of good men with his arms knowledge and had blown a lot of the North Viets away in search-and-destroy missions. The next time Bolan had seen him was in the United States where the Swede had been quietly working with the U.S. government during an anti-Mafia cleanup.

Then Lars had gone to work for his own government, consulting about weapons, expediting international purchases and sales. Sweden did a big arms business to support their independent industry, and Lars knew the private dealers and all the nations dealt with inside out.

"Boll is a new company, a brokerage," Lars explained, puffing on his pipe. "We don't often get new brokers, and almost never new suppliers or manufacturers."

"You mean they're a front. We figured that already, but a front for who?"

"Sorry. Not a ripple."

"Who would know, Lars?"

"That's what I was considering." Lars turned the pipe in his hands. "It's a long shot."

"Tell me about it."

Lars nodded. "All right. This begins with a secret Soviet sale that included SAM-7 antiaircraft missiles and launchers. A big sale of advanced weapons, eighteen million dollars' worth."

"A regular deal?"

"Yes. A commercial transaction involving banks and insurance companies in several countries. The telex order was for thirty-five items."

"The buyer?"

"Iran."

"Iran?" Bolan was surprised. "Not even Gorbachev trusts Iran. The Ayatollah is so unpredictable." He stopped suddenly, understanding. "Then it was strictly for cash. The Soviets need cash."

"Right. The arms came from a Warsaw Pact arsenal in Poland. A French broker chartered some DC-9s in Israel to transport them from Israel to Poland to Nicosia and then to Tehran. A Swiss broker had the cargo—331 cases—misidentified as industrial equipment and spare parts and labeled with North Korea as the destination. The North Korean embassy in Vienna issued an end-user certificate guaranteeing that the weapons were destined for Pyongyang, North Korea. A dummy West German company handled delivery. Final directions came from Soviet officials at the Perenosny Zenitiny Raketny Kompleks, a Soviet-controlled installation outside Warsaw."

"The bottom line?"

"Altogether the Iranians bought four hundred missiles, one hundred launchers, Soviet antitank grenades and artillery ammo."

Bolan shook his head, disgusted by these unethical, complex deals that ultimately cost the lives of so many people.

"What about the insurance companies and banks?"

Lars smiled coldly. "The insurance inspectors issued a certificate stating that the quantity and quality of the goods corresponded to the contract. The Swiss broker posted a hundred-thousand-dollar performance bond through the London branch of Commerzbank A.G., the West German bank. At the same time the Union Bank of Switzerland issued a letter of credit on behalf of the Iranians for nearly nineteen million dollars, the amount Tehran would pay for the arms."

"And then the bank transfers began."

Lars nodded. "First to Commerzbank, London, where profits and commissions were paid, and then to the West Berlin branch of Deutsche Bank A.G., where the Soviets had an account."

"Big profits and commissions."

"Enormous," Lars agreed. "The Soviets got twenty-five thousand dollars for each SAM-7, but the Iranians paid nearly forty-four thousand."

"The difference went to the banks, the insurance companies and the brokers," Bolan said.

Lars looked at his friend, sadness deep in his eyes, and shrugged. "It's a big job to break chains like that. Maybe impossible. The financial profits are so huge that the cost in human life is insignificant to them."

The two men fell silent.

"This H. Boll, Ltd.—if they're behind deals like that, they'll stop at nothing," Lars continued at last. He held up his pipe in front of the crackling fire and examined its silhouette. His red hair looked almost white in the firelight. "Certainly not for one lone man."

"Doesn't matter," Bolan said as he watched his friend.

"You still have to do it," Lars said, resigned.

"The name you have for me…it must be the guy who gave you the intel on the Soviet-Iran deal. If he heard about it, he's got to be good."

"You're right," Lars agreed. "Remember, Mack, I think Boll is a front all the way, not even a real middleman, just a paper corporation. Someone is behind them. It could be a supplier—an independent or part of a big cartel. It could be a manufacturer like Colt, or Ruger, or Heckler & Koch, or a big consortium like Takeda Industries, or Krupp, or Carlisle International. Or it could be a government—Israel, or France, or the Soviet Union."

"I understand, Lars. Who's your intel contact?"

Lars paused, then took his pipe from his mouth. "André Villela," he said slowly, almost reluctantly. "He's an FNLA commander in the bush."

"He handles the FNLA arms deals?"

"Yes. If FNLA dealt with H. Boll, it was André who did the dealing."

"I'll find him."

Lars studied Mack, his pale blue eyes worried. "I know."

PERHAPS IT WAS the tree branch rubbing against the black nighttime window. Perhaps it was the wind, which howled occasionally. Or it might simply have been that sixth sense, that special hard-earned instinct Mack Bolan had developed over the years, which had warned him of trip wires in Nam's jungles, of Mafia punks behind closed doors, of terrorists lurking in the shadows of airline terminals.

Bolan flipped back the bedclothes. Instantly the bedroom's piercing cold struck his naked flesh. He pulled on his skintight combat blacksuit, thermally lined to protect against the cold. Except for the occasional groaning of the old house in the wind, all was quiet.

He rubbed black cosmetic on his face, masking any glimmer that moonlight might reveal. From his neatly packed arsenal, concealed in one of the hidden compartments of his suitcase, he took Big Thunder—his stainless-steel AutoMag, a pulverizing flesh-shredder with wildcat .44 cartridges.

Still listening, he shrugged into military-style webbing, holstered the gun low on his right hip, drew on thin black gloves, strapped a commando knife to his ankle and picked up a pair of heavy-duty 105 NVD binoculars.

Quietly he turned the doorknob to the Marletts' guest room and checked the long upstairs hall. It was empty, quiet. He padded down the hallway, the aged floorboards creaking occasionally, went down the back stairs, and entered the shadowy kitchen.

Nothing. No one moved in the house except him. He both sensed and knew that.

It was outside. What had awakened him was there, now maybe in the dense forest that surrounded the Marletts' meadow.

He unlatched and slid open a side window. The biting air exploded into the room. He looked out. A light snow dusted the meadow, melting with the last bit of autumn warmth still in the earth. He slipped out into the shadows of moving firs, onto the first snowfall of the Swedish winter.

And then in the pale moonlight he saw the footprints.

The prints of heavy boots were in the slush, between a particularly large pine and the house. His eyes followed the trail, back to the half-timbered home.

He retraced his steps and found the mound of plastic explosive tucked under a bay window, directly beneath the second-floor sleeping wing of the house. Ripping off the explosive, he dismantled it and threw the parts aside.

Fury boiled up in him.

H. Boll! It had to be.

And the next victims of that unholy company would have been the innocent, sleeping Marletts.

The Executioner slipped away, another moving shadow in the meadow where everything seemed to shudder and move in the wind. He hugged cover—snowy trees, boulders, an ancient rune stone. His NVD binoculars to his eyes, he scanned the forest.

The cold wind moaned through the trees. The scent of fragrant pines filled the air. Dark snow clouds moved sluggishly across the charcoal sky, hiding and revealing the stars and the moon.

And then he saw them. Three dark figures spaced widely just inside the tree line, watching the house. Why? Waiting for the explosion? A stupid thing to do.

Bolan angled away, backtracking. He came up on the forest about one-eighth of a mile away, stopped and watched through the binoculars. The guy in the center was smoking. Cocky and stupid!

He pulled out his combat knife and crept forward, using cover, a shadow among other shadows.

The man closest to the Executioner was leaning against a tree trunk, arms crossed, staring at the great dark house sitting in the moonlight in the center of the meadow.

Bolan melted into the trees and circled around. The man was so confident that he didn't even make the instinctive, last-minute turn of so many men who are about to die.

Silently Bolan sprinted the last few steps. With one gloved hand he jerked back the guy's chin. Simultaneously with the other hand he sliced the throat to prevent a death shriek, then slammed the combat knife up under the rib cage and straight into the heart.

As the dying man quietly gurgled, Bolan held him. At last he wiped his knife across the guy's jacket and let him drop into the slush and his own quickly cooling blood.

One down. Two to go.

Again the Executioner melted into the trees, heading toward the next dark figure. The thin smell of his cigarette smoke drifted among the pines.

The smoker was nervous; his head kept jerking toward the forest, even while he concentrated on the house. As he dropped his cigarette butt into the wet duff, Bolan followed his line of sight and saw a flicker of movement coming away from Lars and Majvor's sleeping home.

There was a fourth intruder!

What in hell was the fourth person doing at the house? Bolan had to hurry. His long stride ate up the last few steps to the man who'd just put out his cigarette.

The guy turned. His eyes widened. He lifted his AK-47 and opened his mouth to yell a warning.

But the Executioner was ready. He slipped in close, blocked the Kalashnikov and spun his opponent, stunning him with strength and speed. Again the Executioner expertly yanked back the chin, sliced the throat and slammed the long knife blade up under the rib cage directly into the heart.

And then it hit Bolan—what the fourth man had been doing at the house!

Silence no longer mattered. He needed noise to awaken, warn Lars and Majvor before it was too late!

Quickly Bolan dropped the second guy, wiped his knife and slid it back into his ankle holster.

The third watcher in the forest had spotted the Executioner.

Bolan unleathered Big Thunder.

A burst of AK fire bit into the trees around Bolan, sending splinters, leaves and bark spraying like needles into the frosty air.

Bolan had the advantage of recon. The other gunner was shooting blind, while Bolan could see him. He didn't know two of his partners were already dead.

The Executioner aimed his .44, then squeezed the trigger. The recoil-operated pistol roared. The opponent staggered back, his chest ripped open. The Executioner pivoted, aimed and caught the fourth and last man as he sprinted toward the forest.

The shot was perfect. The intruder flung up his arms, lurched and fell back.

Bolan ran for the silent house before the echo of his gun's last shot had died away through the dark pines. He fired the big AutoMag again up into the cold air as he raced toward the house.

Hear it, Lars! Wake up!

The first explosion echoed against the trees as the side of the house erupted. The second explosion caught the gas tank. Fire engulfed the house in a giant orange-and-red ball.

Bolan stopped and stood in the light snow, Big Thunder useless at his side. The night was now as bright as noon as flames consumed the house. A great sadness filled Bolan as he watched the house burn. He thought of his own family destroyed long ago by naked evil. Now it was Lars Marlett and his wife. Innocent bystanders.

And then he thought about the guilty, about the ruthless new organization, H. Boll, Ltd. He would find the men behind it, wherever they might be.

He strode to his car and started the engine. The Swedish police would be here soon, and he couldn't stay to answer questions. There was a man in Angola he needed to talk to.

CHAPTER FIVE

Brigadier General Arnold Capp's favorite time on the sprawling Texas ranch was dawn. He loved to watch the sun flare above the vast prairie and sere hills, spread its hard pewter light across corrals, flat-roofed bunk-houses and barracks. It shadowed the scraggly mesquite and cottonwoods that lined the creek and picked out the ranch animals and resilient men who met the new day with the oily aromas of San Antonio's hot chili and hotter women still on them.

Dawn started over Beaumont on Texas's eastern border. It needed a full hour to travel the 773-mile breadth of the great state of long horizons, where honky-tonk angels and Coca-Cola cowboys joined Harvard-trained businessmen and Texas-born aristocrats to produce a land alternately drab and dazzling, dirt poor and tycoon rich; where a man like Arnie Capp could rise to accomplish something of significance.

From where, if need be, he could save the world.

Brigadier General Capp, usually of Washington, D.C., reflected now on his adopted state and the future of his country as he stood in the recon tower high above the training camps and weapons-testing grounds that patchworked this isolated chunk of Texas prairie. The training and testing installation had been erected on his orders alone.

Burly and thick-chested, even at this early hour he was impeccably dressed as he raised his binoculars and studied the emerging morning, proudly wearing the maroon beret of the USAF Pararescue Service.

It was this honorable beret that more than a year ago had attracted Janet Lovelace across a crowded room at a Georgetown cocktail party. She'd asked him about the jaunty beret and coaxed him to tell her about the Pararescue Service and about his honors, his battle medals. Only later had he discovered that she was the daughter of his benefactor, David Carlisle.

Within a month he'd made her his most prized, most beloved trophy, his closest helper and aide in his new operation.

The first booms of heavy artillery echoed across the land.

Capp listened, then turned to look at the corrals where the cattle held their heads high and sniffed the crisp, clean air that soon would taste of dust. The animals were accustomed to the noise now, stoically accepted the unnatural trembling of the ground beneath them. They lowered their heads and resumed feeding, their hides brown velvet in the light of dawn.

The tattoo of small arms began. General Capp turned again to watch the men begin their morning training sessions. He was pleased. His men were industrious, expert. They kept their skills razor-sharp while developing and testing the best new weapons the globe had to offer and training new recruits to the highest standards of soldiering.

He climbed down the ladder. Soldiers emerged from the bunkhouses, eyes still sleepy as they headed for their duties. They snapped to attention and saluted. Solemnly he returned their salutes and walked on.

The breakfast smells of fried steaks and eggs drifted from the cookhouse. Jeeps in the motor pool roared to life; horses in the remuda whinnied; someone in the distance bellowed an order.

At his usual brisk gait, General Capp continued alone to the development lab. He disliked a retinue of followers surrounding him. He felt no need to be reassured of his importance.

As he approached his HQ, he looked up. Just below the roofline of the simple structure was posted a long sign: Falcon International. His creation.

He stepped out of the bright sunshine and the last gusts of autumn Texas heat into rooms with fluorescent light fixtures and air-conditioning.

He nodded a curt greeting to his secretary. She gave him a dour smile and continued filing. The woman was overweight, and had plain features and severely styled gray hair, but she could keep her mouth shut and her loyalty was above reproach.

Capp strode past his personal office, as clean and tidy as a monk's cell, to the back of the long building, stopping at a door where a red light flashed and a big sign ordered: Keep Out.

The two soldiers guarding the door saluted. The general returned the salute—the routines of discipline were what kept any unit at its peak at any time—turned the knob and walked into a large room that vibrated with quiet activity. He was surrounded by the tap of computer keyboards, the rustle of paper and the blink of color monitors. Throughout the temperature-controlled, air-filtered room, white-coated scientists labored at various tasks.

Capp stopped beside a young lieutenant whose fingers nimbly worked the keys of his computer. The soldier was a whiz kid, stolen from under the nose of a Navy admiral who hadn't had the sense to recognize the brilliance of the new scientist assigned him. Capp, however, had seen the youth's records, realized he could fill a gap in his operation, traced him and pulled the strings that made the transfer happen.

"I'll call it up for you, sir," the young lieutenant said, responding to a directive from the general. He entered the commands.

Capp studied the computer screen, where a single laser beam divided into three smaller beams, each a different color to symbolize its level of energy. Here was a new method to wage war and win, a method measured in volts, microns and miles per second.

"Straight out of SDI," Capp murmured, not really understanding the technology involved, but firmly appreciating the results. "You say this will do the trick?"

"We hope so, sir. We know a single, immensely powerful laser can burn through the metal skin of a nuclear missile in flight thousands of miles away. But the huge mirrors needed to focus and reflect the laser beam are beyond what we can produce today. It would be like building a road from Dallas to Anchorage with less than an inch of height variation. We won't have that kind of technology for at least another twenty years. That's why phasars may be the solution to long-range defense and attack. They're simply phased-array lasers that couple many laser beams and use much smaller mirrors."

"And if one laser fails," Capp said, "the device keeps working."

"That's right, sir." The lieutenant smiled, but didn't take his eyes off the computer screen, barely tolerating Capp's intrusion and eager to get back to his work. "And it's so strong it'll blast a Soviet missile right out of the sky."

Capp patted the young man's shoulder and moved on to discuss with his other scientists their projects, dealing with less exotic but equally necessary weapons ranging from new SMGs with pinpoint accuracy to enormously powerful, lightweight SAMs.

"General." Capp's dour secretary stood in the door. "Your meeting."

He nodded and strode from the development lab, down the narrow corridor to where voices rumbled indistinctly beyond a door. He opened it on another spacious room, this one grand and imposing, its only furniture an elegant oval Queen Anne table with matching chairs.

His top ten subordinates sat around the table, their cigar and cigarette smoke layering the morning air. With them was a new candidate, a man who came highly recommended. His linguistic expertise would be valuable.

Alert and respectful, the men fell silent when the general entered.

Capp looked around the room, savoring the decor. Unlike the rest of the utilitarian building, this conference room had walls paneled in rich, dark mahogany imported from South Africa. The floor was covered in thick wool carpeting. A gleaming brass-and-crystal chandelier hung from the ceiling, centered over the mahogany table. The effect was spoiled, however, by the coffee cups that littered the shiny surface. Unconsciously the general grimaced at the untidiness.

"Gentlemen," he said.

"General," they murmured, some nodding. All were retired U.S. military or government employees, with experience in almost every branch of the armed services and every war and brushfire since World War II.

"Peru," said the general to retired Colonel Bryan Wright as he studied the new candidate.

"Lima and Callao are under curfew between one and five a.m. because of the bombings of government buildings, military installations and power plants," Wright answered. "There have been massive blackouts."

"Attributed to the Shining Path?" the general asked, referring to the Peruvian Maoist organization.

Wright grinned. "Totally. The people are up in arms over the terrorism, demanding that the government wipe out the Maoists. It's enabled the government to issue twenty-four-hour safe-conduct passes when people arrive at Jorge Chavez Airport, in order to screen out terrorists." He laughed. "We've picked off over a hundred drug smugglers since then. The smugglers are so worried about being tapped for Maoists that they forget to tend to business."

"And the actual damage to the government installations is minimal?"

"Superficial. Our people down there are careful to take care of our friends. Especially since they're paying for our fake-Maoist operation."

Again the general smiled.

The candidate looked surprised, impressed at the devious operation of Capp's unit posing as Maoists to trap both terrorists and drug smugglers.

"Bolivia?" Capp continued.

"Sorry, sir," said Harry Long, once of the Defense Intelligence Agency. "No arms."

"I told you I'd personally take care of that."

"They still haven't arrived."

The general's face reddened with anger. His heart pounded. It was a rebuke, and from a subordinate. From a man he'd bought and paid for with his own glorious vision.

"We need them this week or the whole Quechua operation is off," Long went on, unheeding.

The general breathed deeply, remembering Janet's calming words, the way she stroked his forehead when the idiots in Washington became too much for him. Somehow the supplier, Cordoba Construcciones, had failed in the delivery.

He turned deliberately away. "I'm on top of that. See that your end is ready on the instant." His voice was tight. He was aware of the tension around the table. The men feared his anger. They had reason to.

Capp didn't look at Long again during the meeting. The man was new and hadn't yet learned respect. A man without respect was dangerous. Long would learn that, or he would be dead.

The candidate for membership to this elite group looked stunned as he recognized implications of the anger—and the power behind it. The candidate was smart.

Capp asked for and received positive reports on Falcon International activities in El Salvador, Honduras, Israel and Ireland. In a world where power was bungled by amateurs, Falcon put it back where it belonged—in the hands of the professionals.

Then it was time to take up the candidate. Capp turned to him and waited until everyone's eyes were on the new man. "You speak six languages," the general said. His smile was easy, reassuring.

"Fluently, sir." The former State Department official in clandestine operations was a man in his midfifties, divorced and without children after a tragic accident. There was no room for him now at State; he was a man on the shelf just when he needed his work more than ever. He continued, "I can speak fifteen reasonably well."

"Do you know what we do?"

"You're private," the man said, an excited edge to his voice. "You take on security missions abroad so that American boys won't get killed, or if they do, there'll be no fuss."

Foreign governments paid for most operations, but Capp knew that eventually U.S. companies and the government would buy in, too. He had longtime friends in high, untouchable places. Particularly David Carlisle, Janet's father. The old man had financed this ultrasecret ranch operation and was now reaping a handsome profit.

When the meeting ended, Brigadier General Capp had a new head of linguistics. He was well pleased with Falcon International's overall progress. His power base was growing. Soon he would have the respect of the entire country. Of the world.

MARTHA CAPP SAT in the luxurious living room of her Pueblo-style home and looked out the large window that framed her dusty pink oleanders. Once she'd sat in this comfortable chair and knitted to keep her hands busy and her mind vacant. But now the worry was too great.

She was beginning to suspect that Janet Lovelace, the infamous tart married to the junior senator from Montana, was carrying on with Arnie. She was beginning to suspect that she, Martha Webster Capp and the general's wife, wasn't the only one who didn't know what Arnie was doing down here—maybe no one back in Washington did, either.

All of that was terrible enough, but what turned her blood ice-cold was the new look in Arnie's eyes. It was a gleam, as if he could not only see the future, but could create it.

Arnie had changed. She didn't know why or how, and she was terrified.

CHAPTER SIX

Mack Bolan fell through the night.

Stars blanketed the inky Angolan sky, the moon behind the black wall of the mountains. On the eastern horizon, the modified twin-engine Cessna disappeared with a fading hum as Bolan dropped alone through the darkness, pulling the rip cord at the last possible second. Soon he would meet Angola freedom fighter Carlos Matamba, who would escort him to weapons expert André Villela. Villela's key role in his country's struggle for freedom caused him to keep a low profile. His location at any given time wasn't generally known. Brognola's connections had arranged the rendezvous with Matamba, who would conduct Bolan to Villela if Bolan passed his skeptical screening. Villela, Bolan hoped, would have the key to the power behind H. Boll, Ltd.

Bolan maneuvered his shroud lines. The camouflaged chute above him arched and mushroomed. His descent through the humid air slowed. Through his night-vision goggles, he studied the dense treetops that spread like a vast, dark sea beneath him.

There was no signal.

With every foot of altitude lost, his maneuverability decreased geometrically. Soon he would have to sight for a landing or risk being trapped and broken in the unseen claw of some tree.

As dark and unseen as a shadow in his combat blacksuit, Bolan pulled on the parachute lines again. His Beretta 93-R was leathered under his left arm, a Fairbairn-Sykes dagger rigged beside it. Soot blackened his hands and face. Two ammo belts crossed his muscular chest, and a half-dozen frag grenades hung from his D-rings. An M-16 was slung over his shoulder and tied for easy access. His imposing frame balanced the equipment as easily as if they were extensions of himself.

Calmly he closed in on the treetop dangers of the pit below.

Then he saw it. First one blue flicker, then another, then a third.

He humped the shroud lines, angling the chute farther north.

The three lights made the points of a triangle. In the center of the triangle would be the protected area for his invisible landing in the Angolan night, an open spot in the hills and thick forest. If the signal was from Carlos Matamba. If not? Well, any war was dangerous, and a secret, invisible war was the most dangerous of all.

Bolan plunged sideways through the sky, aiming for the center of the black triangle. Suddenly close now, he saw, thanks to his night-vision goggles, a shadowy circle of men moving catlike through the foliage around the drop zone. Too damn many men. Matamba would have one, maybe two with him for this secret rendezvous. But there were a dozen down there, they were closing in, and they were armed.

Soldiers!

Bolan's feet grazed leaves. He lifted his knees.

Gunfire erupted below. It was an attack. A dozen against maybe two. Red muzzle-flashes exploded all around the drop zone. Sudden death sliced through the trees and hammered across the clearing.

Return fire now came from only one point of the drop zone triangle.

The attacking soldiers hit the dirt, pinned down by the deadly reply of the solitary defender. They crawled in on the end of the DZ triangle. That would be Matamba, who was reputed to have survived a hundred battles. But the freedom fighter was in trouble now. Out here he'd be facing the MPLA, the Angola government army. Or, even worse, Cuban regulars.

Bolan unhooked his M-16 and cradled it. The shadowy trees blurred past, the hot air whistling in his ears. The gunfire grew louder, concentrated.

Bolan shoulder-rolled onto the high grass and hit the release button. The chute harness fell off. He was on his feet and running, two grenades in his hand.

Bolan pulled the pins, lobbed first one grenade, then the other into the middle of the attackers. He threw himself flat and laid a withering fire with his M-16 to keep them pinned down.

The explosions came in seconds. The ground trembled. Cartilage, bone and blood sprayed into the air.

And Bolan was on his feet again, running. One had escaped. One guy in an MPLA uniform, slipping into the forest to warn others, to get help.

Bolan skirted the smoking ground, leaving behind the mangled bodies and the smell of burned flesh. He entered the timber at a different place, stepping carefully, silently.

Soon he heard it, the scuff of leather on stone.

Bolan padded toward the sound. He tracked the guy softly, bearing left and away into the moist shadows of mahogany and musuemba until at last he bore hard right again.

The Angolan's face twisted with surprise and hate as his eyes were caught by the cold stare of the Executioner. The guy lifted his new Uzi, finger on the trigger.

The 5.56 mm rounds from Bolan's M-16 punched four instant holes in the man's helmet. The guy froze, astonished. Blood poured down his face. Then he pitched forward, the Uzi blasting uselessly into the brush.

Mack Bolan whistled low, two longs, one short as he melted back through the thick, dark forest toward the DZ. Damp leaves brushed his face. Insects clicked and sang. One small animal, then another rustled through the underbrush, still terrorized by the battle in their usually quiet environment.

Bolan repeated the signal until at last came the answering whistle. He found Carlos Matamba squatting warily at the edge of the open DZ over a body with a mortal chest wound. As Bolan approached, the half-Portuguese native nodded at the mangled bodies of the Communists killed by Bolan's grenades.

"You're as good as they say," the freedom fighter murmured.

"Do you know how they heard about the rendezvous?" Bolan asked.

"Government patrol." Matamba shrugged. "They go out all the time. Sometimes they get lucky."

Bolan nodded grimly. "We'd better get out of here. You can fill me in later."

He handed the Uzi and ammo to Matamba. The two men moved quickly from one dead soldier to another, gathering weapons and ammunition. Carlos collected canteens, watches and jewelry, too. Guerrillas never had enough armaments, and the watches and jewelry would buy more.

They piled the arms—Uzis possibly from the stolen Angola shipment from H. Boll—in a tunic stripped from a body, tied it and slung the bundle over Matamba's back.

Bolan nodded at the corpse of Matamba's partner. "A relative?"

"My sister's husband," Matamba said simply. "I buried the chute. Path's over here."

Matamba led Bolan at a fast clip through the timber. Bolan had the dead freedom fighter slung over his shoulder. For hours they pushed along one narrow, winding trail after another—up, down and around the hills. They stopped only to drink from their canteens and to exchange their loads.

At last, as the sky was paling with dawn, they saw below them a small, impoverished village of thatched huts. Cooking fires trailed thin wisps of smoke into the sky. Naked children stepped from some of the crude buildings, rubbing their eyes.

"Hurry!" Matamba warned.

The sun would soon be fully up, and Mack Bolan and the FNLA soldier feared being caught in the open by daylight. In spite of the weight of their loads, the two men double-timed down the hill and trotted to a hut at the edge of the village. They slipped inside.

A woman with soft brown eyes and pale skin looked up from her sleeping mat. As her gaze focused on them, shock spread across her face. She opened her mouth, but she didn't scream. She only stared at Matamba and the strange Caucasian, and at the body over Bolan's shoulder.

"He died quickly," Matamba told the woman.

She gave a slight nod and waited quietly as Bolan placed her husband's corpse on the mat beside hers. Then she knelt and pulled the body to her. She sat there in silence, rocking slowly, waiting for the two soldiers to leave. She had seen many die and wouldn't cry until they were gone.

There was nothing they could do for her.

"We will have the funeral tomorrow," Matamba told her. He beckoned to Bolan. The two men moved quietly out into the dirt compound.

Angola was a poor country, engaged in a civil war for more than a quarter of a century, beginning when Moscow-supported insurgents took up a limited terrorist action against the Portuguese colonists. Then Cuban troops and more ComBloc "advisers" moved in, encouraged the war to spread, leaving the people poverty-stricken, hungry, often ill and without hope.

Bolan and Matamba passed two of the thatched huts and entered a third. A thin, handsome man about thirty years old, dressed in loose white peasant trousers and tunic, sat inside. His face was dark, his hair black and curly. He was holding a bowl that had been pounded out of scrap metal, maybe from a jeep fender. He stared at them, then resumed stirring with a long-handled wooden spoon.

"They say you are good," he told Bolan, his voice cool. "A good soldier, a good man. But you eat well, dress well, fight with the best weapons." He continued stirring the bowl, his eyes suspicious. "We wear tire sandals, use grass ropes, homemade ammo, patched rifles, anything we can get our hands on."

"It's wrong you should have to fight and live this way," Bolan agreed. "The government in Luanda intercepts a lot of the supplies sent to you—food, clothes, weapons. But it's true we don't send enough."

Both Angolans nodded, appreciating his honesty, but they still studied him. They had learned to be suspicious. The Marxist government they fought was propped up by rich international oil companies. With that kind of financial backing and the support of ComBloc nations, their enemy was powerful. To survive and fight on they had to be constantly wary.

"I need your help," Bolan said.

"Help? How can *we* help you?" Matamba scoffed.

"I need to talk to André Villela," Bolan said.

There was sudden silence. Matamba and the other man looked at each other. That wasn't a request they liked.

"Eat." The villager passed his bowl to Bolan to make a point.

Inside was *funj*, the congealed, gluey manioc porridge loaf on which Angola guerrillas survived. They had learned from experience that the food turned the stomachs of Westerners.

Bolan dug in expressionlessly, swallowed, then licked the sticky stuff from his fingers.

"Who is André Villela?" Matamba said as he watched Bolan eat.

"Your weapons contact," Bolan said. He ate another mouthful. "Probably the guy who nearly pulled off the Uzi steal a couple of weeks ago."

Their faces stretched in astonishment. "You know about that?"

"Some of your guys had a load of Uzis in their hands, maybe these very guns." Bolan nodded at the bundle he and Matamba had collected that night from the dead MPLA attackers. "But then the MPLA pulled off an ambush, killed more than forty of them and took out a Huey."

"How did you know?"

"I'm after the guys behind the original deal. A new weapons broker, and they don't care who they sell to. They sell to anyone with the cash. Capitalists, Communists, revolutionaries, hard-liners, it doesn't matter."

"And you think André can tell you who they are?"

Bolan smiled. The two guerrillas knew André Villela, which proved his intel was right. "Where is he?"

They frowned, realizing what they'd revealed, and exchanged a long, questioning look. "We would do this only for you," Matamba announced at last.

"I appreciate it," Bolan said simply. He put down the bowl of *funj*.

Matamba stood and gestured. Bolan followed him out of the hut and into the forest as the sun rose over the rim of the mountains, which seemed to smoke as the heat of the morning raised steam off the wet vegetation. They humped through a stand of Angolan tacula, huge timber trees, their wood blood-red. Birds sang from high branches, and the sun climbed in the sky. The forest was full of shadows, full of the possibility of another MPLA attack.

Bolan's weapons were ready, as always among friend and foe alike. He had no idea of their destination. "Where are we going?"

"You'll see," Matamba said.

As they moved, Bolan studied the terrain, his gaze sweeping over trees, boulders, and up the steep mountains almost on top of them. Matamba's pace quickened suddenly, and Bolan knew they were almost there.

"Where?"

Matamba smiled. "Here."

The FNLA's headquarters was a series of caves with an entrance low in the base of a mountain west of the village. Boulders and trees blocked the opening so that it could be seen only up close and straight on. From anywhere else in the surrounding hills, the three-foot-wide hole was invisible, the trails to it carefully camouflaged with bushes and vines.

Bolan and Matamba sat down in the large central chamber while guards watched from hidden posts outside on the hill. In the other chambers guerrillas quietly worked on their outmoded weapons, gambled and dozed.

Carlos Matamba laid his forehead on his crossed arms and seemed to sleep. Bolan waited patiently.

Then a tall, imposing older man walked in. Rail-thin, his face pasty, lined, he carried himself with arrogance.

He was followed by a smaller man of medium height, face tanned, as nondescript as the tall guy was impressive.

"André Villela," the tall guy said and extended his hand.

Bolan shook it. The grip was strong.

"Let's cut the crap," Bolan said and smiled. "You're not André Villela." He gestured at the other man, the one trying to pass himself off as an assistant. "He is."

CHAPTER SEVEN

Tension filled the guerrilla cave hidden in the Angolan mountain.

A flush reddened the neck of the tall, thin impostor. The smaller, athletic man with the tan face went rigid, his hands raising an old but polished M-16. Throughout the cave's chambers, soldiers reached for their weapons. The waiting was electric with danger.

"Lars Marlett sent me," Bolan said calmly, extending his hand to the real André Villela.

Villela blinked at the mention of the weapons expert. His gaze dropped to Bolan's hand. Slowly he extended his own. They shook.

"Sit," Villela invited, breaking the tension. "You have come to talk." He nodded to his assistant. "Fernando," he ordered.

Fernando went to the chamber's entrance and leaned against the stone wall, arms crossed. His narrow face turned hard, set immobile as concrete. The perfect sentry.

"You'll forgive my little charade?" Villela said politely, but his tone indicated Bolan's opinion was immaterial. "You are smart to have figured it out. We fool everyone. How did you know?"

"André Villela is an active man who lives outdoors with his troops. Fernando has the wrong coloring."

Villela laughed. "Hear that, Fernando? You're too damn white!"

Fernando roared, and suddenly his thin, lined face rearranged itself into a clown's mask. Fernando was a natural-born actor, the perfect impostor for Villela in offices and drawing rooms, seldom called upon to do the job in the field.

Villela turned back to Bolan. "You have a reputation."

"I want Boll."

"Personal?" Villela wondered. "Of course, with Mack Bolan, it's always personal. Do you think you can save the world?"

"Nothing happens when people just stand by and watch."

Villela took out a long, thin cigarette, hand-rolled. "Well said, Mr. Bolan, but it is not always so simple in the real world. Here we must make deals, compromise, settle for less than we want or need, for what we can get." Villela, the descendant of Portuguese settlers, lighted the cigarette. He was stalling.

Bolan nodded. "Sounds like you don't much like doing your business with companies like H. Boll, but sometimes you have to, eh? How hard is it doing business with Boll?"

"It has its ups and downs." Villela drew on his cigarette.

Bolan smiled. The guerrilla, intent on stalling, on not revealing too much, had just made a tactical error and revealed exactly what Bolan wanted to know. Villela not only knew enough to steal from the company, he'd made a buy or two as well. That meant he had a name or names, a phone number, maybe an address other than that of the sham Hamburg headquarters.

"So, you've done real business with Boll, not just one hijacking. You can tell me what I need to know."

"You didn't know?" Villela said, surprised. He appeared annoyed at his slip, but he quickly recovered. "My mistake."

"We all make them. Who's really behind H. Boll?"

"I never found out."

Villela's reply came so fast that Bolan believed him. "You've got to have a contact to do business with."

Villela smoked and watched Bolan. A small smile played on his lips as he sat silent in the cave headquarters.

"It's in your interest to tell me, to let me handle Boll." Bolan told him. "You may be doing good business with Boll now, but that's only because you're useful to them, you have the money to pay them. When you're no profit to them, that's the end, and if you cross them again they'll pull the plug. They'll get you if they have to, just like they got the Uzis back. You thought you had a steal, then there was a leak, and then they made sure the Uzis went to the hands that paid for them—the MPLA. You lost the shipment, a lot of good men, and if you hadn't come up quick with the cash to buy more guns you'd have lost Boll, too."

Villela exhaled smoke and went on staring at Bolan, but there was anger in his eyes now, and annoyance, and something else. Bolan thought it might be pride.

"It'll happen again," Bolan told him. "You'll run out of money, have to hustle your arms and supplies. If you try another steal, they'll kill you, ruin your operation, maybe end any chance your guys have to make this country a democracy. Boll can't afford to forgive a second time. Not in its business."

Villela's eyes flickered. Bolan's words were making sense, and the pride in his expression was taking over from the wariness and suspicion. "What do you want to know?"

"I want to know everything you know about the company."

Villela removed his cigarette with thumb and forefinger and flicked ash on the stone floor. He looked at it curiously, then back at Bolan. "You assume a great deal," he said. "You assume I know more than I do."

"Your intel is so good that you found out about the Soviet-Iran arms sale."

Again Villela was surprised. He fingered his weapon with rough hands, then glanced at Fernando to make sure the assistant was still there and alert. "Lars talked a lot. That was out of character." His eyes said that Bolan could have gotten his information somewhere else. From H. Boll. From the Soviets.

"He talked to me," Bolan said simply. "We knew each other and trusted each other, had no secrets when we needed help."

"So?" Villela put the cigarette to his mouth, leaving it to dangle from the corner of his broad lips. He squinted through the smoke, a muscular man with a will of steel. He was deciding whether he should, or could, trust Bolan as much as Lars Marlett had.

Suddenly the ground shook. Violent explosions, distant yet pounding, hammered Bolan's and the guerrillas' ears. Some of the freedom fighters fell to their knees, their hands over their ears with the pain of the shock waves. Chunks of rock dropped from the ceiling of the cave. The floor rolled like a small ship in a high and angry sea. Somewhere on the mountainside an avalanche of rocks thundered down, echoing inside the caves. Dust clogged the air.

The stunned FNLA guerrillas coughed, then grabbed their weapons. They stumbled through the dim caverns toward the cave's small entrance.

Bolan ran with them. Another blast and another shook the mountain. Now he could hear the distant roar of jet engines.

"Air attack!" Villela shouted at Bolan as they passed the tall, thin Fernando.

"That was no government ambush last night!" Bolan shouted.

"Boll? At your rendezvous?"

"What else?"

"And now they're here?"

"Or they alerted the MPLA."

Understanding widened Villela's eyes. Bolan was right. H. Boll, Ltd., was playing all sides against one another. They sold the arms to the Angola Marxists, helped arrange Villela's hijack, triple-crossed Villela by warning the MPLA, and now Boll was helping the MPLA to finish off Villela's group by locating their hideout and sending in jets!

And all the time they were selling arms to everyone.

"Hurry!" Villela said grimly, anger and hate in his voice toward the safe and secure "businessmen" who dealt only in death, believed in nothing but profit—profit for them.

They reached the exit where they had come in—and saw nothing but a thick wall of fallen rock still spewing dust. The opening had been blocked by the bombs and avalanche.

"Take the other passages," Villela commanded.

The guerrillas divided into groups, heading in different directions. They were so well organized Bolan knew they were operating under an evac plan. The cave would have other entrances and exits; no guerrilla group would set up headquarters where a raid could trap them. But using the emergency exits wouldn't be easy.

Soon Villela split off, leaving Matamba to lead others in a different direction through the maze of dark tunnels inside the bombed mountain.

"This way!" Villela shouted at Bolan as flashlights beamed on and torches blazed throughout the caverns. A guerrilla shoved an American-made flashlight into Bolan's hands.

Bolan, Fernando and a dozen freedom fighters followed André Villela. The Angolan leader weaved through passages and small caverns, past glistening stalactites and stalagmites, into the cool and quiet of the mountain's heart.

He moved fast now in the light cast by their flashlights, Bolan at his heels, the others panting behind. Bolan gratefully inhaled the clean, cool air far from the dust raised by the bombing raid at the cave's mouth.

They seemed to penetrate deeper and deeper into the mountain, and Bolan guessed that the exit would be far away on the other side, so distant from the base camp no government troops could connect it. The farther away, the safer, and the big guy hurried along with the others, confident now that Villela and his men would get them out in safety.

The soldiers slowed, and Bolan saw the glistening black surface of an underground lake. Some of the men hesitated as they started around the dark, almost invisible water. They stepped cautiously onto a narrow ledge. Ahead, where the ledge ended, Bolan could see the black hole of yet another cavern. The inky, bottomless lake water lapped below. The air was dank, the rock walls slimy.

No one spoke as they felt their way along the ledge. Their flashlight beams sliced erratically through the darkness, hitting the low ceiling, soaked up by the black lake, lost in the shadows across the warehouse-wide cavern. They couldn't hold the light beams to the narrow path, for they needed both hands to balance on the ledge.

In the distance behind them came the muffled sounds of the bombing, which was still going on. The ground trembled, and the black, icy lake water surged like the maw of some great monster.

And then Villela slipped.

It seemed a minor misstep, until suddenly the guerrilla leader was sliding like ice on a hot rail off the ledge and down the slimy cave wall.

Bolan grabbed for Villela's shoulder, his shirt, an arm, anything. Grabbed again, almost slipped off the treacherous ledge himself. And missed.

"*Comandante!*" Fernando cried out.

The compact, muscular leader bellowed with fear and frustration as he plunged down. His arms waved wildly over his ammo belts, and his eyes turned up white and terrified in the dim light as he disappeared into the depths.

"Comandante!" Fernando cried again as he peered into the jet-black water, coils of silver rolling away from where Villela had vanished.

The cries of horror echoed back from the walls, reverberating again and again in the great cavern.

But there was no answer.

The guerrillas knelt on the narrow ledge, leaned over and shone their lights into the lake. There was no splashing now, no sound to show where Villela had disappeared.

The men began to shrink back from the edge, crossing themselves and looking at one another. Fernando himself stared down at the silent water, then inched back.

"He doesn't swim," Fernando said, looking at Bolan. "He is dead."

Bolan struggled out of his equipment and kicked off his shoes. "There's still time, hurry!"

Fernando didn't move. "There is no way. Nothing can be done."

The tall, thin second-in-command was already heading toward the passage that led to the next cavern and escape from the deathtrap that this mountain had become.

"He'll float up, dammit," Bolan said. "If we dive now, we can find him."

Fernando shook his head. "The *comandante* carried too much ammo. Too much weight."

Bolan stared at the second-in-command, at all of them huddled away from the edge. "You're afraid. All of you! You're scared of monsters living in this hole."

The ground suddenly trembled again, and the guerrillas looked fearfully at Fernando, at Bolan, at one another. Afraid of the unseen bombs, afraid of being trapped inside the shaking mountain, afraid of some prehistoric man-eater lurking in the lake.

Bolan shook his head with disgust as the soldiers recoiled against the cave wall, avoided looking at the water below. He stripped quickly out of his blacksuit.

"Keep your flashlights aimed down there," he shouted. In rapid succession he directed the flashlights in a circle around where Villela had fallen in. "If any of you even think of leaving, I'll come back after you myself. You won't live long enough to be glad you've escaped this hellhole."

He glared at the men. They were brave enough to fight Marxist guns and bombs with the most rudimentary arms, but their culture was still primitive, and what they imagined—ghosts, spirits and lake monsters—could quickly become real to them and defeat them.

"Fernando," Bolan ordered, "that goes double for you. Take charge, and you'd better be here when I come up."

The tall, skinny guerrilla seemed to take a deep, shuddering breath, and drew himself up even taller. "Yes, sir!"

The men watched in awe as Bolan leaped off into water so black it seemed to have no surface. As he fell toward the dark lake, he felt a qualm himself. What could be there under the inky surface? He didn't know, but he had to find André Villela, and alive. Villela held the key to H. Boll.

CHAPTER EIGHT

"Report."

Philip Carlisle drummed his manicured fingers on the big walnut desk in his opulent office as he snapped at his chief assistant. Behind him, through the floor-to-ceiling window, Johannesburg bustled with noonday fervor, doing business around the world in gold, diamonds and securities. The arrogance in his voice and in everything he did came from knowing that a good part of that business was influenced simply by the existence of his powerful company, Carlisle Mining.

Michael Jones didn't seem to notice the arrogant tone of his boss. He closed the door and sauntered to a lounge chair. "Report on what—Houston? Maybe the Saudi Arabian deal? How about your safari with Manucher Ghorbanifar? You can bet he'll come, dragging three wives, six concubines and a telex machine. It'll be the social event of the continent." Jones dropped his hard six-foot body into Carlisle's soft leather lounge chair. "Or perhaps you'd like to know the latest on your illustrious brothers?"

Philip Carlisle glared while his number one employee's restless eyes scanned the penthouse as if he wished it were the grassy veld. Only out there was Jones really happy.

"Don't push it too far," Philip warned coldly.

Jones said nothing. He returned his gaze briefly to Philip, acknowledged the threat, then directed his attention to his own concerns, as if nothing had been said to him.

Jones's lack of fear fascinated Philip. That fascination, and Jones's unique skills and usefulness, were the only reasons Philip allowed the former soldier to get away with his insolence. "Where the hell is Bolan?" the magnate demanded. "Is he dead?"

"Not yet. He's in Angola."

"You let the bastard get that far!"

"A bastard, maybe," Jones agreed with a shrug. "But he's also one hell of a soldier."

With the billions of dollars from his gold mines in South Africa's Witwatersrand Reef—and his various private business dealings that only Jones knew about— Philip Carlisle liked to remind himself that he financed kings and named presidents. Chairmen of international corporations sought his advice and support. Movie stars wanted the prestige of having their photographs taken with him on one of his famous safaris. He had power, influence and fame.

Now Mack Bolan threatened it all.

"Where's the famous Michael Jones touch? You idiot, this is costing me a fortune!"

"I told you getting Mack Bolan would be tough."

"What in hell am I paying you for—pansy jobs?"

"You're paying me," Jones said evenly, "because I do this work better than anyone else, and you damn well know it. As for your question—the MPLA is bombing the hell out of a secret FNLA hideout right now."

"So?"

"So Mack Bolan's inside. He won't come out alive."

Philip Carlisle smiled, then laughed aloud. "Now that's more like it."

AT SEVEN A.M. IN CARACAS the sun was up and the mild warmth that characterized much of lush Venezuela was spreading through the valley of the Rio Guaire. The serrated skyline rose in steel and glass along the Guaire, once a scenic river flowing through clean, grassy banks, now dark, polluted and girded with concrete.

Caracas was one of the fastest-growing metropolises in the world. It was a hectic, traffic-clogged nightmare by the middle of the day, but a glittering, inviting valley at night.

Because of Venezuela's rich oil fields, incredible wealth had poured into Caracas, demanding new houses, offices, skyscrapers, warehouses, roads, shopping centers, government buildings and monuments. As Caracas burst at the seams, construction boomed, and most of the building market went to Roberto Carlisle's Cordoba Construcciones S.A., founded just ten years before. Now Cordoba Construcciones had spread beyond Venezuela to Brazil, Colombia, even Argentina. The rowdy city had made Roberto personally rich—and discontented. The only thing that would satisfy him now was to run Carlisle International itself.

"Louisa, send in Harter." Roberto Carlisle released the intercom button and waited for the first of the day's long line of employees and favor seekers who waited outside his office door. This was Latin America, and Roberto—born Robert Cabot Carlisle on Boston's posh

Beacon Hill—had learned to do business the Latin American way.

Roberto greeted Harter politely as the mercenary entered the office, then waited until he stood in front of the vast, glass-topped desk.

"You have news?" Roberto asked.

Harter, lean and craggy, held his straw bowler in his hands. "Yes, Roberto. It is as you suspected. Your brother, Philip, tracked Mack Bolan from Paris to Sweden."

"And Philip's men?"

"Dead. Bolan killed them."

"When they tried to capture him?"

"Philip sent them to kill Bolan."

"Philip's an idiot," Roberto said. "A man like Bolan will have information, be useful. He can be killed later."

Harter bowed his head in agreement. It wasn't his place to say aloud what they both knew—that Philip Carlisle thought too much of himself and Carlisle Mining, of his power and importance.

"And now?" Roberto prompted.

"We have lost Bolan, but I expect intel any moment. Our new man will report."

"You're sure of this one?"

"He hates Philip and loves money. He wants out." Harter smiled smoothly, his craggy features rearranging themselves into mock kindness. "As you know, and as our inside man knows, it is dangerous for anyone to leave Philip. But our man also knows that with you he will find sufficient cash and appreciation to make the risk worthwhile."

Roberto nodded, pleased with his new employee. Harter was a good man who knew his business. Too bad Philip wasn't as smart. Philip was a blowhard who believed the globe hungered for his attention, his wisdom. Hungered just to be seen with him. But Roberto knew that people took his brother's favors and then laughed at him, though never to his face. They feared Philip's power and cruelty.

"Tell me what this new inside man reports," Roberto said.

Harter related the events in Paris where Hal Brognola and Bolan had met, and where Bolan had killed Philip's agent from Puerto Rico.

"In the hotel hallway?" Roberto said. "There was no one around, and still the guy couldn't get Bolan?"

"We are not sure, but we think he tried to surprise Bolan. Bolan must have heard him, maybe surprised him first."

"Bolan has that reputation, always on alert," Roberto said, growing more interested in the man he would someday order killed.

There was a silence in the office high above the bustle and noise of Caracas. Harter's face revealed nothing but the detachment of a professional soldier making his report. Roberto Carlisle's expression showed he was torn between anger at the loss to a Carlisle company, and amusement at his brother's failure.

"Bolan has eliminated several of my brother's finest," Roberto said, his voice full of irony. Philip had yet to learn that throwing money at a problem was no guarantee of a solution. "Tell me when our contact reports in. I want to know where Mack Bolan is, what Philip's plans are."

"Of course." Harter bowed and stepped back.

"You've done well," Roberto said.

Harter's head drooped even lower, acknowledging the praise, then he raised himself to his full height and strode to the door.

As Roberto watched him leave, he thought about the company he'd built—Cordoba Construcciones S.A., of the difficult early days when Carlisle International's name and influence had been a major factor in keeping him in business as he'd fought for contracts, eliminated competitors, paid bribes, to the *caraqueños* who ran this wealthy old city.

Roberto had arrived from Boston with no local connections, but now he was a full member of Carcas's Spanish elite, personally running a multimillion-dollar company with spreading influence throughout Central and South America. This achievement had impressed his father, David Carlisle, who ran Cordoba's parent company, Carlisle International, a multinational cartel with subsidiaries around the globe. The notice was exactly what Roberto had wanted. Someday his father would retire, or die, and Roberto would be ready to succeed him.

His younger brother, Philip, had chosen an easier route. When their cousin, Victor Carlisle, had died, opening up the presidency of Carlisle Mining, Philip had stepped in and grabbed it, propelled by their father's influence. Roberto had often wondered whether the bullet that killed Victor during a family shooting party had been an accident, or one of Philip's more creative solutions.

If so, then it was the high point of Philip's lackluster career of small-time outside deals and petty pilfering from the family arms business. He had walked into a ready-made, flourishing company. Carlisle Mining was one of Carlisle International's oldest subsidiaries, founded by their great-grandfather in the late 1800s shortly after the first gold strike on Witwatersrand Reef. Old Angus had had vision, and a series of sons and grandsons had benefited from it.

But now, because of the threat of Mack Bolan's penetration, their father, David Carlisle, had ordered all subsidiary companies to curtail their outside activities until Bolan was stopped. And the older man had made it clear that he wanted Bolan stopped fast. By one or the other of them.

The order didn't do much harm to Roberto's operations, but it would greatly affect Philip. Roberto's younger brother looked beyond Carlisle Mining for activities to make him feel smart and superior, to add some excitement to the boring day-to-day management of a company that essentially ran itself.

Philip would be sure to resent their father's orders, and to become overeager to get Mack Bolan. Then he would make mistakes. This was a weakness Roberto intended to exploit as far as he could.

"Louisa," Roberto said into the intercom, "send in Malva."

Malva Gomez was slight and dark, with smooth skin and round hips. She had worked for Roberto since his arrival in Caracas, more than earning her way with her uncanny ability, when called upon, to fade into any office's woodwork or to become vital to an influential bed.

Now she stood in front of his glass-topped desk, her eyes flashing, still trying to seduce him after all these years.

"Roberto," she greeted him, flinging her long black hair over her shoulder. "What a pity to waste a body like that." Brazenly she looked him up and down.

He laughed. "Someday, Malva. When I have time."

Roberto thought of his wife, a Spanish aristocrat with ice water in her veins, who resided in their suburban home, and of the series of women who kept him company in his downtown apartment. If Malva waited long enough, she might win.

"Promises, promises," she said, pouting.

"You don't have enough work?"

"With you it would be pure pleasure."

They laughed together.

"You've brought me news?" he said at last.

"Of course, Roberto. Do you remember that secretary at Boll's relay in Paris whose American lover was killed when his car was bombed?"

"I remember."

"He wasn't only American—" she paused for drama "—he was also a Fed. He worked with the Justice Department."

"Trying to penetrate Boll?" Roberto said.

"Looks like it," she said, pleased with herself and her discovery.

"That makes three then," he said slowly. "The woman who was tapping the KGB phone line in West

Berlin, and the kid tapping our contact's phone in Cartagena, were agents, too." No wonder Mack Bolan was on the warpath. Three federal agents were dead, all within a week, and all had been investigating H. Boll. "Looks like someone's doing us a favor, getting rid of agents."

"Justice wouldn't look at it that way. And I don't think your father does."

Roberto swiveled in his chair and fixed his hard gaze on the beautiful woman in front of him. "The Justice Department doesn't matter, and someday neither will my father. Right now it could be a big opportunity for us. This Mack Bolan seems to make my father nervous, even scares him." Roberto shook his head in a kind of wonder. "I didn't think anything could scare the old man, but Bolan seems to, and that may be our chance. Think you can find out who's our benefactor?"

Malva smiled, showing her small, white teeth. "Love to."

The intercom buzzed. Roberto pushed the button and watched Malva. She emanated sex and violence at the same time.

"Mr. Harter is back," Louisa reported.

Roberto raised his eyebrows. "Send him in."

"Roberto," Malva chided. "I have to leave so soon?"

"Sorry, but business is business."

"I know!" She flung the words over her shoulder as she flounced toward the door. "But what about love?"

She frowned at Emilio Harter as he opened the door, then she stalked through.

Harter closed the door softly, his eyes showing no interest in what had happened in the room while he was gone. He strode toward Roberto's desk.

"The new man called?" Roberto asked.

"Bolan is in Angola," Harter said. "The MPLA is bombing a mountain where he is hidden."

"Will he survive?"

"It doesn't look like it."

Roberto swiveled in his chair and stared at the city through the big window. Already central Caracas was congested. The city suffered from an overloaded phone system, poor drainage in the streets, lousy garbage collection and occasional water shortages. Yet it struggled on valiantly, bustling, growing.

"Damn!" Roberto Carlisle said. "If Philip kills him, the rest of us will look bad." He went on gazing out the window. "And a pity, too. Bolan is a worthy opponent. I would have liked to kill him myself."

IN PARIS, the window of David Carlisle, Jr.'s, quiet office faced the pearl-white dome of the majestic basilica of Sacre-Coeur atop Paris's tallest hill—emerald Montmartre, the Mount of Martyrs.

It was ten a.m. Already tourists were riding up the narrow, winding roads on double-decker sight-seeing buses, crowding the elegant church's stone steps for mass photography sessions, and scrambling up and down the famous hill where artists and revolutionaries of all persuasions had lived, worked, caroused and died, helping to make Paris the center of the civilized world for much of the nineteenth and twentieth centuries.

David Junior reflected on the power and importance of history as he drank his morning *café filtre*. He had just finished reading the stack of morning reports that detailed the vast world of his Société Fabrique de Guerre et Cie, a major subsidiary of Carlisle International, and one of the world's largest legitimate manufacturers of armaments, ammunition and matériel wholesaled and retailed to governments, licensed dealers and private citizens.

David liked to look at Montmartre and remember that so much of Carlisle International had started here in Paris. Because the historic old city had opened her arms to all political ideologies, she had also provided the freedom for presidents and generals to borrow the money to buy the weapons that made war possible—and profitable.

Banking and arms dealing would always be the two most powerful trades in the world, and Carlisle International boasted more than its share of both. Banking had made the Rothschilds, arms had made the Krupps, and both had made the Carlisles.

For twenty years David Junior had been president of Société Fabrique. He had inherited a good company, then shrewdly built it into a great company. He had streamlined and made efficient his original antiquated holdings, acquired smaller manufacturing plants, established new state-of-the-art ones, constantly built outlets for sale and resale of the finest available weapons.

He sensed that soon his diligence and hard-won ability to act at the right moment would pay off. Unconsciously his fingers riffled the pages of one of the reports he'd just read. It disclosed recent unusual events occurring both outside and within Carlisle companies.

Something strange was happening in Carlisle International. It wasn't just the attempted penetration by an apparently well-known former soldier and agent named Mack Bolan, who was now trapped in some mountain in Angola and might already be dead. It wasn't just the executions of three American federal agents and the unknown benefactor who had killed them, apparently to stop their investigations of H. Boll, Ltd. And it wasn't just the stupid ambition, arrogance and avariciousness of his two younger brothers, who both hungered to run Carlisle International. After all, in the end that was what he wanted, too.

No, it was something more, something bigger.

War?

David Carlisle, Jr., smiled, his handsome face and cold eyes calculating the odds. War could be good. But if not war, then what?

He was tempted to call his father and pump him for information. But that would be a weakness. No, he would wait to see whether Mack Bolan survived and could be located and made to answer.

If not, then someone else would eventually lead him to the answer to his question—what was going on inside Carlisle International and all its far-flung operations, known and unknown? Something about H. Boll, yes, but more. What was it? And who was responsible?

IN SPRAWLING, noisy nighttime Tokyo two men sat in an austere room with rice-paper walls and braided mats on the floor. They drank aged brandy and watched the city lights spread through the darkness to encircle the harbor like a string of sparkling jewels. There was nothing in their Western dress to identify who was who, yet there was no doubt that the younger man was the boss.

"Philip is the impetuous one," David Carlisle, Sr., said. "Greedy and sometimes foolhardy, but he gets results."

"He likes action," the older man agreed.

"Robert is levelheaded, ambitious," Carlisle, Sr., said of his son Roberto, creator of Cordoba Construcciones S.A.

"And he will gamble on himself," the other added.

"And David? David is the mountain, yes. He has learned to wait until the moment is right, and then he conquers."

"But he likes to make his own rules."

The two swirled their brandy and sipped it thoughtfully. The older man finally glanced at his employer. "What will happen?"

"We will watch. If Mack Bolan dies, we have an answer. If he survives, then the game continues."

They sat in companionable silence, watched the glittering harbor lights in the distance.

CHAPTER NINE

André Villela's guerrillas watched in terror as Bolan leaped into the underground lake and disappeared. They were so afraid that they couldn't look at one another. The Angolan partisans stared down at the inky water as it exploded into froth and waves that surged away into the darkness of the giant cavern. They leaned forward, slowly, reluctantly, with their flashlights aimed below as Bolan had ordered, their frightened eyes searching the black surface for any sign of the Executioner or their *comandante*. But they could see nothing.

Their fear radiated in the pitch-dark cave. The flashlights they trained obediently on the water trembled as the mountain that surrounded them shuddered with new explosions. The headquarters they had once thought secret, invincible, was still under attack.

The cavern echoed with the bombing, and dirt and small rocks rained down on them as a series of deadly HE bombs and air-to-ground missiles struck the mountain directly above them. One delayed-fuse rocket seemed to bore deep into the mountain, loosing an avalanche of larger rock that churned the surface of the black underground lake.

It was too much.

How long would they have to wait for Bolan to reappear before the whole mountain collapsed and buried them? How long before the mountain crushed them in a giant grave where no one would ever find them, or before the head of some terrifying monster reared up from the depths with Bolan's body crushed in its jaws? They knew Bolan was dead, that their leader was lost forever.

First one, then another, took a tentative step toward the black maw of the next cavern, where escape was uncertain but at least more likely than in this dank cemetery.

"Stop!" Fernando ordered. His voice reverberated with strength in the musty air.

But the men knew him too well, knew his acting and pretenses. He was not the *comandante*. The frightened guerrillas were much too scared by the bombing, the dark caves, the black and lurking menace of the underground lake to be stopped by the command of a man without real power inside him. They took more steps toward the mouth of the tunnel that led out of the vast cavern.

Fernando pulled out his pistol and aimed it at the line of guerrillas. "The American must have the light from our flashlights!" he shouted. "If he is to have a chance to find André—dead or alive—we cannot leave our posts!"

The men looked at the lake, at Fernando and at the escape route beyond.

MACK BOLAN SLICED down through the inky water of the lake. It was cool, silent, deceptively soothing, and it wrapped around him like a shroud. Sheltered as it was in the bowels of the mountain, its temperature probably varied by no more than five degrees any time in the year.

The flashlights above penetrated only a few yards. Bolan's gaze swept the gloom. Granite particles thousands of years old floated and danced, disturbed by the bombing far away outside, by the fall of André Villela and now by Bolan's dive. Small particles, even large chunks of stone, too, were dislodged by the explosions above, but Bolan paid them scant attention.

He had little time, and Villela even less.

The Executioner circled wide, then swam along the wall, through murky pools. His lungs grew tight. The water was colder now.

Dim, shadowy rocks jutted out from the cave wall. Villela could have hit his head on one, knocked himself unconscious. But where was he now?

Too much time had passed already. Had Fernando been right? Had the weight of Villela's equipment dragged him down to his death?

Suddenly the icy water went completely black. No light above him. Nothing.

Where were the guerrillas?

Bolan grabbed at the water, pulled himself up, up. Damn them! He needed their lights to spot Villela.

Breaking the surface, he gulped the cold, dank air of the cavern. His eyes searched for the guerrillas. Before he could call out the lake suddenly seemed to grab him and slam him against the rocks.

Pain shot through him. Darkness cloaked him. He struggled, almost unconscious from the smashing into the wall, caught up by a powerful, rushing current of water. He was dragged under the dark surface of the lake. Alone.

FERNANDO CRUZ, André Villela's second-in-command, was a man who often lied to himself. He told himself lies to make his life seem better, to escape the hunger and poverty of his people, to escape his guilt. After all, he ate regularly while the villagers and guerrillas often went to bed without food in their bellies.

Some days Fernando didn't eat. Comandante Villela would order him to eat, but Fernando would look at the food and feel sick. He felt even sicker when he and the *comandante* went to expensive restaurants for the meets to make their arms deals. Restaurants where every day enough food was thrown away to feed a whole village of his people for a month.

So he made jokes about the rich Europeans who ordered snails at the fancy restaurants, who covered good chicken with smelly sauces, who got fat and bloated and died young from the bad diet. He made everyone laugh, and then he laughed, too, and forgot.

They were little lies. They didn't matter. And they made him feel better. Everyone admired him because he was entertaining.

He lied, too, when he pretended to be Comandante Villela. He was tall and scrawny, while Villela was of medium height, sturdy, muscular. But it was necessary for Villela to be protected. Only Villela could negotiate the deals; only he knew the contacts, knew the dangerous alleys and the best hotels where the contacts could be found, knew how to get the money or how to pretend to have the money.

The *comandante* was a good man, reliable, but he carried all the important information in his head. No one else knew what Villela knew, and so he had to be kept safe. Villela had to be protected, and now he had to be saved by the American Bolan and Fernando.

All these thoughts and emotions flooded Fernando in a split second as he stood on the narrow ledge above the bottomless lake with his pistol aimed at his own men. He could sense their fear growing—his fear growing— as Bolan and the *comandante* failed to appear where the flashlights played across the black surface. He wanted to lie again, to lie now to himself. He wanted to pretend they were brave, that they wouldn't run.

That *he* wouldn't run.

So he stood uncertain, the pistol in his hand as first one, then another of the guerrillas, moved toward him and the cavern beyond. If they were terrified enough, they would run him down, throw him into the lake. He couldn't let them. Mack Bolan's threats came back to echo in his head.

And then suddenly, as if for the first time, he understood. His lies fell away. He had to save Comandante Villela because Villela helped their people. He must be brave, not for himself, but for their hungry, impoverished people. It was that simple.

Strength surged through Fernando. He straightened and quickly raised the pistol. He pointed it at the half-dozen guerrillas who edged toward him.

"Stop!" he ordered.

They looked at one another, at the lake and back at him. Again they moved forward.

"Stop!" Fernando bellowed.

They rushed him, one behind the other, running, pushing.

He fired.

They panicked. They trampled onward and flung him against the cave wall. His shot went wild, smashed the echoing stone wall somewhere across the lake and ricocheted.

Fernando lost his balance and slipped down the wall. Pain throbbed in his shoulder and arm. The spooked guerrillas scrambled and slid over him. Fernando's head spun. He turned and watched with half-closed eyes as their shadowy figures vanished in the dark of the next cavern. Their lights bounced off the stone ledge and walls. And then they were gone.

He felt he was going to be sick. He leaned over the ledge, waited, but no vomit came. He sat back, dazed and confused in the now silent darkness of the great cavern.

Then he remembered the *comandante* and Bolan. He had a job to do! He grabbed his flashlight and pointed it toward the water where Bolan and Villela had disappeared. For an instant he thought he heard someone or something break the surface and gasp for air. He swung the light beam. There was nothing. Only a faint spreading ripple on the black surface where something might have been.

He went on shining his flashlight alone in the cavern.

It was a feeble beam in the vast darkness.

SEMICONSCIOUS, Mack Bolan seemed to ride the speeding gunboat through the swampy Vietnamese waters. The war smells of smoke and burned flesh singed his memory. Death. Punji sticks tipped in poison. Booby traps hidden on corpses. Mines disguised as flowers in the lush swamps.

His head ached and pounded. It slammed against something again. And again. A low-ceilinged passageway the boat was racing through?

He gasped—and swallowed water.

Death by drowning.

More death.

His own?

The vessel sped on.

He tried to cough up water, but only swallowed more. His lungs were bursting. He needed air. What was happening?

He struggled to make sense of it until, at last, the pieces suddenly fell into place.

Water.

Speed.

He wasn't riding on a boat; he was caught by the strong current of an underground river that streamed through the lake in the cave!

Again his head smashed stone, and he realized he was bumping the top of some tunnel the current had carried him into. There had to be pockets in the rock. And where there were pockets there was air.

His eyes snapped open but he could see nothing in the pitch-black water. He clawed his way up and rolled over on his back, his mouth high. He parted his lips. Water rushed in. He gagged and sputtered, but he forced himself to stay up. There had to be air trapped at the top of the tunnel. There had to be. Somewhere.

Again he steadied himself in the current, his mouth pointed up at the ceiling. This time he let his body flow with the rushing water, no longer fighting it.

His lips brushed the cave ceiling. He was patient. At last he felt the first sign—algae. And then the sudden insubstantial dryness that meant trapped air.

He opened his lips and gasped. Air! He breathed deeply, filling his lungs.

And was once more covered with water.

Again he rose to the ceiling and waited for the algae, and the air. He inhaled the stale oxygen, feeling energy and purpose return.

He swam with the stream, not knowing where it was taking him and not able to do anything about it. He stroked with the current to his unknown destination, hoping that he would find the surface before he needed air again.

And then, instead of black, the water on one side of him turned murky brown. It had to be some distant light. It wasn't much to go on, and if he turned he could lose the ceiling and the air pockets, but he had to take the chance.

He pulled against the current, and then suddenly was caught up in it again as it swung to the side. He floundered helplessly. It was going where he wanted, but it was so strong it would crash him against the wall of the tunnel. It might kill him yet.

He fought the stream, pulling himself up, away, exhausting his strength. Then his head was out of the water. There were no rocks walls anywhere. He was floating in the current across another lake.

He took a ragged breath, then another, and looked around. There was a distant pinpoint of light. He rode the current toward it.

VILLELA AWOKE to underground darkness and a red haze of pain. He lay sprawled on gravel, small waves licking at his feet. He was wet, shivering with cold. He ached everywhere. His clothes were torn, his weapons were gone, but the bandoliers across his chest still held cartridges.

A combat veteran, he was instantly alert in spite of the pain. But there was no sound other than the quiet lapping of the waves. The bombing seemed to have stopped. He looked around, trying to figure out where he was, what had happened.

This cave was dark, but not as dark as the other. There was light at the far end, a small but distinct shaft of natural light.

Sunlight. An exit.

No matter how small the exit he would get out! He would make it bigger, escape this hellhole.

He tried to sit up, and groaned. It was too soon. The darkness swept over him again as he fell back, unconscious.

THE POWERFUL CURRENT of the underground stream threw Bolan up onto the flat gravel beach. He scrambled away from the water and sank to his hands and knees. As he inhaled great gusts of air, his gaze found and quickly locked onto the thin shaft of sunlight in the distance.

There was an opening.

He nodded to himself, and again his steely eyes went to work. If the current had carried him here, perhaps...

And then he saw it—a dark, man-sized lump on the beach.

"Villela!"

Was the *comandante* alive? Bolan hurried to the fallen man and felt for the pulse in his neck. The beat was there, steady. Luck had been with both of them. Sometimes luck—and knowing how to take advantage of it—was all that stood between victory and defeat, right and wrong.

He picked up Villela and slung him over his shoulder. The unconscious man moaned. He'd probably hit his head on a rock when he'd fallen into the lake and had then got caught in the same current that had captured Bolan. Only Villela, unconscious, had been caught and carried sooner and faster, and so had survived but in worse shape than the Executioner.

Bolan carried Villela across the quiet underground beach toward the sunlight. He passed rocks, boulders and old logs carried by the underground stream and then cast up onto the shore of the cave.

As he approached the light, its color turned from yellow to white. The air freshened, and welcome heat spread from the opening in the cave's roof. The hole was about a foot in diameter and twelve feet from the floor. Bolan could see the blue afternoon sky outside and hear a strong wind whistling through a forest. There

were no birds' songs. Not yet. The bombing had
stopped too recently for that. Sometimes it took a long
time for the birds to return.

Bolan laid Villela on the ground against a boulder.
Nearby he found a thick branch bleached white long
ago by the sun. He pushed the branch up through the
opening and rubbed it along the perimeter. Sand and
rocks and leaves and chunks of clay hurtled down.

Bolan ducked and jumped out of the way. He went in
again from an angle, working the branch around the
perimeter. The heavy debris spilled to the cave's floor,
missing Bolan, but sand and dust sprayed and clogged
his nose.

As the cloud of dust and debris rose in the cave, Villela, still unconscious, coughed.

Bolan moved the unconscious man to the side, then
returned to work the branch until the hole was en-
larged to three feet.

He rolled a boulder beneath the opening, stood on it
and felt around the perimeter. It continued to crumble;
it wouldn't hold his weight, and was sure to collapse. He
needed more support.

He pushed the branch through the hole, laid it outside on top and across the hole so that each end rested
on at least two feet of soil. Then he tugged on the center of the branch. It creaked and more dust sprayed
down, but it held and the sides of the hole didn't dis-
integrate any further.

Bolan took off Villela's cartridge belts and fastened
them together in a circle. He slid the circle under Villela's arms and carried the freedom fighter to the hole. He
propped him up against the boulder, fastened Villela's

waist belt to the ring of cartridge belts and again stood on the boulder.

Bolan grabbed the branch. Without touching the perimeter, he swung himself up and out through the narrow hole. Sunshine bathed him, warming his cold flesh. He was free of the dark interior of the mountain and the silent underground waters.

The warrior squatted above the opening, listened for any sound of aircraft or gunfire and surveyed the sweeping panorama of the damaged mountainside and the valley below.

Wind gusted through the trees, carrying heat, dust and the faint stink of HE. Brown columns of smoke billowed up from the thick forest. Naked black spots on the mountainside smoked where the high explosives had hit.

There were no jets in the sky, and no sound of firing anywhere. But the planes would be back. There had been two passes so far: the jump-off attack and the follow-up when he was under the water. The mop-up was still to come. His estimate said he had five minutes, tops.

Judging by the sun's position, they were on the east side of the mountain now. There was no village in sight, no movement, no sign of either life or danger.

It was time to bring up Villela. He hoped he could get the unconscious leader up and away safely before the jets returned for the coup de grace.

Bolan pulled the waist belt slowly across the tree branch, to protect the crumbling perimeter of the hole. The cartridge belts tightened under Villela's armpits.

Bolan continued to pull smoothly, his muscles straining at the deadweight of the unconscious man.

First Villela's head, torso, then his legs rose. At last he dangled like a rag doll from the heavy bleached tree branch that lay across the hole.

Bolan's muscles ached, but he continued to haul the man up. The ground began to give beneath his feet. Soil crumbled. He had to get Villela out of there fast before the land around the hole collapsed.

Then he heard the jets. Coming in at eleven o'clock, and he didn't have five minutes. Maybe not one minute.

Sweat poured down his face. He walked backward away from the hole, dragging Villela at the end of the belts.

Earth fell into the opening. Villela's head appeared, covered with dirt. More land sheared off.

The jets were louder, lower, no higher than nine o'clock

Bolan ran backward, dragging the unconscious weapons buyer. Soil, rocks and debris collapsed with a roar. But Villela was free!

Bolan strode to him, picked him up and carried him from the treacherous area above the cave as the jets roared in on the far side of the mountain, the HE pounding until the ground shook under Bolan.

Staggering, almost naked, the big guy slipped and slid down the rocky slope until he found a narrow hollow deep enough to have trees growing from the bottom. He deposited Villela under a tree in the gully. The guy was still breathing.

Bolan wiped an arm across his eyes and looked up as the first bomb hit his side of the mountain. Would there be paratroopers after this last run, choppers coming in?

CHAPTER TEN

The private helicopter descended noisily to the concrete pad on the mountain ridgetop as small animals scattered in panic through the thick underbrush. The tall ponderosa pines and Douglas firs that surrounded the landing area shuddered and whipped in the rotors' heavy draft.

In the passenger seat Brigadier General Arnold Capp looked out on the broad sweep of spectacular scenery. Here in rural Montana the air was diamond clear and the mountains pleated into fertile, timbered valleys of rare beauty. He never saw this western country without sensing what it meant to be free and an American, how vital it was to keep that freedom for all good Americans, now and in the future.

When they landed, Capp clapped his pilot on the back and gave him the thumbs-up sign. The general jumped from the chopper into the brisk autumn air, ducked and ran out of the rotor stream as the chopper took off again and swept away to the south and east to the private landing field of one of the patriotic ranchers who supported Capp's worldwide operations.

Then he turned and strode toward the petite form of Janet Lovelace, who was waiting eagerly for him astride her palomino, the reins of the big roan she had given him in her hands.

This was her husband's vast ranch, where his family for generations had run cattle and harvested timber in the shadow of the majestic Mission Mountains. Now Oliver Lovelace was the junior U.S. senator from Montana. He spent more time in the drawing rooms and cocktail lounges of Washington and New York than in the saddle riding the broad lands of his family ranch. The ranch was run by hired help who knew Janet better than her absent husband.

Ollie Lovelace was in Europe now, with the President at a summit meeting of NATO allies to discuss terrorism and the international arms trade. Then he would embark on a sixty-day fact-finding tour of the Middle East. It was an opportunity neither Capp nor Janet could resist.

Janet had a plain, round face, but such intense energy radiated from it that few men noticed her lack of beauty. Instead, they were captured by her eyes and mannerisms. She had a demanding, sexual look that attracted men. She knew this, and enjoyed it. She wore clothes to enhance it. Today she was dressed in a skin-tight brown leather shirt and riding jeans.

"Baby," the general whispered huskily in her ear as he swung into the saddle of the roan. He leaned and drew her to him, their horses rubbing flanks under the high pines.

"I've missed you," she said, and looked deep into his eyes.

Warmth spread through his limbs at the promises in those dark eyes. There were still times when Capp found it hard to believe that this woman was his now, that she wanted him, that she saw him as strong and desirable even at his age. "I'm almost as old as your father," he'd told her the first time they'd gone to bed back in Washington. "No one is that old," she'd laughed, and then had become serious, her eyes intense on his face in the dim hotel room. "You're strong, Arnie, you're doing something about the evil in the world, not just talking and talking like Ollie and the other old women in Congress. You're attacking, not sitting around waffling and wondering if you have the right while the Communists take over everywhere." That had been the beginning; now she was beside him astride her horse under the tall trees of her husband's ranch.

"Come on," he said roughly. "Let's get out of here."

Ruts from winter storms and spring thaws lined the dirt road as they cantered toward the ranch house. They rode a quarter mile through the quiet forest where an occasional deer peered out from behind a big tree. Beavers had dammed the stream above the lake where cutthroat and rainbow trout were stocked. Fishing on the ranch was excellent, and so was hunting for deer, elk, moose and antelope.

Janet was a crack shot. The general had watched with pride the first time he'd seen her bring down an antelope with one clean shot. She was remarkable—beautiful, loyal, smart and as at home in the saddle and behind a rifle as he was. Perfect for him in every way.

"I think we should let the world know about us," the general said, watching her determined profile as they rode up to the main house, dismounted and gave their horses to the ranch hands who came to take them.

"I know, darling. Don't I just wish we could?"

"I'd take care of Martha for life," he vowed. "She'd have nothing to complain about. A quiet divorce, and then you and I could have a simple wedding. Maybe in the chapel at West Point."

"I'd like that."

As they walked toward the two-story shingled house, he began to hope that this time she'd actually agree. Not only would he have her and be free of Martha's worried remarks about his new operations, but David Carlisle would be his father-in-law and the influence and power of Carlisle International would be behind him permanently. With power like that there was no limit to what he could do!

But Janet sighed and stopped on the porch. She looked up at him and wrapped her arms around his thick bull neck.

"My darling, I can't do that to Ollie. He's up for election next fall. A divorce now..." Her voice trailed off, and Capp filled in the information they both knew.

Divorces were no longer the kiss of electoral death they had once been, but there was always the chance that the press might discover Janet's affair with Arnold Capp...or the true nature of Oliver Lovelace's promiscuity. How could the Montana voters return to office the young senator they believed represented them so well—a savvy, virile cowboy who always got the girl, the legislation and the votes—after they found out he couldn't hold his wife, and didn't really want to?

No. Oliver Lovelace had been cuckolded, hoodwinked, fooled. If a senator couldn't manage—couldn't satisfy—his wife, then how could he be man enough to manage—and satisfy—a state, a country? That's what they'd say in Montana. Not aloud, not in public, but in their homes, in the bunkhouses and saloons and private clubs where men still gathered. And if they knew the rest, Ollie Lovelace might not even be allowed to stay in the state.

Son of a governor, inheritor of millions, the last male in his proud pioneer family, young Senator Lovelace would lose his second term and probably wouldn't even be able to get elected dogcatcher. But then, the general decided again, as he had when Janet first told him her husband's secret, Lovelace didn't deserve to serve in the U.S. Senate's august body.

General Capp studied Janet. She was good, pure. Every time he looked at her, he wanted her.

She had confided in him, had told him about Oliver Lovelace's abuses, about the secret life he led. Lovelace went on lecture tours so that he'd be able to stay in strange towns where he could have his boyfriends meet him discreetly. There were rumors in Washington that some male pages refused to deliver personal notes to the handsome senator's private offices. For years Lovelace indulged in homosexual orgies at his Montana ranch.

Through it all, Janet held her head high, a proud, brave woman.

"Let's go inside," Capp said, wrapping his arm protectively around her small waist and urging her toward the heavy, timbered door.

When Capp had met her, he'd seen she was a scared doe, big-eyed and uncertain of her place in the world—even though her father was David Carlisle, Sr., Capp's most loyal benefactor, a great patriot and one of the richest men in the world. She was uncertain because she was Carlisle's daughter, not his son. She was afraid, too, of losing her husband, afraid to hurt him. She wanted to make him and the world right.

Gradually the general had convinced her no one could make well a man as sick as Oliver Lovelace, and that she deserved to be happy for herself with or without her husband. If she had to stay with Lovelace, he, Capp, would understand, but he was determined to have her, and someday he would have her permanently and in public. For now he would have her in private, and in her husband's house where they stood now inside the great doors.

The living room was paneled in warm Douglas fir. The furniture was bentwood and overstuffed, scattered haphazardly throughout the enormous room. A fire crackled invitingly in the massive rock fireplace. Once the center of a ranch house, the living room was now the heart of a hunting lodge, and Arnie Capp felt at home there.

"What are you thinking about, Arnie?" Janet said, running her fingers up over the buttons on his shirt. "You're so quiet."

He looked down. Her lips were full, round, pouting. Her eyes were dark and sultry. She tossed her head as he watched, and her dark hair cascaded over her slender shoulders.

He smiled, and passion flared in her eyes, responding. It took his breath away. He picked her up, cradling her in his arms like a baby.

"Arnie!" She laughed, struggling and pushing against his chest. "Put me down!"

He carried her up the long stairs. She was light, no more than a hundred pounds, but all curves and roundness. He buried his face against her throat and inhaled her hot woman scent.

She gasped, breathed raggedly. "Darling..."

He carried her along the upstairs hall, over the braided rugs, past the Lovelace family portraits, to her room that was only Janet. It was decorated by her, filled with her. It smelled of her. Her bed was there.

She kissed his face, his neck, his ears, his mouth.

He strode into the room and kicked the door closed.

THEY AWOKE NAKED in the bed, the sheets twisted and flung about and still wet. Her head was on his chest, his hand on her round bare breast. She sighed.

"What would I do without you?" she murmured.

He chuckled sleepily. He was in love. Sometimes he wondered if he had ever really been in love before. He wondered what the passion had been that had made him marry Martha. He remembered wanting sex, which in those days he could get only from prostitutes or a wife. Prostitutes were expensive, and they didn't know how to respect anyone or anything. Prostitutes had been for other men, not Arnold Capp.

And then he'd met Martha, daughter of a general, who knew the Army life and understood a man's need to serve and rise. She'd admired his intelligence, competence and modesty. She'd told him he had all the right qualities to be a good officer and maybe a great soldier. And she'd been willing to gamble her future by marrying him.

He'd heard that she told her girlfriends she was crazy in love with him, because he was so handsome, so dashing, so very much like her father must have been when he was young. Her father had been a fine officer, who won a Congressional Medal of Honor in World War I.

Well, Arnold Capp hadn't let Martha down. He didn't get the medal, but he had three Silver Stars from Korea and Vietnam. Making brigadier without a major war was no small accomplishment. Martha had been to the White House, had command posts, had traveled a lot, had been safe and secure all her life. What more could she want?

He held Janet close to him, felt the firmness of her breast beneath his hand.

"You'd do just fine," he told her. "You'd have to. You're David Carlisle's daughter and my woman."

"Survival goes with the territory," she said.

He could hear the teasing smile in her voice. He chuckled again. She made him feel happy, tender.

"That new whiz kid, the scientist," he said, changing the subject, "he's doing great things with phasars. Looks like we're getting close to a breakthrough on laser weapons."

"I'm glad, darling," she said. "It was clever of you to steal him from Admiral McAdams. And how are the new men doing down at your base? Are they training well?"

"They're turning into real soldiers," he said proudly. "They'll be ready for any operation we need them to do in the future, ready for whatever the country will need."

"Wonderful."

He looked around Janet's sun-filled room. Unlike the rest of the house, the walls were papered and hung with watercolors in soft pastels. The curtains and bedspread were pink chintz, the carpeting thick, plush lavender. The room was like her. She wore sexy clothes, often black, but inside she was soft and womanly, just like this room.

Suddenly he heard a tone of worry in her voice. "What about Hal Brognola and Mack Bolan?"

"Brognola is hard to keep track of. Access to his staff is near impossible, but I'm sure he has his people on the H. Boll problem your father is worried about." He smiled, thinking of his contact in the Justice Department. "He's got Bolan investigating the killings of those three agents."

"Good. But be careful he doesn't stumble onto Falcon," she said, "discover your strength, your capacities, your successful missions around the world. Brognola's such a blind fool he wouldn't understand and could ruin all your good work."

The concern in her voice warmed him. It was concern for him, for the United States. She had respect. Which was more than Hal Brognola seemed to have. Sometimes he wondered if Brognola had some secret connections no one knew about. Connections with other people like Mack Bolan, who sounded like little more than a terrorist himself.

"I wonder if the President knows how narrow Brognola is, how much power he holds, how afraid he is of Congress and of breaking any damn rules," the general continued. "He just about runs his own little empire, you can't work with him. He thinks like all the old fools who can't see the real danger of the enemy we face, the hoodwinking of our allies and the rest of the world that can be dangerous as hell.''

"I know, darling," Janet said. "Thank God we have you to see the way the world really is. Thank God *I* have you." She moved tight against him, kissed him and lay touching him with her eyes closed.

He held her in the silence of the room with the wind whispering in the pines outside. He liked this house. There was quality here. It was quiet, sturdy, built to last. It should be a house full of children again. Not Ollie Lovelace's children, but his. As he was considering this, he heard a telephone jangle in the distance. It wouldn't be for him. No one knew he was here. And he would be gone again in a few hours.

There was a soft, tentative knock on the door. Janet must have left orders not be disturbed. Which meant that the call had to be very important. Could someone have found him here? He looked at Janet.

"Sorry," she said, and patted his chest, then called "Yes?" to the closed, locked door.

"For you, ma'am," a servant said with a Montana drawl.

"Damn." She fell back on the bed and groaned.

"You'd better get it, honey," the general told her, relieved that at least it wasn't for him. "We want to keep everyone happy. At least for a while."

"Oh, all right," she said petulantly, and stood, her breasts swinging.

He watched and felt the heat go to his groin again. Here he was, more than fifty years old, and acting like a tomcat. He had to hand it to her. She was one hell of a woman.

She pulled on a fluffy robe, tied it tight and flounced to the door. She yanked it open. "I told you I didn't want to be bothered by anyone! Can't you take a simple order?"

"Sorry, ma'am. But it's the senator."

Janet turned her face back into the room, and rolled up her eyes in disgust.

The general laughed. "Anytime you want out, just let me know. We'll get the divorces and the preacher the same day."

She smiled and padded from the room.

The general lay back to wait. He'd have one more go-around with her when she got back. There was plenty of time. He sighed in anticipation of the pleasure.

"IT'S HIM?" Janet said quietly to the leathery-faced old woman who had knocked on the door. "You're sure?"

"Yes, ma'am. He said his name was Tripper."

Janet nodded and ran down the hall to her husband's den. She closed and locked the door and picked up the phone. "You've found him?" she asked breathlessly.

"In Angola," the man said. "Your brothers know, and your father knows. The MPLA has an air attack on the mountain where he's hidden. When that's over, they'll send in ground troops."

"You think he's finished?"

"He ought to be."

"I want to know as soon as they have the corpse. If he gets killed, we'll have to make other plans."

There was a pause at the other end of the long-distance call. "This will cost you."

"Darling," she drawled, "if I've got one thing, I've got money."

CHAPTER ELEVEN

The mountain shook with the third wave of the MPLA aerial assault. Mack Bolan squatted at the bottom of the narrow, wooded hollow and watched the jets slice low through the blue sky just above the treetops to fire their air-to-ground missiles and drop their bombs all across the mountain headquarters of the guerrilla group.

The aircraft looked like MiG-21 Fishbeds and MiG-23 Floggers. The Soviets supplied those jets as well as Mi-8 Hip and Mi-24 Hind D helicopters to the Marxist Angola air force.

The HE pounded in, delayed fuses slamming into the mountainside to blast out caves, heat-seeking missiles homing in on fires and electronic installations if there were any. Trees and boulders exploded. Fires ignited. The deafening thunder of jets and high explosives filled the air.

Bolan watched, listened and calculated. The attack was intense, its pattern methodical. The bombs and missiles sectored the mountain with a deadly precision that left no area on the south slope unscathed. The last time he'd seen such a neat, expert, thorough job, he realized grimly, was in Vietnam by the USAF.

The attack was a pro job, and looked like the work of ComBloc fliers. Like Afghanistan, Angola had become a military training and testing ground for Marxist pilots. The strike today was an opportunity for Soviet, East German and Cuban fliers to hone their air combat and ground attack skills.

Bolan heard screams of pain, anguish and fear from the far side of the mountain. The guerrillas were dying. But safely at Bolan's feet lay what he knew had to be one target of such a massive raid on so small a group— the key to H. Boll, weapons buyer André Villela, unconscious but still alive after the wild ride on the underground river. And Bolan didn't have to do a lot of hard guessing about the ultimate reason for such a hotshot operation in this remote area. It had to be the Executioner himself the Marxists were after. Well, the bastards weren't going to get him.

All he had to do was figure out how to get himself and Villela safely out of there—with no weapons and damn little clothing and no gear! It could be a hell of a lot more difficult than escaping the underground lake and the bowels of the mountain.

As he looked at Villela, the man's eyes opened slowly. "What...? Where am I?" he asked.

"Take it easy," Bolan told him. "We're on the other side of the mountain. It's an air attack. It'll be over soon."

Villela groaned, put a hand to his head and winced.

"Lie still and get your strength back," Bolan said. "We'll have to get out of here soon."

Villela seemed to study him, then suddenly grabbed for the weapons he no longer carried. He looked down at the torn rags of his clothes. "What the—"

"You lost it all in the river, soldier," Bolan stated quietly, trying to bring the guerrilla chief back to reality slowly.

"River? There's no river...."

"Inside the mountain. We were attacked, sealed in your HQ, and had to muck it through the caves."

Villela stared at him. "Do I know you?"

"Damn."

"You look familiar, but..." Villela's face was puzzled, his eyes slitted as he tried to place the Executioner.

Amnesia! It was the last thing Bolan needed. His only source of information couldn't even remember who he was. "I'm Mack Bolan. I came to talk to you." The name appeared to mean nothing to the Angolan.

"What's your name, soldier?" Bolan asked quietly as the jets continued to hammer the shattered and smoking mountain. The pass would end soon, and then it would be time for the Executioner and the guerrilla chief to get out of there as fast as they could.

"Don't you know who I am?" Villela responded.

"I do, but do you?"

Villela opened his mouth to answer, then closed it. The puzzlement on his face slowly turned into defeat. He closed his eyes. "Good God! I don't know my name!"

Bolan sat on his haunches and studied the freedom fighter. Pain creased his face. He lay limp on the ground. His sturdy, muscular body, which had once vibrated with energy, was now useless after his ordeal inside the mountain.

Amnesia, probably from hitting his head on the underwater rocks. The sudden blow, fear, strain. Bolan had seen combat amnesia many times in Nam. He hoped to hell it wasn't total amnesia. Combat amnesia was a temporary trauma. Even so, there was still no way of telling when Villela's memory would return. They had no time now to wait.

"Do you know where you are?" Bolan asked.

"In the mountains, obviously." There was a touch of sarcasm, some of the old Villela spirit. A good sign.

"What country?"

Again the pause as Villela tried to remember. "I don't *know*!"

Bolan looked at him a moment longer, then made a decision. He didn't have time to coddle Villela. He had to get him up and moving as soon as the air strike was over. Ground troops would be coming in.

Bolan had decided paratroopers were unlikely. By all logic, the FNLA mountain hideout had to be too small a job for expensive elite forces. Ground troops would be bad enough. The MPLA had a strength of about forty-five thousand troops. Added to this, of course, were the "advisers" supplied from the Communist bloc. In Angola there were some three thousand Soviet military and civilian advisers, fifteen hundred other Eastern bloc advisers, between eight and ten thousand Cuban civilian advisers and an estimated thirty thousand Cuban combat troops. All highly trained, well equipped, and bored by the inaction of fighting a hit-and-miss guerrilla war.

The MPLA could easily send a company to finish off the guerrilla's hideout. An enthusiastic company.

"You're André Villela," Bolan told him. "Ring a bell?"

Villela frowned. "Don't think so."

Bolan showed him the cartridge belts. "What are these?"

Villela fingered a cartridge, took it out and looked at. "Bullets." He looked up. "Mine?"

"Yeah. Know how you got them?"

Villela shook his head.

Bolan started talking. He told Villela what he'd learned from Lars Marlett of the freedom fighter's reputation and work, his place in the Angolan war, his guerrilla hideout inside the mountain, the air attack, and how he and Bolan had ended up here in this tree-lined canyon with HE pounding down around them.

As Bolan talked, Villela sat up, grimacing with pain. He took in the information quietly, occasionally rubbing his temples. His eyes seemed to be clearing. The pain must be subsiding. But he still sat there in the hidden hollow, listening as if he was hearing the story of a stranger.

When Bolan had finished, Villela was silent a moment, then said, "You want something from me."

"That's it. Intel about a giant weapons dealer with HQ in Hamburg, West Germany. The company's obviously a front for something much bigger—and as crooked and dangerous as hell." Bolan paused, looked expectantly at Villela. "The name's H. Boll, Ltd."

Villela thought a while. "Damn," he said at last. "Seems familiar, but I still can't place it."

Bolan closed his eyes, frustrated. What damn rotten luck! His only intel source had amnesia, and he had no way of knowing when the amnesia would clear up—if it ever did.

Now, when the jets finally let up and before the ground guys could move in, he had to get the man out of here with no help or weapons. Survive and, maybe, find someone to help Villela get back his memory, or hope that the guy would remember on his own.

Bolan looked up. The explosions had stopped; the screams of jet engines and wounded men could no longer be heard. He checked the sky. It was clear and empty. The last jet run was over.

"You still know how to fight?" he asked.

Villela bristled. "Listen..." Then confusion covered his face. He looked uneasily at his square, powerful hands as if to ask them who he was, at the tattered rags he was wearing.

Bolan smiled. "Good. Let's get the hell out of here."

They moved up through the trees into the heavier mountain brush, Bolan clearing a path as Villela followed. Villela was a stubborn man of action. The basic personality was never lost. Bolan was counting on that to help get them through and bring back, in time, the guerrilla chief's memory.

"I don't know where to take you," Villela said, realizing he should know.

"You don't have to take me anywhere," Bolan said. "I have friends."

"A rendezvous?"

"Something like that. If they're still there."

They headed over a high shoulder and down the mountainside. Bolan turned left halfway down. At night he'd have to use the stars to guide him, and hope he could be exact enough.

"Zaire?" Villela said tentatively.

Bolan looked at the guy, at the surprise on his face at having remembered that the country bordering Angola on the north was Zaire. Another good sign. His memory could be returning.

"We're going north, but not that far," Bolan said.

They crossed devastated bald spots on the lower slope of the mountain, flat, charred and still smoking from the HE that had cleared them of all vegetation, chewed up the blackened brush and shattered rocks and boulders. The air stank of smoke and explosives. An unnatural silence cloaked the damaged forest as if nothing there wanted to live or grow again.

Suddenly Bolan sprinted forward toward the cover of some undamaged timber. "Come on."

Villela picked up his speed without a question and hurried into the cover of the mahogany trees. "What is it?" the guerrilla asked, panting. Already he was exhausted, his energy depleted by his long struggle with the underground river.

Bolan hit the dirt, motioned Villela down beside him and stared down the slope through a natural clearing and across the open terrain at the base of the mountain, terrain burned and flattened now by the jets. Villela's gaze followed. Instantly the freedom fighter was alert.

In the forest they saw figures melting from tree to tree.

"Who?" Villela whispered.

"MPLA," Bolan said grimly. "The ground mopup."

He watched the troops moving almost carelessly across the open burned and blasted areas. From what he could see they were Angolan government regulars. Behind them he saw the ComBloc trucks that had brought them in along the single narrow road from the southwest.

"Looks like regular troops. Just about what I'd expect for this operation. What do you say, *comandante*?"

"Standard," Villela said. "But that jet pounding wasn't so standard. I'd say—" The guerrilla broke off and stared at Bolan.

The big American grinned. "Coming back to you, *comandante*?"

Villela nodded almost eagerly, started to speak again and then stopped. They both heard it at the same instant—the sound of jet engines low and clear to the northeast. Different jets, slower, more ponderous, droning higher in the evening sky and closer and closer. They looked up.

Bolan shaded his eyes and wished he had his binoculars. "Antonov AN-24s, ComBloc short-range troop carriers."

"Short takeoff transports for unpaved airfields," Villela said. "It's what the Marxists use."

They both continued to watch for what they knew would come next. High above, white parachutes opened and puffed into a spray of billowing mushrooms.

"Damn!" Bolan said.

"Paratroopers." Villela nodded grimly. "And dropping to the north, American."

Bolan glanced at Villela. Again the freedom fighter had come up with an unexpected piece of information straight out of his background. But Bolan had no time to dwell on this bit of good news. It was the bad news he had to deal with now. Villela had said it—they were dropping to the northwest, cutting off any escape toward Zaire, and catching the fleeing guerrillas in a squeeze between them and the advancing ground troops.

But that was only part of the immediate problem. Paratroopers, elite troops, maybe even Cuban, definitely meant someone had paid MPLA a big "donation" for this operation, or was calling in all the old debts. It looked like H. Boll, Ltd., was determined to get Mack Bolan, no matter what the cost.

Rifle fire erupted close by on the lower slopes of the devastated mountainside. A battle between some of the advancing MPLA ground troops and what had to be a pocket of Villela's guerrillas.

Suddenly explosions fell on either side of where Bolan and Villela lay hidden. Trees and rocks burst. Wood splintered into the air, showering Bolan and Villela with needles. Rocks pelted them.

"Grenades?" Villela wondered.

"Looks like it," Bolan replied.

"Maybe AGS-17s," the weapons expert said, naming the devastating automatic grenade launchers supplied by the Soviets. He smiled grimly. "I guess I really am starting to remember."

In the sky the paratroopers descended toward the forests to the north and west. Below, the MPLA troops closed in on the guerrillas.

"Let's go!" Bolan jumped to his feet to scramble low to the ground down the hill.

They ran a weaving course from cover to cover, but took the shortest and straightest route toward the sound of the firing. When a battle was close and time was short, there was no point being so careful you got there too late. Run to the sound of the firing, a Bolan law. Especially when he needed weapons. There were only two places to get them, from friends or enemies—from the guerrillas or the MPLA soldiers.

Rifle fire and grenades tore the trees and brush, bracketing Bolan and Villela as they raced down the hill.

They ducked behind trees, fell behind rocks, crouched behind boulders and brush.

Villela's skills were coming back. He was tired, but Bolan could tell his adrenaline was pumping.

They ran and rolled through dust and rifle fire toward the pocket of defending guerrillas still holding off the government troops. The attacking MPLA people knew the paratroopers were coming, and had no stomach for a dangerous frontal assault.

The three guerrillas saw Bolan and Villela and increased their fire to keep the MPLA attackers distracted and pinned down.

The MPLA men saw them, too.

Bullets whizzing past, Bolan and Villela dived headfirst down into the deep gully the guerrillas were defending.

"Comandante!" one of the men cried, amazed. He stared at the ragged Villela, and at Bolan in his shorts and barefoot, both men streaked with sweat-caked dirt and black charcoal from the blasted mountain. Then relief flooded the guerrillas' dark faces. With the *comandante* there, they suddenly felt safe, as if winning was now possible.

"It is the *comandante*!"

Villela looked at Bolan. Bolan shrugged. None of these men had been in the group Villela had led through the mountain in hopes of escape. None of them knew that Villela and then Bolan had disappeared into an underground lake. But then Villela didn't know that they didn't know. Villela would have to decide whether to tell them his memory was mostly gone, or to pretend with them that his presence made the situation manageable.

"Hang on, soldier, we'll get out of this," Villela said, gripping the man on his shoulder.

The guerrillas beamed and returned to their work of picking off the MPLA soldiers who stood between them and escape so that they could continue their fight for their nation's freedom. In the hollow, dug in under heavy tree cover that had escaped the savage jet assault, they had not yet seen the paratroopers descending through the evening sky.

"Villela," Bolan said quietly as he sorted through the pile of old, damaged arms the guerrillas had brought from the cave.

Villela stared over the rim of the hole. The white parachutes had landed, vanishing into the trees. Soon the troopers would descend on the courageous band of freedom fighters. Villela's men, and Mack Bolan, were caught in the jaws of a closing vise.

CHAPTER TWELVE

Bolan grabbed two old M-16s from the pile of weapons at the bottom of the small ravine where the guerrillas crouched. He tossed one of the M-16s to André Villela, and the weapons buyer turned it over, examined it eagerly and critically as if it might unlock his memory.

Bullets sliced over the guerrilla position as Bolan dug through the pile again and found a half-empty belt of ammo clip pouches. Two guerrillas looked at him and shrugged. Almost all the ammo was half gone or worse. There wasn't enough to make a really solid stand, maybe not enough even to make a decent escape.

Villela leaned against the rim of the gully to watch, aim and fire at the movement back up the mountainside. The other guerrillas watched and listened, rising occasionally to squeeze off rapid shots when the MPLA troops in the forest downslope moved closer.

The Marxist company was moving forward slowly and carefully. The fight was essentially only a containing action for them; they weren't pressing in for the kill. They didn't have to. All they had to do was keep the guerrillas pinned down in the hollow and wait for the paratroopers to arrive and overrun the small position, or sit back and wait for the guerrillas to attempt a breakout, and mow them down in the open. Sooner or later one or the other, probably both, would happen, and all the regulars had to do was keep up containing fire and wait.

Bolan and the Angolan freedom fighters were sitting in their hole, waiting to be surrounded, overrun and killed. The rest of André Villela's guerrillas from the mountain headquarters were long gone by now, dead or trapped and fighting in other small pockets throughout the area.

The grenades started coming in again.

"Damn!" Bolan muttered under his breath.

Villela looked at him anxiously, waiting to be told what to do. There was fear in his face, and unconscious surprise that he was afraid. The other guerrillas looked at their *comandante* for orders. Bolan realized he was going to have to take over without making Villela lose face with his men, or the guerrillas might panic and blow the whole damned show. What was left of it, that is. He'd seen it too often, the loss of a tough but fair commander destroying the backbone of the troops and the whole operation.

Bolan wasn't sure he could to it, but he was sure of one thing—they were all dead if they stayed here. The warrior squatted at the bottom of the hollow and got their attention. "All of you hear this—you want to live, you do what the *comandante* and I tell you. We worked it out before we cruised in here, right, *comandante*?"

Villela stared at Bolan a moment, then nodded.

"Okay," Bolan said, and rapidly divided up the weapons, the ammo and the few grenades. Then he started to give the men their instructions.

ON THE SILENT EDGE of the underground lake, where his panicked comrades had all deserted him, Fernando Cruz crouched for what seemed like hours, his solitary flashlight trained on the black water. He listened to the bombing thunder outside the mountain. Listened to it end and start again. Still he sat there waiting and hoping.

Until the bombing ended once more, and he knew it was time to give up. The *comandante* and Mack Bolan weren't going to break through the still surface that shone like a black mirror in the beam of his single light, to greet him, laugh, climb up to join him and fight again. They were both dead, or had miraculously escaped some other way.

Fernando didn't really think they could have survived—he didn't believe in miracles—but he had been a guerrilla long enough to know that survival was often unexpected, and there was always hope if you fought hard enough and never gave up.

So he gathered up Bolan's clothes and weapons into a tight bundle and turned back the way he and Villela and the others had come. The bombing was over. He knew three sweeps was standard operating procedure for most air forces; he was certain the Marxists would be no exception. He had two reasons for retracing his steps: sometimes doing the unexpected was the best course of action, and he didn't trust the soldiers who had deserted the *comandante*, and run forward, for they would have reason to not want to see him.

So he stumbled back through the now silent mountain until he found an exit tunnel near the destroyed headquarters cave, and emerged cautiously into the late-afternoon sunlight on the blackened and burning mountainside.

The devastation stretched on every side—splintered and smoking trees, torn and bloody bodies, ripped-off limbs. There was a reek of explosives and blood. In a daze he wandered down through the shattered timber, stunned, confused, clasping the bundle of Mack Bolan's discarded clothes and weapons to his chest as if they were a shield that would ward off death.

Trees had literally exploded from the earth, their roots naked and shattered. Animals and birds had died instantly, their broken bodies littering the ground. Some of his fellow guerrillas were only charred lumps of flesh.

There was deathly silence.

Fernando staggered on.

He knew he had to get out of this hellground before the predatory animals began to move in, and before the Marxist ground troops came to mop up and enjoy the destruction their jets had wreaked. His instincts drove him downhill. From the long years as a guerrilla, he knew he had to go all the way downhill, and then climb again onto the next mountain, which no bombs had touched.

If there was time.

Even to his own ears his footsteps sounded heavy, echoing in the quiet like thunder across the denuded slopes. Consciously he slowed and tried to lighten his noisy tread. He used what cover was left, moving among the splintered and blackened trees instead of taking the easier more direct route over the smoking earth cleared by the bombs.

Fernando thought about the *comandante* and knew he would approve of the wariness and alertness of the irregular fighter he had taught so harshly and well. But the *comandante*, whom Fernando loved and respected more than any other man in the world, would approve of nothing now. The *comandante* was dead, a tragedy beyond any Fernando had ever known—and he had known many.

Why should he, Fernando, survive? Why even try to escape, to go on?

Because the *comandante* would want him to, he told himself. Because Villela would want the battle to go on, to never stop until it was won. It was a battle for life itself; it had to go on.

Yes, Fernando had to live and find a way to help his people.

Then he heard the sound of an engine.

He hit the burned earth in the reflex of the guerrilla, and lay motionless, listening.

The engine had stopped just ahead, and he heard voices—casual, relaxed, laughing voices that spoke in his own native tongue mixed with Portuguese. The speakers sounded as if they were out in the open, standing on one spot and in no hurry to move on.

Fernando snaked forward, Bolan's weapons and clothes cradled, and looked down over a rise at a small truck filled with MPLA regulars. The truck had stopped, and the officer and noncoms were out on the dirt road talking and laughing as the rest of the dozen soldiers waited in the truck.

He assessed the situation coolly, enjoying the feeling. His mind seemed to need something to do, to stop remembering the past and get on with the future. To take action. To do battle.

He had his weapons and Mack Bolan's. That was good.

There were twelve of them, and one of him. That was bad.

But the more Marxists he stopped here, the better for his people. It was time to stop running, stop remembering, and act.

He lifted his Uzi, took careful aim and fired.

IN THE DEFILADE POSITION in the draw, Bolan, Villela and the three guerrillas moved to the top of their cover at the lip of the hollow. Bolan was counting on surprise, hoping that the Marxist soldiers below wouldn't expect so foolhardy an action as the freedom fighters exposing themselves to fire all at once and escaping straight across the front of the enemy.

They each had two weapons, as much ammo as they had left and two grenades.

"Let's do it," Bolan said quietly. "Now!"

They all leaped over the rim and hurtled toward the soldiers below, at the same time angling across toward the thick forest of unburned trees some fifty yards away down the slope.

Surprised, the attackers hesitated. It was enough. Before their fire became more than ragged and ineffective individual rounds, the guerrillas were halfway to cover in the thick trees.

Bolan hurled one grenade, then another.

Villela flung his grenades.

The freedom fighters tore across the last of the open space, blistering the Angolan position with a hosing fire that might not do much damage but would keep a lot of heads down and give the grenades a chance to do their deadly work.

The grenades exploded.

Cursing and screaming, the Marxists increased their fire. The bullets sang around the freedom fighters.

Hit in the arm, one of Villela's men spun and dropped. The man next to him grabbed him, yanked him to his feet and dragged him forward.

At last Bolan and the guerrillas fell into the safety of the trees. But the trees weren't safe. It would be close contact now.

The Marxists surged toward them, rifles hammering.

Bolan crouched and returned fire. He saw two Marxists go down, picked off as they came out of the forest. Then a third, a fourth.

Beside him Villela fired, the ways of war returning before memory. Action before thought, the instinct of all men. But his face had changed; now it was full of fear.

Villela's guerrillas were spread out, their orders to get the hell out of there any way they could, to live to fight tomorrow. There were too few of them to take on successfully a company of well-trained, well-equipped men. But they could get rid of a few, and survive, and win the war.

An MPLA soldier came out of the trees behind Bolan. Bolan swung his rifle, but Villela picked him off first. Two descended on Villela from the front. Bolan got one, then the other.

"Move!" Bolan shouted.

They zigzagged, fired and were fired upon. The afternoon heat and stink merged, explosives and sunshine. Violent death and the fight for life.

Marxist blasts killed two of the guerrillas as they were escaping down the mountainside. The two were dead before they hit the ground.

The survivors ran past more Marxist corpses. Bolan saw that some of them were Cubans killed in their Fidel Castro uniforms.

Then Villela and Bolan were running alone in a silent forest, neither friends nor enemies anywhere. They had done it! They were out of the pinned-down hollow and through the Marxist troops and away. Now all they had to do was reach Bolan's rendezvous.

"How far?" Villela panted as they settled down to a steady, ground-covering dogtrot, his eyes clear now, the memory of who and what he was deep in his steady gaze.

"Maybe twenty miles."

"The paratroopers?"

"We go south."

"Good."

Then there was gunfire directly ahead of them.

Bolan swore.

The new battle had the sound of desperation.

"One man," Villela said, listening, his military judgment fully restored now. "Against many."

Bolan angled toward the small battle ahead. It was important that he and Villela survive and escape, but someone was fighting and in trouble, and Bolan couldn't leave a freedom fighter to die alone. Villela hesitated. He knew the job he had to do. Then he shrugged and followed Bolan.

They passed a stand of quiet, lush forest, and then more destroyed patches of vegetation that smoked and reeked, all under the perfect blue of a tranquil afternoon sky.

They found the battle at the edge of a dirt road.

A squad of Angolan regulars were circling around some guy trapped by the closing arc, or rather, what was left of a Marxist squad. Bolan could see four Marxists dead. About eight were still alive, firing on the lone man who lay prone behind a downed tree trunk.

Villela saw the single fighter. "Fernando!" The *comandante* stood up in the open. "Fernando! What are you doing! Have you gone crazy?"

"Villela, stop!" Bolan shouted.

But Villela had his memory back. He knew who Fernando was; he knew what the skinny second-in-command meant to him—as close as family, his only friend, the only person he fully trusted in a world where he dealt constantly with greed, death, lying, cheating and a grim, unsafe future.

Bolan looked at Villela. He knew in an instant the Angolan leader had remembered all the information Bolan needed, but he also saw that the recent experience had changed Villela. He wasn't the old hard, tough arms buyer anymore.

"Hang on, Fernando!" Villela yelled and ran down the slope, firing his old M-16 at the startled Marxists as he ran.

"Villela!" Bolan shouted again.

It was no use. The arms buyer and hard-bitten guerrilla saw his last and only real friend in danger and there was no stopping him now.

Bolan fired his M-16, blasting at the targets to his left and right. Villela held the information Bolan needed. He had to get the guerrilla through this alive.

Then Bolan ran out of ammo.

From the trees to his right a Marxist stepped out, and raised his rifle at Villela's back. Bolan rushed the ambusher, his feet raising powdery clouds as he swung his last weapon, a long Angolan knife.

The enemy looked at Bolan. Surprise covered his face at the sight of the white man dressed only in shorts. The hesitation was enough. Bolan was on him. The guy reared up, and Bolan swung the long knife and took the man's head off in a single powerful sweep. Hot blood splashed Bolan's hand. The warrior pushed the body away and turned to find Villela.

"Comandante!" Fernando shouted. "Go back!"

"Villela!" Bolan yelled. "No!"

But Villela raced across the last few feet, firing his M-16 as if he were his old self again, the wily guerrilla leader who had survived hundreds of battles, the cosmopolitan arms buyer with the impeccable Portuguese background who was equally at home in the drawing rooms of Austrian castles and on the hellgrounds of war. Villela was doing exactly what he wanted, what he was driven to do, what he had to do in the end.

The three remaining Marxists couldn't believe their eyes at the fine target he presented. They turned their rifles on him and they riddled him with bullets.

A cry of anguish split the air. Fernando jumped up and blasted at the Marxist soldiers with the M-16 rifle Bolan had left behind so long ago to dive into the underground lake to rescue Villela.

Bolan snapped up an AK-47 from the ground. The Marxists opened fire on Fernando. Bolan pivoted, and with smooth precision fired at the three Marxist soldiers.

They never knew what hit them. One moment they were going to wipe one more Angolan scourge from the earth, and the next moment their chests were ripped open and they were on the forest duff bleeding to death.

Fernando dropped to his knees beside Villela. He threw aside Bolan's rifle and grabbed his *comandante*'s shoulders. "André," he said softly. "André?"

But Villela was dead. His muscular body lay sprawled on a bed of dry leaves in the shadow of majestic mahogany trees. His lifeless eyes gazed at the crystal-blue sky. In the distance more rifle fire sounded suddenly, but here all was quiet, unnaturally tranquil.

Fernando said nothing more, just stared down at his fallen leader. Bolan stood with him for a time, then began to put on the clothes Fernando had carried with him all the way from the mountain interior. That seemed not just miles away but years ago now. He picked up the weapons with the clothes.

"We have to go," Bolan said at last.

Villela had been a good soldier, a good leader, had fought for many years in this thankless war for freedom. And now that he was dead, the war would, must, continue.

As must Bolan's war.

Now he had even less time to lose. He had to get out of here, but where to now that his only source of intel was dead?

"Know where this road goes?" Bolan asked, back in his blacksuit.

Slowly Fernando nodded. "West to Luanda."

Bolan leathered his Beretta 93-R under his left arm and rigged the Fairbairn-Sykes dagger beside it. He slipped on his ammo belts, now almost empty, and slung his M-16.

Fernando picked up Villela's body and slung it over his skinny shoulder. He was stronger than he looked.

"Taking him home?" Bolan asked Fernando.

"The *comandante* would not wish it, but I must."

"I understand," Bolan said. He looked at the second-in-command thoughtfully. Fernando had changed, too, and for the better. Gone was the air of an actor and impersonator. He seemed stronger now, more stable. "You went with Villela on his buys?" Bolan asked.

"Sometimes." Fernando glanced at Bolan, surprised at the question.

"Know anything about a company called H. Boll, Ltd.?"

Fernando shook his head, then started walking down the slope to the silent road, his dead *comandante* over his skinny shoulder. He would go to Villela's village, arrange his funeral, a burial for a hero.

"What about the Uzis you swiped, the ones the Luanda soldiers came and took back? They killed a lot of your people for them. You lost a Huey in that steal, too."

Fernando turned back. "We almost had the Uzis. But somehow the supplier must have found out we'd pulled a switch."

"The supplier? You mean the actual shipper of the guns? Who was it?"

"A company called Trans-World Arms, Inc. I saw the letterhead," Fernando said bitterly.

Sometimes it happened that way—you finally asked the right question of the right person. So simple, but you had to go down all the other wrong roads first to find the right one at last. That was why those who gave up easily often lost a round that, if they had persevered, they could have won.

"Where are their headquarters?"

"In Monrovia." Fernando took a few steps, then stopped as if suddenly shocked. "I know their telephone number," he said wonderingly. "And their postal box. I wrote and called them many times for André." Without hesitation he recited the two numbers for Bolan. Then he grinned at him.

"You know more than you think," Bolan told him.

"I begin to see that now," Fernando said. "I can try to do what André did. We can go on!"

Together they humped on down the hill, the tall, skinny new leader and the Executioner.

"I must find the rest of our men and rally them. André would have wanted that. We will fight and we will win."

They would give André Villela a soldier's funeral, and then they would continue their country's fight for freedom.

Mack Bolan trotted to the road, got into the truck and tried the engine. It started. He would drive it a few miles east and south, then walk to his meeting place with Jack Grimaldi. He only hoped the flyboy would still be waiting for him at the small, remote landing strip.

CHAPTER THIRTEEN

Dusty, tired and hungry, Mack Bolan dragged himself up the last mountain rise before the pickup point. It was twilight, and he was worried. The sky over the mountains and forest was empty as far as he could see. Not a sign of Grimaldi and the Cessna.

With the aid of the Angolan army truck and his compass, he had reached the rendezvous area and had found this final rise much more quickly and easily than he had expected. He was due for a break.

He hoped to hell that the usual bad luck of the grunt wasn't about to set in again. Even though he'd made a lot better time than he could have hoped, he was still late, and Grimaldi could be long gone. The ace pilot *should* be long gone, because that was the SOP of any pickup, and because it was dangerous to take off in the falling darkness. That would leave Bolan stranded in this remote piece of godforsaken wilderness for another long night until the second pickup time, and that would give H. Boll another day's lead.

Bolan hiked over the rise and onto the mountain saddle. He took a deep breath and exhaled slowly. He was thankful for good friends.

Grimaldi stood beside the specially modified Cessna, arms crossed in the gloom. "Took you long enough," he said in an easygoing manner that concealed a hard-earned suspicion that had saved his life many times, not to mention the lives of a lot of others, including Bolan's.

"Not too long, I guess." Bolan scowled. "What the hell are you doing here anyway? You should be long gone. You know the rules."

"Sure, Sarge."

Bolan grinned. "Think you can get this shoebox off the ground?" He threw his gear into the back of the Cessna.

"Do bears shit in the woods? Get in."

"Don't mind if I do." Bolan settled into the copilot's seat and leaned back. Grimaldi produced some old field rations and a thermos of coffee. Bolan dug in as if he hadn't eaten in two days—he hadn't. He would eat whatever was on hand, and then sleep during the flight.

"Looks like you had a party. What now? Back to Zaire?"

"Monrovia."

"Liberia? Geez, Mack, nothing's there. No one goes to Liberia."

"I do," the Executioner said simply and closed his eyes.

PHILIP CARLISLE SAT BACK in the soft glove-leather seat of his luxurious 747, listened to the quiet hum of the giant jet engines in flight. Attention to detail was his hallmark—this aircraft had been built and outfitted to his exacting specifications. Not only did it run perfectly, it was opulently comfortable.

Carlisle was feeling good, very good. His hard work was paying off. He smoked a hand-rolled cigarette with his monogrammed gold tip and thought about the news.

Mack Bolan was dead. Killed in the mountain in Angola.

Philip had already sent the message to his father. Brognola's threat to the secret H. Boll operation was ended. Now the old man would have to recognize his youngest son's brilliance and move him ahead of everyone else. Philip liked a fight, liked to beat his rivals, especially his brothers, but it was always best to move up peacefully, with the backing of the organization, and it would be best to take over the whole damn business peacefully.

Philip inhaled the sweet tobacco smoke and looked out his window as they passed over the night-black South Atlantic, heading northeast to his country estate in Ireland. In the background the jet's special telephone rang. He turned to admire the handsome cabin his money had bought. He sensed time passing, too much time, but no one had come to bring him a telephone message.

A very long conversation.

That made Philip nervous. What the hell was taking so long?

He was fuming inside by the time Michael Jones finally strolled through the enormous cabin toward Philip's chair. There was a strange expression on the former soldier's face. His lack of fear always fascinated Philip, but there was more than that on the face now. Now it was something like a challenge, a bold dare that Philip do something, or say something, or...

"Well?" Philip said impatiently.

"He's alive."

Philip didn't need to ask who. "You idiot!" he screamed. "Imbecile! Fool! How could you make such a stupid mistake!"

As Philip raged, Jones waited. The patience of the former soldier of fortune infuriated the Carlisle scion further. He bellowed and shouted until, exhausted at last by his fury, he glared daggers at Jones.

"What happened?" the magnate growled. "It better be a damn good explanation, and you damn well better have a solution."

"There were other exits from the mountain." Jones shrugged. "The people we have in Luanda didn't know about them. That's what happens when you hire second-raters. I've told you before. Most of the guerrillas got out, but the Angolan army did manage to wipe out at least half of them once they were in the open. Even got their leader—André Villela."

Philip ignored the criticism from his subordinate, but he wouldn't forget it. He filed it in his mind with all the other insults he'd taken from the mercenary. The time would come when Jones's usefulness would be over, then Philip would deal with him painfully and permanently.

"Villela? We've done business with him, right?"

Jones nodded. "He's the one we let think he was stealing the Angolan Uzi shipment from H. Boll and TWA. Then took them back from him and his guerrillas."

"Ah, yes." Philip laughed. "He was pretty damn mad about that, I expect."

"He'd have gotten over it. They have to buy their guns from someone."

"When we're finished, that someone will be only us, right?"

Jones said nothing, and Philip sat back and imagined his triumph once more. Then he thought about André Villela. The guerrilla had been okay. Gutsy. A man you could deal with. He was sorry about Villela. Why the hell was it Villela who bit it and not the goddamned Boy Scout? "So what about Bolan?"

"Escaped, turned Villela's band over to his second, Fernando Cruz. He's not as smart as Villela. He'll be harder to work with."

"No one's hard to work with when they need our guns."

"Maybe not," Jones said. "Our man inside Villela's old group says Bolan went to meet Villela to talk about H. Boll."

Philip chewed his lip. "You got a positive ident on Bolan?"

"Of course. Something happened inside the mountain to make him leave his clothes behind. He was the only half-naked white guy there in the firefight with the Angolan troops."

Philip Carlisle roared with laughter. "God, I'd like to have seen that." He wiped at his eyes.

"Don't underestimate him," Jones said bluntly. "He's the only one who could have gotten out of that trap, then led those two-bit guerrillas in a breakout."

Philip glared at Jones again. "All right, so where the hell is he now?"

"Our contact says he was picked up and flown somewhere north and west. Not Zaire again. We think he's in Liberia. The guy in the guerrillas said Bolan and that Cruz were talking about TWA."

"You figure he knows TWA is headquartered in Monrovia," Philip said.

"It's his only reason to go to Liberia."

Philip Carlisle had a cruel smile on his handsome lips. "And your only reason to stay alive is to intercept that message to my father saying Bolan's dead, and then to find and kill Bolan. And without any mistakes this time."

ROBERTO CARLISLE stared down from his big office window high above Caracas. He enjoyed the night lights, the sparkling sea of diamonds that filled the valley of the Rio Guaire. So many of the modern buildings there, where wealth was made and spent in this oil-rich country, had been built by his corporation, Cordoba Construcciones S.A.

Emilio Harter had just reported the survival of Mack Bolan, the erroneous message sent to Roberto's father, and Philip's rage and frustration.

Roberto nodded when Harter finished. He spoke to the window, to the city, his words also directed to the trusted man behind him. "Philip is a child. A spoiled, arrogant child. He's going about this all wrong."

Harter bowed his head over the hat he clasped in front of him, reluctant as always to judge his employer's brother. The inherent politeness, the good breeding even in poverty, were qualities Roberto admired in Harter.

"Philip chases," Roberto continued. "We must lead. We must set up a trap that Bolan will walk—no *run*—into. We want him alive, and if not alive, then certainly dead. Pick him up in Monrovia, watch him, and we'll go about this scientifically. I've given the matter some thought, and I have a plan that will work. The Executioner's good luck is about to run out."

THE DRAPES WERE pulled closed in David Carlisle, Jr.'s Paris office. He sat in the overstuffed chair beside the fireplace, where he met with men as powerful as himself, or with his father when the older man made one of his infrequent surprise visits, or with women who were wealthy, sophisticated, educated or elusive enough to tempt him.

He met people of less consequence at his desk, seated in his high-backed leather chair. They sat in low-backed chairs beyond the barrier of the desk. Those who were sensitive to such nuances would deduce their relative unimportance to him from the seating arrangements.

But now David was alone with new reports that had come in. The bell beside his bed had rung, and he had awakened and taken the elevator from his penthouse down to the next floor to read the reports in the privacy of his office, even though the hour was late.

The news was good. Philip was failing. He had lost Mack Bolan and was trying to pick him up in Monrovia. Robert was monitoring Philip closely, working on some secret plan of his own. Robert—Roberto—had a good mind and a steady personality. But he lacked depth of thought, imagination and creativity, the willingness to take big risks on daring lines of action.

David understood the need to gamble in the high-rolling world of international business, and he was gambling now on his knowledge of his younger brothers—on his knowledge and on their greed and ambition. He would wait for their utter failure. If Bolan didn't get them, they would fail anyway, because David would make it appear that Bolan had gotten them.

Then David would take over and remove Bolan once and for all. He had a simple way to end the Executioner's threat. He smiled as he thought about it. That part would be easy. The only tricky part was to eliminate his brothers first.

IN THE DRY, CRYSTALLINE AIR of Lake Tahoe the two older men sat in a comfortably furnished room and looked out on the scenic alpine lake. They had received the reports by phone, and now they sat quietly, contemplating the news.

"Bolan has apparently survived," the older one said. His voice as noncommittal as ever, deferring comment to the younger man, who emanated quiet, complete power.

"Yes," David Carlisle, Sr., said. "The game continues. A deadly game. And the only loser will be Mack Bolan."

The older one smiled. "Precisely."

JANET CARLISLE LOVELACE lowered the telephone in her husband's empty den. A smile was on her lips. Tripper's report was excellent. Philip had fucked up.

Mack Bolan was still alive. And that meant there was still time to do the job she was born to do.

THERE WERE FEWER than ten thousand telephones in Liberia. Mack Bolan thought about this fact as he walked into the Monrovia Transport Authority terminal on the corner of Center and Front streets.

It was early afternoon. Liberia's capital city of more than three hundred thousand inhabitants stank and reverberated with the cries from street fights and of hawkers and half-naked street vendors in from the bush, selling cotton, rice and fish from carts that weaved dangerously among old Thunderbirds and Cadillacs, relics of the days when oil and American investors had made this small country on West Africa's southwest coast prosperous.

The heat and humidity hung heavy in the bus terminal. Caged chickens squawked. Children played and fought. American rock music blasted from a radio. Adults sat listlessly in chairs, leaned against walls, squatted in corners. They were waiting for the buses that would take them to the Liberian hinterlands of Ganta, Gbargna, Buchanan and Harper. The roads were bad. The buses were old, and always ran late.

But the MTA terminal had a telephone. In Liberia it was easier to find a television or a radio than a phone.

Bolan dialed the number Fernando Cruz had given him two days before and leaned back against the wall. He was still tired from his experiences in Angola, exhausted from the hike and search for the rendezvous with Grimaldi.

He'd hiked into Monrovia from a deserted stretch of beach north of the city, thinking about André Villela, who had fought long and hard, only to throw his life away in a moment of instability, and thinking about Fernando Cruz, who had begun to learn about himself and his possibilities. With luck, Cruz would use to good purpose the intel he remembered from working with Villela. He could even become a *comandante* himself.

Bolan let the phone ring twenty times. No one answered.

To put in time, he took a walk around the block. The Republic of Liberia was slightly smaller than the state of Pennsylvania, yet here in Monrovia it seemed as if the little country had all the width and breadth of Africa.

The deserts of the dark continent seemed to gleam on the skins of traders and entrepreneurs from Mali, Niger and Algeria, who brought handmade crafts, jewelry, fabrics and small appliances to sell from colorful booths set up in alleyways and empty lots. Dark and silent mountain forests showed like a silent film in the fierce hunters' eyes of the trappers and timber merchants from Liberia's interior, and from nearby Guinea and the Ivory Coast. Here they came to peddle soft skins, hats, leather goods and cords of wood. And the vast oceans echoed in the foreign tongues of the fish vendors who shouted their fresh catches on Monrovia's congested corners. "Perch! Halibut! Tuna!"

Bolan walked back through the noisy, dirty, teeming streets to the MTA terminal, and dialed the number again.

This time it was busy. At last someone was there. Bolan waited two minutes, then dialed again. He was in luck—it rang. But then it rang and rang. No one answered, though he again let it ring twenty times. He wondered whether he'd just had the bad luck to call right after the answerer had left.

He took another walk. Throughout the long, humid afternoon, he repeated the process. Several times the number was busy when he dialed. Then he would keep dialing until the busy signal no longer sounded. But there was never an answer.

And there never would be.

He realized suddenly that someone was certainly there at the other end of the telephone, but he or she would pick up the phone only after coded rings, such as two rings, then hang up and call again. And whatever the secret combination, if Bolan happened by sheer luck to guess it, he would still need a verbal ID—a code word or phrase—to get the person there to talk to him.

He had wasted a whole afternoon. Damn!

He walked out of the terminal and down the sidewalk to Broad Street and the main post office where stamps were sold, mail picked up and visas extended. It was a busy place, the poor, the middle class, and the servants of the wealthy jockeying for service.

He located the rows of brass-fronted postal boxes and found the number Fernando Cruz had remembered. Villela had done business with TWA—Trans-World Arms, Inc.—through the mail as well as by telephone, through the very postal box he was now studying.

He checked his watch. Almost five o'clock. Not much chance a company would send a messenger to collect mail this late in the day. Still, he would stick around, reconnoiter, keep his eye on the box and be prepared to spend the day here tomorrow.

Then Bolan spotted the Englishman.

The Executioner stepped back against a wall and faded into a shadowy doorway behind a row of public lockers. He watched the man stroll idly around the post office, like any interested tourist, as if eagerly studying all the new sights and sounds. He grinned. It was quite an act. But Bolan had recognized the man instantly: Paul Stone, MI6. The blond Londoner, dressed like a tourist with camera around his neck and expensive camera bag over his shoulder, postcards sticking out of a pocket of his Banana Republic photographer's vest, was acting the part of a bluff-looking, good-natured tourist.

In Monrovia?

"Stamps, or did you come here for your visa extension, Paul?" Bolan said as he stepped from the doorway to amble alongside the Englishman.

Stone did a double take. "Mack, old chap! What a surprise!"

"I know what you mean."

Stone casually turned and moved toward a wall. Unconsciously he lowered his voice. "So what brings you to this part of deepest, darkest Africa?"

Bolan just stared at him.

Stone sighed. "Oh, very well. I heard about the killings of federal agents. I suppose that's it."

"Good thinking. What about you?"

Stone shrugged. "Got a little time off, needed to unwind, eh? So here—"

"In Liberia?" Bolan smiled. He'd always liked Stone. The guy never gave up.

"Good climate here," Stone offered.

"If you like torrential rains, or days hotter than hell."

"Fine beaches—"

"If you like riptides."

Stone looked balefully at Bolan.

"Trans-World Arms, Inc." Bolan waited for the reaction. He got it. Stone's pale eyebrows went up ever so slightly.

"I'm at the Nevada Hotel at the corner of Benson and Gurley. Let's have a glass of mango wine," Stone suggested.

"Beer," Bolan said. "And stay out of the bars on Gurley. A nice ripe tourist like you will get mugged."

"Oh, stow it. Meet you in an hour."

"No way," Bolan said. "We'll walk over together. Wouldn't want you to get lost before we could talk, now would we?"

CHAPTER FOURTEEN

Bolan and Stone sat in the corner of the Lazy Suzette bar on Gurley Street, drinking Watney's ale, listening to American blues and eyeing each other. Bolan was still on just about every national wanted list around the globe, and he was sure Stone knew it.

The only question was, was Bolan on MI6's wanted list?

"That mess in Abu Dhabi a while back," Stone said. "I think MI5 would really like to talk to you about that."

"Am I on MI6's list?" Bolan listened to a great horn on the canned music.

"Not that they've told me," Stone said dryly. "It seems the Iraquis were really quite put out when their fake ayatollah was shot down before he could get to Khomeini."

"He was a triple agent, Paul, working for the Iranians and the KGB, too. Out for himself all the way. He would have blown the Gulf wide open."

"Can I tell that to MI5?"

"Be my guest."

"Thanks."

"Now," Bolan said, "let's get down to brass tacks. TWA. What about them?"

"Suspicious outfit," Stone said solemnly. "Very suspicious, don't you know."

"Obviously, or you wouldn't be here. How did you learn about it?"

"Can't tell you, you know that. Have a burner?" Stone offered his pack of Player's to the warrior. "The Liberians couldn't make a good cigarette if their Cadillacs depended on it. Not that they can make much of anything except a nice cushy living for the old slave elite who came over from the States way back when. At least that's what our PM says."

Bolan shook his head. "Okay. Let's try this one for size—we exchange pieces of intel. One for one. Fair enough?"

"Speaking of our dear lady PM, she's in one grand uproar about the international arms business," Stone continued, as if he hadn't heard Bolan's offer. "It's getting so loyalty no longer exists. Everything's gone to hell in a hand basket, as you Yanks say. Next thing you know, the goddamned opponents in a war will be selling arms to each other to finance the war. Where's the morality in that?" He leaned forward, chin jutting in anger. "And morality to hell, where's the bloody common sense?"

"Sounds like something's happened. You Brits take a bath somewhere?"

"A bit of one," Stone said, his face flushed with outrage. "We put through a large defense order with TWA to help out the government in Burma, and what happens? It ends up in the hands of the Marxist guerrillas. It looked like a straight steal. The Marxists had pulled one over on us, and we had to pay the bill."

"Then you find out the Marxists had a little help, and on the inside."

"You bet they had help, and TWA got paid twice."

"Meaning," Bolan said, "that TWA was double-dipping. They double-crossed you by taking your money, then delivering the goods to the Burmese Marxists who also paid for the shipment."

"God-awful mess. I mean, we won't do business with TWA again, but in the arms and ammo world you never do know exactly who you're dealing with, and now we don't know if we can trust anyone." Stone looked with disgust across the room as if it were filled with double-crossing, double-dealing weapons sellers.

"Just the Burma stunt, or are you running into that kind of business elsewhere?" Bolan asked quietly.

Stone lowered his eyes, then looked up again. "I suppose it's no secret. Probably why you're here. We're seeing it around the globe. Our boys have friends who have friends—you know all that—and the friends are saying it's getting less and less that they can buy from a company and know they won't get screwed, or ripped off, or the intel for delivery won't get sold to someone else. It goes on and on. Weapon sales used to be a relatively honest business as long as you paid and kept your mouth shut. Had to be, or those who bought the guns would turn on those who sold them. Now someone or something is upsetting the balance."

"Someone or something so enormous that it thinks it can get away with it."

"Enormous is right. Something like the old Krupp empire, Carlisle International, the Soviets or even you chaps. You know what that could do to the balance of power?''

"Agreed," Bolan said. "And we've got to do something about it. Have you heard of H. Boll, Ltd.?''

"Yes," Stone said slowly. "They're new boys. We've had some dealings. No problems I know of. They deliver on time, have good prices." He studied Bolan. "You think they're connected to this TWA down here." It was a statement, not a question.

"Looks like it," Bolan said simply.

"Ah," Stone looked thoughtful.

"Now what about our deal? What do you know about TWA?''

"Not bloody much," Stone said.

"Don't con me, Paul, I need the intel. You been watching the P.O. box?''

Stone emptied his bottle of Watney's into his glass and studied the bottle. "Two bloody days."

"And?"

"If TWA's come in to collect their mail, it hasn't been while I've been there," Stone said. He drained his glass slowly. "Watney's do make a nice ale, don't they?''

Bolan shook his head at the closemouthed Englishman. "Quit holding out, Paul. What do you have?''

Stone sighed. "Anguilla, British West Indies," he said reluctantly. "The checks from TWA seem to be drawn on a bank in Anguilla." Stone gave Bolan the bank's name and address. "Now, old chum," Stone continued, "the rest of our deal. What do you have that I might use?''

"A Monrovian telephone number for TWA."

"Nice. Very nice."

Bolan repeated the number and added a warning. "You'll need a code."

"I'll have my second come in with the code team and work at it from that angle."

"And you?" Bolan asked, downing the last of his ale.

"Off on another lead. Seems we've had some quiet word of a possible IRA connection with TWA. Tenuous, but one never knows. My assistant will come in here, watch the post office and try to figure out the code for the mysterious telephone, while I go chasing around among the bogs and leprechauns. And what about you? Can we double on this one?"

"Maybe later, Paul, when I know more. Right now I'd better play it alone."

Bolan's thoughts were already racing. Tonight he would sleep. Tomorrow he would check once more at the post office to see whether anyone from TWA came to pick up mail. If not, and Bolan didn't think they would now, he would go to the airport and buy a seat on the next airplane to the British West Indies.

ROBERTSFIELD AIRPORT was thirty miles from Monrovia. The terminal was quiet at this time of the morning, the air already hot and humid, promising another uncomfortable day. Grimaldi wasn't available to fly Bolan privately to his next area of investigation, so Bolan had gotten up early and made his way to the airport.

Since there was no direct flight from Liberia to the British West Indies, Bolan bought a ticket via London. As he stood in line at the luggage check-in, he felt rested again, ready to get on with the job, to use TWA to lead him back to H. Boll, Ltd., and put a stop to the secret, shadowy arms broker, and whoever was behind H. Boll.

Concentrating on the problem of the elusive arms company, Bolan only absently noticed that the third man ahead of him in line had two suitcases, but put only one on the scale. The other—a gray Samsonite overnighter—he set casually to the side of the desk where the attendant couldn't see it, and where it would be out of the way, not particularly noticeable by either passengers or attendants.

There was nothing out of the ordinary about that—except the smooth, efficient, almost rehearsed way the man did it. What the man should have done was pick up the overnighter as soon as the big suitcase was weighed in, and then carry the smaller suitcase with him on board the aircraft.

But when the clerk was finished with the paperwork and gave the smooth man his baggage check, he strolled off, leaving the suitcase behind. He had forgotten it. Or had he? Bolan stared at the innocent-looking suitcase, sitting there almost hidden by the counter and the scale and the people in front of him. Then something else happened.

The two people ahead of Bolan, who had been in line between him and the guy who had left his suitcase, stepped out of line and hurried away as if they'd suddenly realized they had forgotten something. Without looking back, or talking to each other, the two men almost ran toward the door to the parking lot.

Bolan could have moved right up to the desk then to check through his suitcase, as any ordinary passenger would have done. He would have been right on top of the abandoned suitcase. But Bolan wasn't an ordinary passenger.

He fit all the pieces together. The suitcase abandoned by the desk, the two guys hurrying away, Bolan's chance to move right up to the desk. He thought of what else had happened to him as he had pursued H. Boll. The killer in Paris who had stalked him and Hal Brognola. The killers on the ferry and in Sweden. The attack on the mountain HQ of the Angolan freedom fighters. And now a suitcase left behind.

"Clear the area!" Bolan shouted.

It was another ambush. The suitcase contained a bomb, a bomb set to explode while Bolan waited for his bags to be checked through. It would kill not only Bolan but a lot of innocent people.

"Bomb! Clear the area!"

He didn't wait for the shocked travelers to move, or for the police or airport security to go into action. After shouting, he raced toward the swinging doors where the two men had disappeared. He'd already lost any trace of the man who had left the suitcase, but he might still be able to find the other two.

"Security!" he bellowed. "Clear the area! A bomb's going to explode! Everybody get out! Security!"

People began to scream, confused and frightened, they ran, stumbled over one another and fell. Uniformed and plainclothes security men seemed to come from everywhere then, clearing people from the terminal. Even in Liberia, airport teams had been trained to deal with terrorism and bomb threats.

"Stop!" they yelled at Bolan. "Stop where you are!"

But Bolan barreled through the door and out to the concrete where taxis, cars and limos cruised slowly along the street that separated the terminal from the parking lot.

One of the two men was straight ahead, hitting fenders as he weaved between moving vehicles on his way to the parking lot. The other was gone, and Bolan didn't have time to go looking. He tore after the one he'd spotted.

The man had crossed the street. Now he glanced over his shoulder as he reached the parking lot. He saw his pursuer and began to run faster.

Bolan chased through the street, weaving between the moving cars and taxis.

The man ahead pulled a Walther from under his arm.

Bolan was almost on him, but he was unarmed. You couldn't go through airport security toting guns, knives and ammo. His weapons were hidden in the secret detector-proof compartments of his suitcase, and his suitcase was back in the terminal at the weigh-in counter.

The Executioner had no choice.

He hurtled over the hood of a parked Bentley and lunged straight at the killer. The man raised both hands in a fist from which the deadly Walther protruded.

Bolan slammed into him the instant he fired. The bullet tore through Bolan's jacket under his arm and exited harmlessly out the back.

The Walther went flying.

Bolan's momentum carried him over and past his target, who had dropped at the last second. Bolan slammed into another car and sprawled on the concrete.

His opponent was up, scrambling after the Walther. Stunned, Bolan forced himself to stagger to his feet. The man had almost reached the gun. He wouldn't miss this close a second time.

The Executioner shook his head clear as he leaped in and slammed a lethal karate kick into the guy's head just as the killer's hand closed on the Walther. The would-be bomber went down like an axed steer, twitched once and lay still.

Bolan waited, but the man didn't move. Blood trickled from his gaping mouth.

The warrior bent down. His kick had caught him flush on the temple the way it was supposed to. Unfortunately the guy was dead. He'd wanted him alive. Bolan went quickly through the dead man's pockets.

Then he was surrounded by Liberian airport guards, guns out. "Don't move," the commander said as the guns pointed at the Executioner's head. "You're under arrest!"

The security guards were grim. Bolan groaned inside. He couldn't explain who he really was and what he was doing. He would be thrown in prison for murder. And there wasn't a damn thing he could do except try to talk his way out.

"The bomb," he said quickly, "did you clear the terminal? Get everyone out? It'll go off—"

"It's clear," the officer snapped, "not that we believe you, my friend. What did you want? To panic everyone so you could murder this man and get away with—"

Inside the terminal the bomb went off. The roar was tremendous. Wooden beams and siding, plastic tables and chairs, metal supports, all splintered toward the sky. There was a tremendous suction. The ground rocked.

On the street and in the parking lot people fell to the concrete and wrapped their arms over their heads to protect themselves from the terrifying sight and ear-shattering sound.

"Jesus!" the commander whispered, and lowered his weapon from Bolan's head. He stared at the destruction in the terminal and watched as the debris rained back down on people within fifty yards of the terminal.

"Help people!" he ordered his guards. "Now!"

His men spread out to look for the injured, to call the hospital for doctors and ambulances if they were needed, to help the uninjured to their feet and calm them.

The commander looked at Bolan. "You saved a lot of people." He slowly holstered his pistol. "You want to tell us what it was all about?"

"I just got lucky, did what anyone would have," Bolan said. "I saw a man leave the suitcase at the counter, saw this guy and another get out of line fast. I'd just been through De Gaulle in Paris, didn't like how it looked."

"Ah, yes. Very tight security there."

"When someone leaves a suitcase, they pick it up and take it to their explosion room."

"Alas, we have no explosion room here. We're much too small. I'm very appreciative that you noticed and called our attention to it."

"Uh-huh."

"Still," the commander said, looking down at the dead man guarded by two of his men, "I must ask to see your identification. You killed this man."

"Of course," Bolan replied. He reached into his pocket for the fake IDs he carried—the international driver's license, the U.S. social security card, the credit cards, the insurance papers. "I'm a black belt. He had a gun. I had to act fast."

A new and quiet voice came from behind Bolan. "Of course you did, Mr...?" He was a tall man in a three-piece gray suit who had approached from across the parking lot. "Kevin, why don't we all talk in my office."

"Our manager, Mr. Keith," the security commander told Bolan. He looked at Bolan's papers. "Michael Blanski," he told the manager.

The tall manager shook Bolan's hand. "This way, please."

In Keith's air-conditioned office, Bolan again explained that he had simply seen the abandoned suitcase and had jumped to the correct conclusion.

"Ah, do you have anything to show what your business was in Liberia, Mr. Blanski?"

"In my suitcases."

"Yes." Keith nodded. "I'm afraid they went up with the bomb, eh?"

"Did they?" Bolan said innocently. "That's going to cost the company. You can call them in New York—

Atlas Furniture. I was sent to look at some of your hardwood timber.''

Bolan gave them the telephone number. It would reach Hal Brognola and would check out long enough for him to get out of the country. Keith nodded solemnly, his quick eyes appraising Bolan. He asked a few routine questions that would fill in the blanks on an official report, tape-recorded the answers, including detailed descriptions of the other two men, and stood up.

Bolan didn't think Keith had bought his entire story, but the man didn't sound as if he was going to give Bolan a hard time.

"We're very grateful to you, Mr. Blanski. We'll put your information to good use. What flight had you planned to take?"

Bolan told him.

"London, eh? Out of the frying pan and into the fire."

"They have more than their share of terrorists," Bolan agreed.

"Well, Mr. Blanski, I hope the rest of your trip is safe and uneventful. Kevin will stay with you until your flight leaves. We want to protect you from any attempt at reprisal by those two who escaped. Meanwhile, we'll get to our work and find out which terrorist group is responsible. Maybe we'll even get lucky and find the other two who left the bomb."

They shook hands all around. Kevin escorted Bolan from the office. It was all much easier than Bolan had expected. Was it simply the good luck of dealing with someone who appreciated Bolan's help, or was something else going on? Had Keith guessed who and what

Bolan was? If so, which side was he on? H. Boll wouldn't want anything about the incident to come out in an investigation others could hear of. They might think it better to let Bolan get away this time, than to risk any public notice. It was more than possible.

Bolan spent the hour until his flight took off under escort by the very protective Kevin. They weren't going to leave him alone one more minute in Liberia. Was it protection or containment? Keeping him safe or keeping him under guard? Bolan didn't know, and as he waited for his flight, he felt as if a thousand unseen eyes watched him.

CHAPTER FIFTEEN

Northernmost of the British Leeward Islands, tiny Anguilla had shining white coral beaches, an eighty-degree year-round perfect climate, no cities, no rivers, few palms because of the arid weather and no income tax.

Anguilla Island, beautiful and pastoral, had only seventy-five hundred residents and a burning ambition to become a tourist mecca. But there were just too few rooms to rent, too little nightlife and tourist entertainment, too authentic a rural and placid native life without the hype to attract the bored, restless and superficial of Europe and the United States. Too few people had heard of the island.

Still, Anguilla had banks, partly as an act of faith in the tourist boom to come, and partly from the lack of income tax: here stood Barclays Bank International, Anguilla National and Caribbean Commercial. In the mid-1980s an FBI agent accused a part owner of Caribbean Commercial in a sworn affidavit of having set up "shell corporations," listing himself as company president, and opening bank accounts on behalf of reputed drug traffickers to launder their money.

Bolan had picked up a taxi at tiny Wallblake Airport. It took him to The Valley, the largest community on the sixteen-mile-long island, and the only one with a traffic light. He ordered the taxi driver to stop in front of the simple white stone facade that announced it was Leeward Island Bank & Trust.

He paid the driver, then strode into the bank, carrying the large black leather bag that held his hidden weapons and combat clothes, which he had replaced in London before the flight here, via St. Kitts.

"Manager, please," he told the beautiful woman behind the receptionist's desk, and handed her one of his fake business cards.

She was slight and dark, with smooth skin and a brilliant smile. She looked him up and down, fluffed her black hair and strolled away, round hips swinging suggestively. The nameplate on her desk said Malva Gomez.

The manager came out to greet him, a small-town bank's courtesy to a stranger, and took him back to his office. The receptionist with the inviting smile gazed after him.

"What can I do for you, Mr. Blanski?" The manager was a short little man with sharp, furtive eyes and a nervous shoulder twitch.

"As you can see from my card, I'm a bank investigator from Council Bluffs, Iowa, U.S.A.," Bolan said. "I'm here to make a request. We've got a company with a branch factory back home that may be involved in some illegal activities. We think the parent company, an international firm, may not even be aware of the irregularities."

He paused and watched a frown cross the little man's face when he heard the word *illegal*.

"Yes?" the manager prompted.

"We're concerned that the SEC may have to be called in. In order to decide on a course of action, we need one more piece of evidence the parent company might be able to give us, and it looks like that evidence is in an account the company has at your bank. Since there's been trouble at other...local banks—" he was referring tactfully to the uproar caused by the FBI agent a few years before "—I thought you might answer a few questions for me. Nothing confidential, of course. Maybe just names and addresses of signing officers for the company so we can talk to them personally and off the record."

The manager's frown deepened. "Well, I'm not sure, but if no confidences are broken, perhaps—"

"I'd like to take a look at your records, to be sure it's the same company, and see who they're doing business with, withdrawals, deposits, dates, that sort of thing."

"The company name?" The little man's shoulder twitched nervously. He didn't like the smell of this.

Bolan saw there was no sense in any more beating around the bush. He had laid all the groundwork he could. This would either work, or it wouldn't. It depended on how nervous, and how dumb, the little man was.

"Trans-World Arms, Inc.," Bolan said. "Commonly known as TWA." What he saw in the manager's sharp eyes wasn't anger or nervousness, but fear.

The manager's right hand moved beneath his desk, and Bolan knew he was in trouble. The little bastard was hitting a silent alarm, and the police would be here shortly.

"Sorry, I don't recognize the name," the manager lied, a smile pasted across his tiny features, as he stalled to give the police time to arrive. "You must have the wrong bank, Mr., er, Blanski, is it?"

Bolan leaned over the desk, his face inches from the pasty manager's. "Want to check your records, friend?" he said coldly. "Just in case?"

"Really, there's no need..."

Bolan grabbed a fistful of the little man's shirt, tie and collar, and yanked him up out of the chair. The manager's breath stank of cheap wine and sausages.

"Listen, pal," Bolan said, his voice arctic in the warm office. "You probably don't even know what's going on. You're just a greedy little bureaucrat doing what the big boys in this bank and at TWA tell you. So let me put you in the real picture. TWA is a slimy octopus that sells guns and bombs to anyone who'll pay the freight, so they can get rich. They live on the blood of good, decent people, and you've just helped condemn a bunch of innocent people to die because you don't have the backbone or the morals..."

He looked into the guy's uncomprehending eyes, and stopped. What was the use talking to brainwashed robots like him? He was just a pawn, taking orders, or bribes, and Bolan didn't have time to educate him. He needed to get the hell out of there, or he'd be in jail, where no amount of bribes or orders would get him out before H. Boll slipped someone in to kill him.

Bolan dropped the man into his chair and, without a backward glance, swept out of the office, past the tellers and the receptionist to the front door. There he paused and turned to survey the bank.

He noted that only the receptionist was looking up from her work, watching him. The others all pretended nothing was happening—they saw nothing, heard nothing.

The tellers worked in their cages. The bank manager sat stunned in his office chair, his mouth open, his shoulder twitching. He would need a lot of glasses of wine tonight to get over the day's fear and shock. Only the exotic brunette smiled at Bolan. Bolan smiled back. Maybe she would be the way to get what he needed from the bank about TWA.

He moved fast out the door, noting the bank's closing time on weekdays—noon. An hour to wait, and an hour to stay out of the hands of the local police. His bag was a dead giveaway, so he turned into a narrow dirt side street of the tiny excuse for a town and slipped the suitcase in a recess under the dilapidated porch of what looked like an empty house. He took off his suit jacket and hid it with the bag, slipped off his tie and shoved it into his pocket.

In his open-necked shirt, he blended with the other casually dressed pedestrians, as he strolled with them along the main street of The Valley, hands slipped comfortably in his pockets. He gazed in store windows, nodded at the barber who was leaning against his doorframe taking the air. As the sound of running feet pounded toward the bank, Bolan wandered around the corner, and down an alley.

The police had arrived. Finally. Nothing moved fast on Anguilla.

If he was correct, the little manager would alert TWA after the police were gone, and TWA in turn would go to H. Boll. The manager would want the police only for short-term solutions—he would be far more interested in making sure TWA knew it had a problem. Once TWA knew, and told H. Boll, then H. Boll would send someone else after Bolan.

He hailed a taxi, asked the driver to take him to the nearest beach. On an island where most strangers were tourists, and therefore had money, the cabbies often doubled as tour guides, companions and, of course, pimps. When Bolan suggested a swim, the driver smiled gladly, imagining a handsome tip and a paid hour or two in the shade while his passenger enjoyed the fine Caribbean water.

Also, Bolan reasoned, the beach was the last place the police would look for a fugitive.

Once on the gleaming white sand, he stripped to his shorts. Few people were on the beach of the small cove, for most islanders were at home or at jobs. He swam for thirty minutes in the warm, buoyant sea, then sat on a rock to dry in the sun, while the cabdriver rested in the shade of his car, the radio tuned to a rock station. When the cabbie returned him to The Valley outskirts, Bolan tipped him handsomely. The driver went away whistling; the generous Yank had made his day.

Bolan waited down the street from the Leeward bank. It was exactly noon when the receptionist stepped out the door. She wasn't one to spend a minute longer than required at her desk. She waved cheerfully back into the interior, and then, her hips swinging, she strolled off, heading away from Bolan.

He crossed the street and tailed her from the other side. She turned down a side street. He followed until at last she walked through a gate in a white picket fence and into the yard of a whitewashed clapboard house, where purple bougainvillea and pink hibiscus grew in a riot of rich colors.

She continued down a brick path along the side of the house, and disappeared.

Bolan quietly crossed the yard after her. At the back of the house, he found her waiting for him on the bottom step of an outside stairway that led up to a small porch, where colorful geraniums, pansies and snapdragons grew in pots.

"I was hoping you'd come," Malva Gomez said, a smile on her lips, her eyes bold and dancing. "What did you say to Mr. Mather? He had a fit right in the office."

She was a small woman, beautiful and exotic, probably close to thirty years old. She spoke with a slight Spanish accent unusual in this British colony. The heady fragrance of her perfume surrounded Bolan.

"You live up there?" Bolan asked.

"Want to see?" she replied, eyes flashing.

"I'd like to, but I've got work to do."

She pouted. "And here I've been waiting for you."

"Why?"

"Well," she said conspiratorially, "we know Mr. Mather is a bad person, *muy malo*. He alters things in the accounts, and then has Jean—that's his secretary—shred papers and make all new records. That's bad, isn't it?"

"Very," Bolan agreed.

She seemed to preen under his approval. "Jean heard you tell Mr. Mather you're a bank examiner, but he told the police you were trying to rob the bank. I told you he was bad." Her voice had grown grim for a moment; now it brightened with a new thought. "It must be wonderful to travel all around the world and see so many places and people."

"With your accent, you must have been a few places yourself."

"Oh, that," she said. "My parents came from Venezuela years ago. I keep the accent. I don't know why."

"It's a very nice accent," Bolan assured her.

"I'm glad you like it."

"I mentioned my job..." Bolan said. "Would you like to help me? Mr. Mather works for some bad people."

"Oh, my!" Her eyes widened. "I would like that very much. But what can *I* do?" She spread her small hands wide and shook her head at her powerlessness.

"Do you have keys to the bank?"

"Of course. I open in the mornings."

Bolan smiled. "Then you can be a very big help."

She gave him a warm smile in return. "We mustn't go there until tonight. Mr. Mather works in the afternoons. You don't want anyone to see us, do you?" She ran her fingers down the buttons of his shirt.

"Not *we*, *I*," Bolan corrected. "I'll go alone. And tonight will be fine."

"But—"

"Alone," Bolan said firmly. "I'll bring the keys back afterward."

"It's a long time till tonight. Aren't the police still after you?" Her fingers traced back up the buttons to

Bolan's neck. She touched his skin lightly, then withdrew as if suddenly shy.

"Probably. Did you have something in mind?" Bolan figured there were worse ways of putting in time than accepting this lovely woman's obvious invitation.

She wrapped her arms around his neck, her soft breasts pressing into his chest.

He kissed her, long and deep. Heat pulsed through him.

She nipped at his neck.

He picked her up and carried her up the stairs.

THE COOL EASTERLY BREEZE of the island night rippled the thin white curtains of Malva Gomez's bedroom windows. Mack Bolan slipped out of bed and dressed silently. He had the woman's keys to the bank, and would pick up his blacksuit and weapons in town.

"You can't do it alone," Malva Gomez said from the dark of the bed behind him. "There's an alarm that must be turned off from outside with a key."

"There usually is," Bolan replied. "I'll find it."

She lit a cigarette, the flare of the match briefly lighting up her beautiful face, and the dark eyes that watched him. "You're no bank examiner from Council Bluffs, Iowa, or anywhere else," she said, and laughed. "Would I want to shake this place with a bank examiner?"

"What am I, then?" Bolan said, genuinely wondering what she thought.

"I don't know, love, and I don't care. Whatever you are is all right with me as long as you take me out of here." She sat up and blew smoke that wafted away on the breeze. "Whatever it is you want in the bank, let's get it together and I'll fly away with you anywhere."

"Malva, it could be damned dangerous—"

"With me," she said, "you'll be in and out in ten minutes. Without me, you'll be half the night, believe me. You've got the keys, but I won't tell you where the alarm is unless you take me with you."

Bolan studied the woman. She had guts; he liked her. The afternoon had been great, and it was true that the sooner he got off this island the better. In a place this small, companies as rich and powerful as TWA and H. Boll were bound to have the local cops on the payroll. There would be nowhere for him to hide for long.

"Then get your clothes on fast," he told her.

She surprised him, dressing faster than he could have expected, though part of him wished she hadn't put them on at all. But she was right; Anguilla was too small and sleepy and slow to hold a woman like her for long.

They slipped through the night, the only sounds a distant radio, soft laughter behind closed doors, the occasional bark of a sleepy dog carried on the trade wind. What little nightlife Anguilla had was scattered in all directions along the beaches, far from the silent town center of The Valley. Bolan retrieved his hidden suitcase and jacket, slipped the specially modified Beretta 93-R into his waistband, pocketed a pair of smoke grenades in the jacket and headed for the target.

The bank was dark and silent.

"No one's ever even thought of a guard at night in this backwater," Malva said, half laughing and half bitter.

Bolan used the key on the alarm box, cleverly hidden behind a downspout and one of the island's few palm trees, and then opened the side employees' entrance. With Malva's help he quickly located the file on Trans-World Arms, Inc.

Ten minutes later Bolan put down the penlight he'd been using and sat back, his face hard.

"Have you found what you wanted?" Malva asked, her dark eyes questioning and her voice anxious as she looked at the clock and listened in the quiet night.

He nodded grimly. He'd found both more and less than he wanted. Checks had been deposited in the Trans-World Arms account from almost every country and guerrilla army in the world, ComBloc, Free World or Third World, but most of the large checks paid out had gone to only one place—H. Boll, Ltd., at the address in Hamburg that was nothing more than a mail drop.

He knew for certain now that Trans-World, and the Angola double cross, *were* H. Boll operations, but he was no closer to locating H. Boll. The names of the signing officers of Trans-World Arms meant nothing to him, rang no bells.

Then he found it. A name he did know. On a check made out to H. Boll and endorsed over to McMurray Brothers, Inc., was the signature of Sean McMurray himself.

"Let's get out of here!" Bolan snapped.

Malva nodded, and they quickly replaced all the files, checked to be sure they had left no trace of their nocturnal visit and slipped out the side door. Malva locked the door and reset the alarm before they melted into the night, heading for Malva's apartment in the small house.

"Do we leave now?"

"I leave now," Bolan said. "Malva, I like you, but right now—"

"If you go, I go. You think I did this just because I want to help you? Because I'm attracted to you? I want to go somewhere I can *live*, where the action is. Either I go, or you do not go very far, Mr. Blanski!"

Bolan watched her as she strode angrily through the silent night.

"You have a car?" Bolan asked.

"No, but I can get one."

"When's the first flight out?"

"There's one to St. Kitts at 8:00 a.m. At six there's a plane to St. Maarten for those who work there."

"Can we get on it?"

"I can get us on it."

"Get the car, and get the flight," Bolan said.

Sean McMurray and his brother Tommy were the largest cocaine and marijuana dealers on the East Coast. They were also strong sympathizers of the Irish Republican Army, Provisional Wing. They sold dope and they bought guns and they dealt with H. Boll. And In Monrovia Paul Stone had told Bolan there could be a link between Trans-World and the IRA. This looked like the break at last.

The McMurrays were headquartered in New York. There should be no problem keeping Malva Gomez busy in New York.

CHAPTER SIXTEEN

The British West Indian Airways 747 from St. Kitts lumbered low over New York's Jamaica Bay, the Jacob Riis Bridge directly under the wing for Malva to marvel at. The big jet rumbled into JFK International as dusk settled over the marshes of Mill Basin and the vast sprawl of lights of outer Brooklyn, with the great glow of Manhattan to the west.

Malva drank it all in. "Isn't it wonderful? New York! I never really dreamed I'd be here someday. Oh, thank you, thank you." She turned to smile softly at him. "You won't regret it, I promise."

Bolan shook his head, but his expression was serious. "I don't do things I regret, Malva. Only now I've got work to do."

Her face fell. "But...but I don't know anyone in New York. Where will I go? Mack, I..." She stopped and shrugged. "Well, I wanted to come, didn't I? I suppose I'd better be a big girl. But I'll see you, won't I? I mean, I like you for *you*, not for New York."

"Of course you'll see me." A twinkle in his eyes lightened his face. "I'll take you to a great little hotel right in midtown. When I finish what I have to do, I'll take you out on the town. Okay?"

"That sounds divine." She kissed him hard, holding him a moment.

Bolan smiled down at her, and then they joined the rest of the passengers filing out of the jumbo jet. A taxi took them into Manhattan and the small Hotel Dexter in the east Sixties just off Park Avenue.

The desk clerk nodded to Bolan. "Glad you'll be staying with us again, Mr. Blanski. Taking in the shows this time?"

"Only off-Broadway, SoHo and no movies."

The clerk smiled. "You're a hard critic, Mr. Blanski."

After they had checked in, they followed the bellman up to the fourth-floor room. He suggested dinner and drinks in the Dexter Room, and left them alone. Malva placed her single suitcase on the rack beside Bolan's black leather bag and turned to face him.

"They all know you so well here. You think they approve of me, Mike?"

"They approve."

She moved close to him and began to unbutton her black wool travelling dress. "Is the Dexter Room exciting? Should we hurry and go there?" She stepped out of the dress. She wore only a pale rose teddy edged with lace.

"Later, maybe," Bolan said, and put his arms around her.

MACK BOLAN CLOSED the hotel room door softly behind him, after taking a last look at the woman sleeping in the bed. He was dressed all in black now, his Beretta holstered under a black raincoat. He strode quickly along the hall and took the stairs down instead of waiting for the elevator.

On the ground floor he catfooted down a narrow corridor through the nonpublic area of the hotel and slipped out a side door into a dark alley. He thought he saw something move in the shadows of the building on the other side of the alley, but walked to the alley mouth as if he had seen nothing. There he flattened himself against the wall and peered around at the main entrance to the hotel.

The car was parked across the street in a loading zone, its engine running but its lights out, two men in it smoking and watching the entrance to the Dexter.

As Bolan stood there he heard the sound he was expecting, the sound of someone moving up behind him in the alley. The stealthy footsteps stopped behind him. Bolan whirled, to suddenly confront the man hidden in the shadows of the alley.

"What do you want with me?" Bolan snarled.

The man started to snarl back when Bolan lashed out with a hard right and smashed him full in the face. Blood spurted. The shadower landed on his back in the alley filth.

"You motherfuck—" The man pulled a Mauser from his coat pocket, silenced and deadly. He had acted from reflex, but saw his mistake almost instantly. He knew he'd revealed himself to Bolan, and knew what that meant. Fear filled his eyes. Bolan's Beretta was already in his hand and pointed straight at the assailant on the ground. With its sound suppressor and specially machined springs that cycled subsonic cartridges, it was as silent as the Mauser. The Mauser trembled, frozen halfway out of the man's pocket.

The Beretta barked once, no more than a loud snap, the New York traffic noise covering it. The shadow in the alley would never draw a gun again. Bolan leathered the Beretta under his arm again and walked out of the alley in the opposite direction from the car still parked so obviously in the loading zone across from the Dexter. They wouldn't see him, wouldn't even look toward the alley, sure their man there would handle that direction. It was a mistake made by too many field commanders, thinking only about their own narrow sector.

Seconds later Bolan was around the far corner onto the avenue. Before he walked more than a few steps, a taxi cruised silently up and the door opened. Bolan got in.

"What's going on, Striker? What's the woman doing at the hotel?"

"No choice this time, Hal," Bolan said. "Trust me. I gave the alert code with the message to meet."

"They're watching the hotel."

"There's one less now."

Bolan told Brognola about the man in the alley. The Fed studied the dark profile of the Executioner in the gloom of the back seat as the cab cruised through the city, then looked out the window on his side. "H. Boll?"

"Or whoever's backing them," Bolan said. "Got to be."

"What have you got to tell me about that?"

"Nothing."

"Nothing?" Brognola scowled. "That's not what I've been hearing from my field stations. They report you've been moving like a hurricane from Sweden to Angola to Liberia to Anguilla and now here. You've got to be hot onto something, Striker."

"Moving, but going nowhere," Bolan said. It was his turn to scowl out the window at the lights of the great city. "I'm beginning to think it's a snipe hunt, Hal. A wild-goose chase. Someone or something's got me trotting down their trail, doing just what they want me to do."

Brognola was silent, only his thick fingers drumming against the doorframe. "Lay it out for me."

Bolan took a long breath. "I'm following leads fast and hard. They look like solid leads. But when I think about what I've found out, I don't really know anything."

The big guy shook his head angrily. "I'm moving around, getting shot at, picking off all kinds of foot troops, but I don't *know* any more than I did at the start. It feels like one of those chases the Cong led us on that went nowhere except into a goddamn ambush."

"You're saying this is some kind of ambush, Striker?"

"I'm saying I'm starting to smell someone laying down smoke, Hal, pulling strings. Someone *wants* me to track down H. Boll and now Trans-World Arms."

"Why?" Brognola asked. "So they can get a shot at you? What does anyone gain by sending you all over the planet? If they want you, why not just send some guys with guns to find you?"

"It's not me. It's something else," Bolan said. His eyes seemed to pierce the dark interior of the taxi. "Look, it feels like I've been set up to go after H. Boll.

Then, everywhere I go, they're *waiting* for me. Someone wants me to go after Boll, but Boll's always ready for me when I get there!''

Brognola stared at Bolan. "You're saying someone cons us into going after Boll, and then warns Boll you're after them? That's nuts."

"Not if the guys leading me, and the guys warning Boll, are different," Bolan said. "What if someone wants to destroy Boll, but someone else found out and warned them?"

Brognola looked out the taxi window. "That would mean someone had four of my people killed just to make me send you after H. Boll." He stared at the back of his shadowy and silent driver in the front seat. "What kind of men kill people just to work some plan?"

"Soulless men, Hal," Bolan said. "Men we have to destroy."

They rode in silence for a time as the dark taxi cruised around the great city.

"Who?" Brognola said at last. "Another arms dealer? The KGB? Some governments that sell arms? Someone Boll double-crossed?"

"Could be any of those."

"And who warned them?"

"Any of the same," Bolan said. "But it's not just that they were warned, Hal. They know where I am and where I'm going all the time. Someone's *leading* me on. I can feel it. Sending me, guiding me."

"How the hell can they do that?"

"Simple. Spies, agents, planted every step of the way."

"You know that? How?"

"The best way there is—I've got one sleeping in my hotel room right now. Or she was sleeping. My bet is she was up and working ten seconds after I hit the stairs."

"You mean that woman—?"

"She was planted on me in Anguilla. It was just too easy and convenient. She was too damned eager to help me out, to come with me. And on the jet she made a slip. Just before we landed, she called me Mack instead of Mike."

Bolan could see Brognola pale even in the dark of the cab. "And you took her into our safe hotel knowing she—"

"There's no way she could have picked up my connection with you, or tailed me," Bolan said. "I can't let her know I've penetrated her cover. I have to play out the whole operation the way she expects it. Later, she could be damned useful."

Brognola pulled out a cigar and chomped on it as the cab continued to cruise under the dazzle of neon and the glare of theater marquees. "Who is she?"

Bolan shrugged. "All I know is she's working for H. Boll, or for whoever warned H. Boll itself. She was sent to guide me on to the next ambush. She's good. If I hadn't already felt I was being set up like some damned raw recruit, I might have missed her. But once I smelled a setup, I looked close and she was just too good to be real. Like a bottle of first-rate hooch you find in a wrecked house on the line and you know it's got to be booby-trapped."

Hal Brognola stared out the taxi window, thinking. "One thing I still don't get, Striker. If H. Boll was warned you were after them, why not just lie low, hide out, not send people to watch you and lead you around?"

"Yeah, that bothers me, too," Bolan said. "It's as if they want me to come after them. As if *they* were the guys who sent me after themselves!"

"That's crazy."

"Right," Bolan said. "Only I've still got this funny idea—that H. Boll was set up just for me to go after it! That there's someone behind the whole thing pulling strings."

Both men rode in silence through the city, thinking about a power somewhere pulling the strings on it all, wondering what it all meant.

"What are you going to do, Striker?" Brognola asked at last.

"Go on," Bolan replied grimly. "Let them lead me. Sooner or later I'll find the spider in the center of the web, and get some answers." He went on to tell Brognola about the check he had found in the bank in Anguilla and the trail to the McMurray brothers.

"Those rats? You think they're your spider?"

"No, they're another step in the snipe hunt, some sure bait to pull me on to whatever I'm supposed to do."

"They're bad medicine, Striker. They get rich selling dope to kids, and try to make like they're Irish patriots when they've never done a damn thing except feather their own nests."

"I know. They remind me of those white slavers in Nam who degraded their own women and worked on

Hanoi's payroll at the same time. But we'll get them, just like we got those snakes.''

''What's your MO?''

''Infiltrate, make like I'm another IRA Provo. Act the way they expect me to act. Everything by the book they probably have on me. Standard operating procedure for Mack Bolan. I've got to make them think they're fooling me, that their plan, whatever the hell it is, is going along smooth as a pig in a greased pen.''

''What do you need from me?''

''The right papers in the right place. I'm Benny Macklin, brother of IRA martyr Kevin Macklin. An American but a heavy sympathizer of the IRA radical left wing, who works over here to get weapons to the left-wing splinter group provos. I want to deal with the McMurrays for a shipment smuggled into Ulster on their boats. They've smuggled in plenty of their own. They'll jump at the chance to be paid to smuggle more.''

''You want me to plant a dossier on you in our files?''

''Cross-filed with the CIA and FBI if you can swing it.''

''I can swing it,'' Brognola growled as the cab passed the garish lights of Times Square. ''I assume you want the money to pay the McMurrays, too.''

''A hundred thousand should do it. Any more would make them suspicious. The IRA isn't that well-heeled.''

''What about Malva Gomez?''

''Nothing. I'll feed her just enough of what I'm doing for her to warn her control, and then leave her in the hotel. I don't want her touched, Hal. She could be my secret weapon somewhere down the trail.''

"I don't like it, Striker, but okay. I'll warn our people at the Dexter."

Bolan nodded. The two men were silent, deep in thought, while the taxi turned east once more toward the Hotel Dexter.

MALVA GOMEZ TURNED OVER in the bed as Mack Bolan bent and kissed her. She smiled up him, the only light in the dark room coming from the teeming city outside.

"What time is it, Mike?"

"Late," Bolan said. "I've got to move out, Malva, and this time I mean alone. You're in New York. You can handle the rest yourself."

The woman nodded. "I think I can take care of myself, and thanks, Mike." She wound her arms around his neck as they kissed again. "What are you going to do? Is it dangerous?"

"I'm working for the Irish Republican Army, Malva. We're working for freedom, and freedom is always dangerous."

"I understand." She smiled. "Take care of yourself. And, Mike, thanks again for getting me out of nowhere and bringing me to somewhere."

"I hope you see it that way in a year or so. New York is a tough world, and Anguilla can be a nice, safe place."

"If all you want is to be safe, you might as well lie down and go to sleep."

"You won't ever do that."

"No, I won't. When will I see you again?"

"I'll call as soon as this job is over."

"All right." She kissed him again. "If you don't, I'll find you. Believe me, Mike, I will. You won't get away from me so easily."

"No," Bolan said. "I don't think I will." He turned away and walked out of the hotel room.

Malva Gomez sat up in bed. She lit a cigarette, stared at the closed door for some time, then picked up the telephone and dialed 9 for an outside line.

SEAN MCMURRAY WAS AS SMALL and dark and skinny as his brother was big and redheaded and massive. The terrier and the giant. It was the giant who winked at the man he knew as Benny Macklin in the cavernous warehouse on the Brooklyn docks of Bush Terminal.

"You've been one fine busy bully boy, Macklin," Tommy McMurray said, laughing. "Sure and it's a glorious dossier they've got on you at the Company. Almost as good as me own. We'll have to have a go at each other one of these days for the fun of it, eh?"

"Shut up, dumbhead," the little terrier, Sean, snapped at the jovial giant. "You and your 'fun' is goin' to be the ruin of us yet. How many times I got to tell you this is business now, not a fuckin' game. Besides—" he looked Macklin slowly up and down "—I ain't so sure you'd have all that much fun with this one. Mr. Macklin can take pretty damn good care of himself, or I miss my guess."

"You sayin' I couldn't be takin' him in a fair fight, brother o' mine?" The giant looked Macklin up and down even more slowly and carefully and scowled.

"Not even in an unfair fight, me brother." Sean grinned.

"Unfair!" Tommy cried in mock horror. "He's sayin' I don't fight fair, Macklin. What kind of brother is that, eh? Now you wouldn't be fightin' unfair, would you?"

"Is there any other way to fight?" Bolan asked.

Tommy McMurray laughed. "Well, now, what a terrible thing to say, and me as fair as an English judge."

Sean looked at his watch. "Okay, had your fun? Should we maybe get down to some business now?"

"Whatever it is you want, brother o' mine," Tommy said.

The redheaded younger brother strolled off and sat on a crate, his feet swinging as Sean nodded to Macklin.

"Then it's agreed, we supply the arms and the boat, you pay us seventy-five grand in advance, the final twenty-five when we land in Ireland."

"And I come with you," Bolan said, carrying off with flair his role as IRA sympathizer and arms buyer.

Sean smiled. "We wouldn't have it any other way, Macklin. Isn't that right, Tommy?"

"Right as rain, Sean me boy. We like a man ready to work, raise his own sweat, take the risks with the rest of us."

"In Ireland we all stay together until I see the guns in the hands of the IRA people. You don't get another nickel until I do," Bolan told them.

Tommy McMurray looked terribly hurt. "The man doesn't trust us, Sean. Can you imagine?"

"I don't trust anyone," Bolan said. "You live longer that way in my trade."

Sean's dark, flat, cold eyes looked straight at him. "You have my word we'll be with you all the way to the end, Mr. Macklin."

And in the deserted warehouse on the Brooklyn docks the two McMurrays finalized their plans with the Executioner.

CHAPTER SEVENTEEN

Benny Macklin, alias Mack Bolan, lay on the narrow bunk of the small fishing boat off the Irish coast, asking himself some hard questions. Were the McMurray brothers part of whatever was going on around H. Boll? Did they know who Macklin really was, or were they just dope kings and gunrunners out to make a dirty buck with no particular interest in him? No interest, that is, except in his money.

And they weren't any damned rear-echelon by-the-book questions. They boiled down to a plain old gut question: would he have to watch the McMurrays all the way, or could he just concentrate on an attack from the outside—until he paid over the last of the money and the brothers and their gang didn't need him anymore?

He'd have to make up his mind pretty soon. The small freighter that had brought them and the guns from Brooklyn had off-loaded and dropped them into the fishing boat two hours ago. They would be putting ashore just as dusk fell, less than fifteen minutes from now, and he'd have to go on deck and join the brothers and their crew.

Bolan put himself in the place of whoever was behind the whole thing. Would he trust the McMurrays, or just use them and watch them? He knew the answer before he'd asked the question—no one in his right mind would trust the McMurrays. No, the brothers wouldn't be part of it; they would be no danger until the guns were delivered and the money paid.

He could concentrate on outside dangers.

The decision made, Bolan got up and checked his weapons. The Beretta 93-R was holstered under his arm, the .44 AutoMag, Big Thunder, hung heavy in a leg holster strapped down and solid under his pants. He slipped his oilskins over his black combat suit and climbed the ladder to the deck.

"So there you are, Macklin," Tommy McMurray boomed through the wind in the gray Irish dusk, the big redhead holding hard to the running gear of the bucking boat. "Have a good sleep, or was the stomach a bit unsettled?"

The fishing boat rolled and plunged through a hard-running sea, the low coastline not a mile away to port. A dark, stony headland was almost dead ahead. Treacherous rocks jutted barely awash all around them in the white teeth of the driving ocean.

Bolan saw instantly that this was a dangerous stretch of water, an almost impossible passage through visible and hidden rocks to the headland, and probably around it to shelter in its lee. Few boats would land on such an inhospitable stretch of coast, so it wouldn't be patrolled by the Irish Republic's gunboats.

"They seized one of our boats last year," Tommy McMurray said through the wind, looking out at the rocks and the deadly slick that showed where a hidden rock lay in wait. "So Sean went for this place." His laugh blew away on the wind. "No Republic navy boys are goin' to come in here, or the Ulster Queen's revenuers, and we haven't lost a shipment to the fuckin' rocks yet."

Holding hard to the rocking boat of the gunrunners, Bolan thought again—as he had so many times over the years of his wars against the Mafia and the terrorists—of how much good could be done in the world if the brains and effort that went into evil could be turned around. There was just too much profit in corruption, too little morality in too many people, from the slimiest dope peddler to the highest politicians, from the NaziComs to the goldbraid dictators. The battle was endless, and this time it was against the blood-hungry international arms trade.

"Hang on good, Macklin," Tommy McMurray yelled over the howl of the wind and the suddenly loud and heavy pounding of the sea on rocks. "We're goin' in!"

The boat had rounded close under the long, rocky headland, and Bolan saw now the narrow sheltered cove in its lee before another craggy headland. But between the boat and the safe harbor lay a violent turmoil of white water as the sea slammed against and boiled over the rocks that guarded the entrance. Sheets of spray hurtled high into the darkening sky, and treacherous currents swirled across the narrow stretch of open water that was the channel.

"Whooee, here we go!" Tommy cried.

The surf surged through the narrow channel of the entrance in long waves that twisted and turned in the swirling currents, slamming into one another as if in some mad dance of the sea. There seemed to be no direction to the waves once they entered the channel, only a chaos of churning green-and-white water.

Bolan hung on and watched as the captain took the boat out in a wide sweep and then headed straight into the maelstrom of the entrance. The crew, the Mc-Murrays and their gunrunners, and Bolan all hung on as the boat surged into the channel between the rocks, seemed to hang in midair and then suddenly caught a great swelling wave and shot forward, hurtling into the narrow passage like a surfer on his board, hydroplaning, the heavy boat in the curl of the wave.

The McMurrays whooped. The crew held tight. The captain was grim and tense. If they lost the wave, fell back, they could be swamped in the backsurge, or be swept instantly into the rocks by the violent crosscurrents. And then the boat soared in like a bird flying on the wave, into the calm, milky green water of the hidden cove.

The crew relaxed, the McMurray men wiped the spray from their faces and mustaches, the captain lit his pipe, and Bolan looked ahead to where the cove ended in the mouth of a small creek.

The boat moved slowly into the creek itself, continued for almost a hundred yards with the banks closing in and then stopped where a small pier jutted out. In the clearing around the pier two trucks and two black sedans were parked, waiting.

As the boat was tied to the dock, four men climbed out of the trucks and cars. They wore ordinary city suits, caps and slouch hats pulled down against the chill, and they all carried ugly little Uzis as they walked forward to meet Sean McMurray. He jumped down onto the dock and strutted toward them.

"That'll be Rourke and his cell," Tommy said, leaning on the railing beside Bolan. "They'll be convoyin' us to the border where an Ulster gang'll take over the escort. Proper army procedure and all that shit. You'd think they were fuckin' real soldiers."

The newcomers and Sean McMurray were deep into some argument, gesturing at the trucks, the cars and the boat, where the crew was already unloading the crates of arms and ammunition.

"Where do we make the final delivery, and pay you off?" Bolan asked.

"Somewhere over the border. We never know exactly where. And no group knows for sure who's in other groups. You won't spot anyone you know until we hit the border, if then. That way no one can set up an ambush, can they?"

The argument broke up, and Sean McMurray came back, swearing to himself. He gave orders to his two men to help the boat crew unload and help the IRA men load the two trucks, then walked over to Tommy and whispered furiously. Tommy laughed and came over to Bolan as Sean went back to supervise the work.

"The 'soldiers' showed up a man short," Tommy told Bolan, grinning. "Bloody clowns, they are. Probably one of them had to stay and mind Dad's shop or something. I'll have to drive the rear car for us."

"Why? There's four of them."

"Rourke never drives. He's the commandant," Tommy sneered. "They have to ride two in the lead car, so one can tell where they're going. That leaves two to drive the trucks, and me."

Bolan thought about the sudden change. It could be something, or it could be nothing.

"Let's get sweaty," Tommy said. "We don't want to be here the whole fuckin' night. When the deal's over, I'm goin' to take you into Belfast to some dives and dames you won't believe."

There was something about Tommy McMurray that Bolan was beginning to like. The guy was a dope dealer and a killer, but there was an honesty about him, an "I don't really give a shit about the money or the power" attitude. Just a big slob who liked action and an exciting life and who'd gotten into the wrong company— mainly his ratlike brother, Bolan guessed.

An hour later they were loaded and moving out of the clearing along a rutted dirt track to a narrow blacktop rural road. On the road the whole convoy turned north: Commandant Rourke, his driver and Sean McMurray in the lead car; Rourke's other two men driving the trucks; the McMurrays' two men riding shotgun in the trucks; Tommy McMurray and Bolan bringing up the rear.

Tommy whistled and talked all the way to the border, Bolan answering but not really listening. The Executioner watched the trucks ahead, and the road, and the rearview mirror. The ambush, if it was going to come, would probably strike before the final delivery of the arms to the IRA in Ulster.

The how and when of the strike probably depended on who was involved—Rourke and his men, the IRA in general, or only H. Boll without the IRA. If Rourke and his men were part of it, Bolan was safe as long as they were with the column. If it was the IRA in general, they might not care about Rourke and his cell, but they'd want the arms to be safe. If it was H. Boll only, they wouldn't care what happened to Rourke or the guns.

He watched and waited and listened to Tommy McMurray through the whole long night. Then they were at the border, and across into county Down—Ulster, where the British Army and Royal Ulster Constabulary patrols swarmed over the countryside and anyone could be stopped at any moment by a roadblock or a search party.

The convoy turned almost at once into a dark farmyard and stopped. Bolan eased his hand onto the Beretta under his arm and watched the trucks and the car with Rourke and Sean McMurray in it, and the black car that had been waiting for them in the farmyard.

"The Ulster mob," Tommy said in disgust. "They'll probably hold a fuckin' ceremony—changin' of the guard, salute and all that shit."

"At least they'll have a driver to relieve you," Bolan said.

But they didn't.

Sean McMurray came up. "You believe these clowns? Short a man, too, you'll have to keep on with the driving, Tommy."

Tommy swore this time; he was getting tired. All the other drivers were relieved by the Ulster IRA men. But there was nothing he could do. Muttering his discontent, Tommy followed the last truck as the new drivers quickly drove out and headed north through the dark again toward the main customs post at Newry.

Bolan was alert. Once, maybe, but twice? To be short a driver twice in the same night in two different IRA cells? It couldn't be a coincidence, but what was the purpose? To get Tommy McMurray to drive? To make Bolan and Tommy ride together? *To make sure none of their men were in Bolan's car?*

His hand on his Beretta, Bolan saw it all, just as the convoy slowed, almost imperceptibly to anyone who wasn't driving.

"Why the fuck are they slowin' down?" Tommy growled.

A dark car was parked at the side of the narrow country highway in the middle of nowhere, a black sedan without lights or anyone around it, and no sign of a house or a side road or even an open field. Just a dark car. Parked and waiting.

Bolan sensed the slowing, saw the car, all in a split second.

"Tommy! Get out!" And Bolan was out of the car, slamming hard against the road, rolling. He came up, fell, rolled.

The bushes closed over him as he pitched down into a ditch, the night exploding in a great roaring flash of orange light as bright as noon.

Hotter than noon.

Shattering the trees.

Searing the blacktop.

Flinging bushes and debris and pieces of cars across the highway and the night.

Two hulks burned in the darkness that was as light as day. Two gutted, shattered cars, torn and ripped open and burning furiously in the silent night—the car that had been waiting on the side of the road, and the car Bolan had been riding in.

Two cars flaming across the night, and men running back along the road. Running from the two trucks and the surviving car back toward the burning hulks. A small figure leading, racing back with horrified face and eyes in the glare of the flames.

"Tommy! God in heaven, they've killed Tommy!"

In the thick bushes of the ditch, cut and bruised and bloodied but without any serious damage, Bolan lay flat. He held the .44 AutoMag unleathered in both hands, and watched the small, weasellike figure of Sean McMurray run toward the flaming wrecks, his two men behind him.

Following them were the four IRA men from Ulster. The tallest in the lead had to be the commandant, a thin, pale-faced man with wild dark hair and an Uzi in his hand.

He shouted, "McMurray! Leave him! The whole bloody British army'll be down on us in minutes!"

Sean McMurray whirled and stared at the skinny provo. "You! You set it up! It was a trap."

"It's a war, McMurray. Out of here now!"

"For Macklin! That's who you wanted, Macklin! You could have told us. You—"

"Five seconds," the tall leader said, looking at his watch.

"You killed Tommy just to get Macklin! That's why you were short a driver! You bastard, you—"

The leader dropped his arm and nodded to his men. The four Uzis sprayed the burning night with their lethal message. Sean McMurray and his two men sprawled in their own blood in the bright light of the burning cars, a final look of astonishment on the face of the ratlike dope peddler and gunrunner.

"Move," the IRA leader snapped.

He and his men vanished out of the circle of light into the darkness.

Seconds later Bolan slid out of the ditch and went silently after them.

THE FOUR ULSTER IRA men sat hidden among the stones of a ruined church on the top of a knoll with a view of the countryside for miles around. They smoked and passed around a whiskey bottle hand to hand. It was their first stop in more than ten miles, and from the ruins they could see any hint of pursuit long before the pursuers could see them.

No one could have followed them; no one could sneak up on them now.

Except Mack Bolan.

They had traveled with amazing speed across the rutted, broken countryside with its stone walls and hedgerows, had changed direction many times, twisted back on their own trail, taking neither rest nor pause until they reached the ruins on the knoll.

Like the jungle cat he had learned to be so long ago in Nam, Mack Bolan had floated after them the entire time, as silent as a ghost. They had moved along the narrow paths, and Bolan had followed, off the path, the way he had learned to follow the Vietcong through the jungle—sometimes flat and crawling and only inches away from their feet as they backtracked on their own trail, unseen and unheard and unsuspected, but always there behind them. A human panther.

Now he lay just at the edge of the knoll behind a large weathered stone of the ancient church, ahead of them, not behind. He listened, the AutoMag in his hands. Sure of their escape now, they smoked, drank and laughed among themselves, lax and careless in the success of their bloody mission.

"Well, lads—" the leader raised his glass and smiled "—to a job well done then."

"Hear, hear!"

"Piece of cake. That Yank never knew what hit him."

"Neither did Tommy McMurray."

There was laughter, followed by silence as the bottle was passed.

"I don't know, though," one of them said suddenly. "Did we have to hose down the McMurrays?"

"Yes," the leader said, "we had to. If they were picked up by the RUC, or even the Brits, one of them would have sung like a nightingale when they realized we'd had to set up Tommy McMurray, too."

"Why did we have to waste Tommy at all? Was it really necessary?"

"We couldn't suggest Macklin drive himself, now could we? Even the Yank would've smelled a rat then. And we didn't want one of us to go west, did we?"

The other three were silent, drinking.

"It had to be done, boys," the leader said harshly. "With what we're going to be paid for this night we can expand our work more than we'd ever hoped. We can blow the Brits back to their own island, and the Protestant buggers with them.''

''It's that much, Charlie?''

''More,'' the commandant, Charlie, said. He took a long pull on the bottle. ''More money than you or I have ever seen or ever hoped to see, believe me. These people have the money to pay for what they want.''

''When do we see it, Charlie?''

The skinny commandant looked at his watch. ''In about half an hour, I should say.''

Two of the others murmured excitedly, their eyes eager for the money they would get for their night's work of killing both friends and enemies. But the third pulled on the bottle thoughtfully, wiped his mouth and looked at the commandant. ''And is it worth blowing up and shooting down four of our friends, Charlie O'Neill?''

The commandant exploded. ''Friends? Scum like that aren't our friends, Matt! The McMurrays and their hired thugs were neither friends nor patriots. Nothing but filthy drug dealers trying to buy some respectability by calling themselves IRA men. You think we didn't know where their money came from? Corrupt and stupid, both of them. So stupid they let that Macklin come right into the heart of our operations without ever finding out he was really an American agent named Mack Bolan! For that alone they deserved to die.''

''Bolan?'' one of the others said. ''I've heard of him. A tough fighter, as I recall.''

''And on the wanted lists of half the security forces, police and governments of the world,'' the commandant said. ''Just the kind of man the McMurrays would work with, a killer and a fugitive.''

But the man named Matt wasn't backing down so easily. "And what is this one we did the killing for but a slimy arms dealer trying to buy some respectability by helping out real freedom fighters?"

"True, Matt, true," the commandant said, "but he's paying so much more!"

The others laughed, and even Matt had to smile.

"So much more," Charlie continued, "we can put hundreds of good men in the field and at last drive the Protestants back across the Irish Sea where they came from." His voice rose in fervor.

The others all nodded eagerly as the commandant looked at his watch and stood up. "Saddle up, it's time to collect our pay."

Each took a final pull from the bottle, the last man tossing it into the darkness of the ancient ruin. They moved out down the knoll not ten yards from where Bolan lay hidden. Overconfident and careless in their own territory, and perhaps a little drunk now, he thought. Liquor and fighting didn't mix. Not if you wanted to win and stay alive.

Close to their objective, and full of whiskey, the four IRA men made more noise and took less care as they hurried on through the night. Like sharks that could smell blood, they moved toward their reward for the night's killing, with Bolan a little closer behind them and a little bolder now, too.

It was a straight walk over the green Irish fields and hills on the ancient path until, as the moon rose in the dark sky, the four IRA men climbed a ridge and slid hurriedly down the far side.

Bolan reached the crest of the ridge and peered over. He stared. A great stone castle stood on a small spit of land thrust out into a lake, which was silvery in the moonlight. Surrounded by water on three sides, the squat stone structure must have dated back to the Middle Ages. Bolan half expected to see the lord and his knights gallop up on great war horses, brandishing their lances, looking out fiercely from the steel helmets of their suits of armor as they followed the narrow road that led to the only entrance.

But the lord who rode up to the castle gate wasn't on a horse, and didn't brandish a lance.

As Bolan lay on the ridge in the night now bright with moonlight, he saw a long, sleek, silver-gray Rolls-Royce glide up along the road and stop outside the gate. A man got out and stood in the moonlight, big and athletic. Even from a distance his smooth, oval face looked boyish. His hair looked recently barbered and blow-dried, and there was a cruel twist to his thin lips as he waited for the IRA cell to reach him. In his hand he held a briefcase, not a lance.

Bolan didn't know the name of the man with the Rolls-Royce, but he knew instantly that he was the enemy.

From the ridge he watched as the IRA men reached the arrogant owner of the Rolls, who got back into his car. They all went through the gate into the castle, the IRA men walking ahead of the Rolls and its driver.

CHAPTER EIGHTEEN

Brigadier General Arnold Capp received the summons at 7:00 a.m. It came over the unlisted private line in his office on the Texas ranch where he trained the men for Falcon International's worldwide operations. He immediately called the main house and told his wife he had to return to Washington at once, then he used the same private line to call Janet Lovelace.

When he had completed both calls, he took the thick Falcon International operations file from his personal safe in the office and had his aide bring his civilian clothes and alert his driver. Dressed in an unobtrusive dark blue suit and white shirt with Air Force tie, he strode out of the office, after leaving instructions for the staff to continue full training in his absence, and was driven to the small airstrip for the helicopter ride into San Antonio and a commercial flight to Washington, D.C.

He bought his ticket under an assumed name, using a credit card issued in that name, and made sure no one who knew him saw him get on the jet. On the plane, in an inconspicuous seat, he tried to study his papers as the jet winged eastward. The summons was important to him and to his work—the worldwide operation that was going to make him a hero of the free world. But, oddly, he wasn't thinking now about the impending meeting, or about the papers in his lap. He was thinking about Janet Lovelace.

He wondered when she would tell her father about him.

LONG AFTER HER HUSBAND, in his civilian clothes, had left in the helicopter, Martha Capp sat in the elegant living room of the Pueblo-style mansion Arnie had built for her. She wondered for the thousandth time where he had gone. She wondered for only the second or third time what he was really doing, and if anyone in Washington knew what he was doing. She wondered for the first time how he had acquired the vast ranch and the opulent house where she lived.

One doubt had led to another, and now all at once her whole life seemed to be endless doubt. Where did Arnie go so often? Did the government know about Falcon International? How *had* he come to own this ranch on a brigadier general's pay?

Some of his trips were to meet with Janet Lovelace; she was sure of that now. Hadn't she wormed out of the air traffic controller on the base that Arnie's last trip had been to Montana?

But it wasn't Janet Lovelace or her husband's probable infidelity that really worried her. Infidelity was something a lot of Army wives had to become accustomed to or find new marriages.

No, it was her sudden fear about what else he was doing. The changes she saw in him terrified her: the sudden ruthlessness in his eyes, the gleam of something close to madness. A madness that seemed to her to hold

an ambition and a lust for power she had never known
in him before. An isolation that sent a chill through her.

Arnie had always been a team man, a dependable
subordinate, a brilliant and valued staff officer. But
now he had that wild light she had seen only a few times
before in the eyes of men who burned to command, to
lead, to make their mark on the universe.

It froze her blood, and terrified her, and she knew she
had to do something about it.

Two hours after Capp had left in the helicopter,
Martha Webster Capp, wife and daughter of generals,
packed a small suitcase, left instructions with her personal maid to feed her cat, got into a Jeep and drove
herself off the sprawling ranch to the highway that
would take her, too, into San Antonio, and, eventually, Washington, D.C.

SOME THOUSAND MILES to the north in Montana, Janet Lovelace looked out a window at a sweeping view,
but she was neither chilled nor terrified. She was angry
and annoyed. She didn't want to leave Montana just
now. She was expecting reports on the whole Bolan operation, and wanted to be alone to plan her next moves.
Damn Brigadier General Arnie Capp.

She didn't damn her father. David Carlisle, Sr., was
only doing what she would do under the circum-
stances, what he had to do to oversee and operate and
protect and increase the worldwide family business—a
business she was going to operate someday, or at least
the Carlisle family's personal part of it. That would be
enough; she wasn't greedy like Philip and Roberto. She

knew how long the entire enterprise had existed, what it required to exist always.

But she damned Arnie Capp as she gave instructions to the staff on what to do while she was away, and dressed in her East Coast establishment clothes: trim black skirt, soft gray leather low boots, white silk blouse, oversize thick burgundy man-styled jacket. The foreman, who didn't like her because he liked her too much and she had let him know he wasn't good enough for even a one-night stand, drove her to the landing pad and the waiting VTOL jet.

In the air headed toward Washington, she swore at Arnie Capp once more. He needed the constant inoculation of sex to keep his resolve firm, his commitment to her solid. The moment he'd told her of her father's summons, that he had to go to Washington and couldn't come to visit at the ranch, she knew she had to be in Washington, too. She had to be waiting for him the moment he left her father, waiting to bring his mind back to her. Nothing kept a man like Arnie Capp's mind on exactly what he needed as much as a good shot of the kind of hot, violent sex his wife had never given him. The kind of sex she gave him. She laughed—the kind she gave him and quite a few others, but Arnold Capp didn't know that.

Under it all, Arnie was an innocent Boy Scout who still believed in women and codes of honor. That was her main problem. She didn't like at all having to depend on a goddamn Alamo type who *believed* in all the codes and principles, who believed he was *right*, for God's sake! Who cared that what he was doing was *good* for the world?

My God, she said to herself as she watched the country pass far below. Arnie thought the world worked the way it was supposed to, that the good guys were all patriots and played for the good of God and country.

It would be funny, except that it made Arnie the weak link in her plans. He could tell the old man about them anytime, blow the whole thing. He was so goddamn *proud* of having her, of fucking her. It was all she could do to keep him from shouting it out, divorcing his wife, making an honest woman of her. She had to tell him over and over that her father could withdraw his support from Falcon International if he knew. That love and business and international affairs didn't mix in her father's view. Even when she told Arnie that, he still could barely hold back.

That was why she had to be there in Washington the moment he left her father, to keep his mind on her where it would stay quiet and in line. Where it would work for her.

WHEN THE CROWD of passengers had all left the jet, Brigadier General Arnold Capp took down his heavy briefcase and mingled with the departing crew.

No one seemed to notice him as he walked to a taxi and told the driver to take him to his downtown athletic club. Then he sat back and watched the city pass. He smiled to himself. There had been a time when the city and its power had intimidated him. Now it only fascinated him. It was his city, the capital of the world, and where he belonged.

At his club Capp used his key for the private VIP members' side entrance, undressed quickly at his locker and stepped into the steam room. No one had seen him. He sat in a corner where it would be unlikely that anyone would join him, closed his eyes and let the heat and steam scour his pores, penetrate deep into the tension that seemed to be always with him these days, except for those brief moments when he was in bed with Janet.

There were moments he wanted to shout to the world, but moments his newfound power told him he had to keep silent about for the good of the free world. He loved those moments, yet he hated them, too. Loved her, and hated...

"General Capp?" The voice was almost in his ear. "Arnie? Is it you?"

Cursing inside, Capp opened his eyes and looked straight into the smiling face of Senator Paul Beck, Foreign Affairs Committee vice chairman and noted liberal. He was an implacable enemy of the President's policies and Arnold Capp's beliefs, and a longtime personal friend of Arnold and Martha Capp.

"Paul." Arnie Capp smiled through the steam. "How have you been? Any good investigations lately?"

Senator Beck didn't laugh. "You know it had to be done, Arnie. We have an elected government."

"We have an elected President who has good men working for him and doesn't need to be told how to best serve the country and the free world."

"An elected President answerable to Congress and the people. One man among many, Arnie."

"We know what the people want, Paul."

"Yes, I know. Maybe that's the trouble," Beck said. "Let's forget the trenches. How are Martha, the kids?"

"Fine, Paul, all fine."

Beck nodded. "We haven't seen much of you and Martha around Washington lately. You still live out in Arlington?"

"Of course," Capp said. "I've just been really busy and so has Martha. You know how she loves her gardening."

"I know how she loves to party, and I didn't think NSC was so busy now, after the investigations. Don't tell me we haven't trimmed your sails, after all."

"Castrated us is more like it," Capp said. "And the President, too, if you want my view, which you don't. You have a closed mind, you liberals. You're back in the old days when wars were fought by rules. We live in a different war now, Paul. There's evil out there that wants to rape the world and eat it whole."

Beck nodded slowly. "Perhaps we haven't castrated you well enough yet. Maybe another investigation of NSC and the rest of the White House troops would be a good idea."

"Investigate and be damned," Capp snapped. "We'll get the job done that has to be done despite you and your sob sisters."

Beck nodded again. "Nice talking to you, Arnie. My best to Martha. Tell her we miss her, wherever she's hiding."

Capp said nothing, too angry at the blind fools who couldn't see where the danger to the world lay, who still thought you could talk to the NaziComs and the hoods and the terrorists.

He watched Senator Beck leave the steam room, and for a time no one else came in. Then two congressmen he recognized but didn't know entered and sat for ten minutes before leaving. Alone again, he waited, and a tall, dark man walked in, sat down near him, stared at the floor and spoke out loud.

"Softball is all pitching. Blue."

Capp stood and walked out. He showered, dressed at his locker and left the club. Some blocks away he picked up his Mercedes at a parking garage and drove out of the city on the parkway that would lead him south and west through Virginia and eventually to the Blue Ridge Mountains.

The softball had been the identification code. Blue had been the place where he was to meet David Carlisle, Sr.

THE DIRT ROAD wound deep into the mountains, switchbacked up a steep ridge near the crest and ended at a large timbered lodge behind a high iron gate. As Arnold Capp reached the gate, it opened silently, and he drove on to park beside the lodge. He got out, stretched and found himself staring into the almost yellow eyes of a slim, cobralike man in a black ninja outfit.

"Come."

Capp fell into step behind the man, who seemed to move without any sound. They went around the huge lodge to a small side entrance.

"Wait here."

"You know who I am?" Capp asked.

"If I did not, you would not be alive."

The cobra vanished almost by magic, returned in what seemed like a split second, then motioned for Capp to enter the side door. Inside there was a long carpeted corridor hung with hunting scenes. They looked like originals.

"Come in, Arnie."

The man who stood up from his seat on a high-backed thronelike chair with carved arms, and waved Capp to a long couch covered with soft tan glove leather, was an original, too. Well over six feet tall and with broad shoulders despite being almost too slender, he had silver hair that was thick and worn longer than was usually thought proper in business circles.

His long tanned hands seemed to move with a life of their own, supple and quick, and his knifelike face had the austerity of a father superior in a medieval monastery, with deep, almost hooded dark eyes.

He repeated his motion to seat Capp, the hand peremptory the second time. The general sensed instantly there would not be a third gesture. He sat down at once.

"The usual, General?" David Carlisle, Sr., asked quietly.

Capp nodded. Somehow, though he was accustomed to a lifetime of command, his voice seemed to fail him in the presence of David Carlisle. Or maybe it wasn't his voice. The older Carlisle seemed bigger than life, part of time and history and the planet itself.

The cobra materialized with Capp's Jack Daniel's and water. In the years he had been meeting David Carlisle, Capp had never seen him with any servants, aides or assistants beyond the ninja and the older man who also now sat silently in the room, Sam Walsh, whose title in Carlisle International Capp didn't know—if Walsh had any title other than friend of the boss.

"So, Arnie," David Carlisle said, "tell us what Falcon is doing."

Capp opened his case, took out the fat file, had a long gulp of his Jack Daniel's and reported. He told the two older men of his operations in Peru, where Falcon International's secret private efforts had seriously discredited the Maoist guerrillas, shut down over a hundred drug smugglers and helped make the friendly government more secure while being paid well for it all by that government.

"Very nice. Self-sufficiency for Falcon is a goal." David Carlisle, Sr., nodded.

The general reported on Falcon's work with the Salvadoran army against the Marxist rebels, their project training antiguerrilla forces in Honduras, the ultrasecret work with the Israelis to infiltrate the Syrian and Iraqi security forces to further equalize the Middle East conflict, the gunrunning to the moderate IRA provos in Ulster to help bolster them against the Marxist wing of the IRA, the beginnings of a project to destabilize the standoff in Fiji in favor of the more conservative native Fijians, secret support to the rebels in East Timor who were at last ready to attack the Indonesian government oppressors, and the dispatch of skilled career soldiers to train the weaker side in some dozen other small conflicts throughout the third world.

"You've been busy, General," Walsh said dryly.

"I think Mr. Carlisle will find his money well spent," Capp said with pride.

David Carlisle smiled. "Our money is always well spent, Arnie. It is simply a matter of knowing exactly what you want and then spending the money to ensure that it comes about.''

"I only meant, sir, that you can feel certain that your generous support to the President's cause through Falcon is doing a great deal to secure the free world against the ComBloc and third world terrorists.''

"I'm sure it is, Arnie," David Carlisle said.

"What about your weapons development work, General Capp?" Walsh asked.

The general took out another sheaf of papers. "The phasar ballistic missile killer system we're working on looks more than promising. It should fit well into the President's SDI plans and silence most of the critics who say the system will never work.''

David Carlisle looked at Walsh. "See, Sam, I told you there was room for us.''

"But can we sell it?" Walsh asked.

"If we can make it, we can sell it. Go on, Arnie.''

Capp completed his report with details on the progress of Falcon's work with new SMGs and the powerful, lightweight SAMs, plus the constant combat testing of all manner of new weapons from across the world. He closed the file.

"That's it, Mr. Carlisle. And as I said, your money is doing a lot of good everywhere, and the President is grateful.''

The two older men seemed to be digesting the report. In the silence the general thought about how David Carlisle had heard of his plan to use the power of private sources against the ComBloc, Marxist and terrorist countries and groups all over the world, and had come forward with his enormous financial support, without strings beyond these periodic reports, which were secret so that there would be no publicity.

He thought of how he had come to realize that men like David Carlisle, and great corporations like Carlisle International, were the real bulwark against the insidious spread of Marxism and terrorism. They were the only real power that could save the world from destruction. The Western democracies were too blind, had so many outmoded laws that blocked the swift action needed, that they were literally committing suicide.

There were too many who refused to see the truth, or who were actually working for the forces of darkness, and used every legal and political trick to stop the truth. Only men like David Carlisle, with their power and money, and like Arnold Capp, with his dedication, could save America and the world from disaster.

"The President," David Carlisle said slowly, "was not to know of our arrangement, was he, General?"

"Oh, no, sir, not the details. Only that I have private financing for all my projects."

"You report your projects to him?" Walsh asked.

"No, but I know he would approve them all. They all fit his stated objectives as well as yours."

"Of course they do," David Carlisle agreed. "And before you go back to Washington, the leaders of some of our subsidiaries have suggested particularly dangerous places for democracy and freedom where much could be done with money and a few good men, that couldn't be done with armies and nations. Sam can give you the details, eh, Sam?"

The older man nodded, and David Carlisle leaned back in his chair and glanced at his watch. "We have time for another drink, I think, Arnie. The same?"

The cobra man, whom Carlisle called Bulba, appeared as magically as ever, and soon the three men relaxed in the comfortable room with their drinks. David Carlisle smoked a thin cigar, which he studied thoughtfully as he asked, "How is my daughter working out in your operation, Arnie?"

"Very well, Mr. Carlisle. She's a lovely, bright woman."

"Yes, she is. Unfortunate about her husband, but we all make mistakes. I hope she'll find a better man the next time."

Capp paled. "I . . . I wasn't aware she'd broken with the senator, sir. I'm very sorry. She—"

"I didn't say she'd broken with Lovelace, Arnie, but they have no marriage, as I'm sure you and most of Washington know. She's a headstrong woman, and tough, eh?"

Somewhere a telephone rang. Bulba appeared again and whispered to David Carlisle, who got up and left the room.

"You're married, General?" Walsh asked.

"Yes, for many years."

"I hope not too many," the older man said.

Before Arnold Capp could ask what Walsh meant by that, David Carlisle returned. His face was pale and angry at the same time.

CHAPTER NINETEEN

Bolan came down from the dark ridge through the silver moonlight, as silent as a shadow in the damp Irish night. He circled away from the road and made a quick visual recon around the castle on its narrow peninsula in the lake.

The people who'd built the fortress so many centuries ago had known what they were doing. Although it wouldn't stand up to an attack by even a well-armed squad today, against one man with only handguns it was as solid as ever.

The Executioner needed a weak spot, a flaw, something the builders in the old days couldn't have foreseen. Or that the present owners had overlooked.

He found both.

Where the keep almost touched the water, there were two windows no more than twelve feet up. The castle builder hadn't allowed for an attack from the lake; knights and men-at-arms favored land assaults.

Later, a tall chestnut tree had grown right smack next to the water, so that its branches almost reached the windows.

It took Bolan two minutes to swarm up the tree and through one of the windows, which was even open! These days no one expected a castle to be attacked, front or rear.

The warrior found himself in a dusty room piled with old furniture. He slipped out the unlocked door into a back passage that curved with the walls of the huge keep. A single heavy wooden door opened out of the circular passage, with a straight corridor ahead and another massive iron-studded door at the far end.

As Bolan catfooted along the stone corridor, he saw the wall slits through which archers had shot from the rooms on either side at anyone who tried to reach the interior of the keep, the last bastion of defense in those days. They were empty now, the rooms and the slits, but they wouldn't have helped an enemy to stop Bolan anyway. No one, then or now, had imagined an attack from inside the keep.

Once through the iron-studded door, Bolan moved along a wider paneled and carpeted hallway, in the part of the castle where people still lived. He heard voices not far away, loud, laughing voices faint through thick walls and somewhere below the wide corridor where he stood listening.

Bolan moved toward the voices.

"Who the hell are you?"

There were two of them, armed with the ultramodern Heckler & Koch G-11 assault rifle, but they were making a careless walkaround with no expectation of meeting an enemy. In short, they were asleep at their posts.

Then they were dead.

Bolan had unleathered the Beretta before they could even start to raise their rifles. He shot them both dead center before they knew enough to be afraid.

They slammed back against the corridor walls and slid in their own blood to the carpeted floor.

Bolan listened to the faint echo of his shots, listened for any reaction in the great castle. Sudden noise or sudden silence.

There was nothing.

No outcry, no running feet, and the voices somewhere ahead and below went on without missing a beat. The Beretta was effectively silenced, and the two dead men had made no sounds except the thud into the wall and the slide of their limp meat to the floor.

Bolan moved on.

The war was always the same, only the terrain changed. Now it was indoors. He tracked through the corridors alert for more guards, zeroing in on the voices. Voices now almost directly below.

The Executioner stood outside a door. The voices seemed to come from both under his feet and inside the room, maybe even louder inside the room behind the closed door.

He opened the door. With the Beretta in both hands, he entered and swiftly surveyed the room. It was empty. Yet the voices were in it—somewhere ahead where narrow horizontal slits cut the stone wall at just below shoulder level. Bolan padded to the wall and looked through the slits.

Outside the slits was a balcony. A narrow door on the right opened onto it. And below the balcony was a vast living room, full of old furniture and suits of armor and ancient silk tapestries on the walls. The ceiling of the great room was higher than the balcony itself. The slits in the stone wall gave a total sweep of the towering two-story room. It was another internal trap where soldiers with crossbows could devastate anyone below.

And something more.

The voices below came through the slits as clear as over a loudspeaker. Bolan remembered the Whispering Gallery in London's St. Paul's Cathedral, where if you stood in the right spot on the walkway under the dome and whispered, your voice was loud and clear to someone listening on the other side of the huge dome.

A trick of acoustics, but Bolan had a hunch that this trick wasn't any accident. The lord of the castle had probably rigged up the acoustics so as to hear everything that was said below. They were sneaky and devious in those days.

Just like today.

Whether planned or accidental, the listening room was something Mack Bolan could use, to eavesdrop on the men who sat around the enormous room below, maybe find out what was really going down.

Bolan recognized the tall, slender Ulster IRA commandant and the other three IRA men. Four armed men he had never seen before were ranged around the walls. The big, boyish-looking, athletic man with carefully blow-dried hair who had gotten out of the Rolls-Royce earlier at the gate was also present, and one other man Bolan didn't recognize.

It was this last man Bolan stared at. He didn't know him, yet he knew him too well, had come up against his type often through the years. A solid six-footer, dark and rugged, hard and muscled. Forty or so, restless, an outdoor man. An old soldier like Bolan himself, a pro and a fighter, but one who hadn't made Bolan's commitment—to fight evil.

He stood a little apart, this last man, leaning against the mammoth fireplace, a faint sneer on his handsome face.

The big blond man with the cruel mouth was lounging on a long couch, sipping brandy. He was obviously the boss, and the cadaverous IRA commandant leaned forward in a hard wooden chair and talked only to him. The other three IRA men watched and listened, and the four armed guards looked half asleep.

"So there it is, and now we'll have the cash, if it's all right with you, Mr. Philip Carlisle."

The big blond boss asked, "You've got proof he's dead?"

Philip Carlisle! So there was the answer. One answer, anyway. Carlisle International, one of the largest multinational corporations in the free world, a three-hundred-year-old conglomerate that had gotten its start in banking and arms manufacturing.

There were a lot of Carlisles, which one was this? Bolan knew the American head of the family was David Carlisle, Sr., who had three sons. One of them was named Philip, but was this guy *that* Philip Carlisle? And what was his connection to H. Boll? Was he the real supplier behind Boll? Or the one who'd lured Bolan after Boll?

"No one could survive that bombing, for God's sake!"

"No body, O'Neill, no money."

The hard soldier at the fireplace said, "You don't want to see a bombed and burned body, Philip."

"I damn well want to see something," Carlisle insisted. "We missed him every time in Sweden, blew it in Africa and got screwed in Anguilla. You still don't know how he got into the bank and out of Anguilla, do you, Jones?"

"A woman," Jones said. "We haven't identified who she works for yet, but I've got a hunch."

"Roberto?" Carlisle asked.

"I hope so," Jones said. "I hope not your old man."

Both men were silent as they seemed to think about who else the woman could be working for. The IRA men had no interest in the woman, whoever she was, or whom she could be working for.

"Look now, your Mack Bolan's dead as Paddy's pig," O'Neill said. "We earned your, ah, donation to the cause of Irish freedom, and we'll have it now and be off. It might do you to be off as well, eh? The British army isn't made up of damn fools. They'll be on our trail sooner or later, and that means they could be camping on your doorstep within the next few hours. So let's finish it now."

Jones came away from the fireplace. "Did you take photographs?"

"You must be loony," another IRA man said. "You think we carry cameras? You think a photograph of a bombed and burning car is going to show anything?"

"It might show two bodies," Jones said. "Can you swear you saw two bodies in the car?"

"It was burning, lad," the oldest IRA guerrilla said. "Like a bloody torch and hotter than three hells."

"Why didn't you stay until it stopped burning so you could confirm the two bodies?"

"You want us to wait to do a clog dance with the British army or the Royal Ulsters?" O'Neill answered.

"Too risky for you?" Jones sneered.

"No," the commandant said, "too stupid. We're not fighting to show how brave we are, lad, just to free Ireland."

"Look, O'Neill," Carlisle said. "I'm not doubting you think you killed him, but the bastard seems to have nine lives and I've got to be sure. It's not the money, you can have that right now, but I have to know for sure."

The commandant thought. "Well, we could wait a few days and then send someone in to check the morgue."

"How about one of you goes back now to check?" Jones suggested. "One man should be able—"

"I'll not send any of my men. The British will pick up anyone even going near the scene for the next few days."

"Listen—" Carlisle began.

A door was flung open at the end of the enormous room, and an armed man ran in, his face pale, his hands and H&K G-11 bloody. "Someone's shot Morgan and Ted," he cried. "They're dead! Up in the hall outside the keep!"

Philip blinked. "Shot? What are you talking about, you fool? We didn't hear any shots."

The man shook his head in disbelief. "One pill dead center for both. Probably had a silencer, too. I tell you, they're dead, and they never had a chance. Their G-11s weren't even fired."

The other four guards gulped and looked nervously around them, assault rifles ready.

"Bolan," Jones said. "A modified Beretta. He uses one."

Philip Carlisle whirled, looking for the IRA commandant. "You stupid asshole! You let him get away again! You missed with a whole fucking bomb! You—"

Carlisle stopped and looked around the room. So did the other three IRA men. The tall, skinny commandant was nowhere in the room. Jones pointed to a door opposite the one the guard had come through to give the alarm. It was open.

"Two of you!" Carlisle yelled at his four guards. "Go find that son of a bitch and bring him back!"

The four looked at one another. Reluctantly two hurried out the door. They didn't like the idea of splitting up when there was a killer somewhere in the castle who killed with one shot dead center. They were right.

Mack Bolan stepped out onto the small balcony above the great room. He held Big Thunder in his hands this time. Its first booming round slammed one of the two remaining armed men fifteen feet across the room to sprawl on his back, a mangled mass of red flesh where his chest had been.

The others dived for cover, clawing for their weapons, without taking the time to spot exactly where Bolan was and find the best position for fighting back.

Only Michael Jones stood long enough to see Bolan high on the balcony at the side of the long room. Out in the open, Jones pulled a mini-Uzi from under his windbreaker. The mercenary fired a sharp burst at Bolan, making the warrior shift his stance at the last moment as he fired at Jones. The wildcat .44 Magnum round missed Jones by no more than an inch.

Bolan ducked inside the balcony door, giving Jones time to take cover at the far end of the room behind an angle in the wall that ran directly beneath the balcony. From there he could keep Bolan pinned down with minimum exposure of himself, and the stone wall was thick enough to stop even a .44 Magnum.

Bolan nodded with admiration. The guy knew his combat skills, a damn well-trained soldier. He wasn't going to be easy to take out. The others, he smiled grimly, were something else.

First, the IRA man behind the high-backed wooden chair. Bolan leveled his AutoMag, stepped out and blasted a hole through the chair and the guerrilla behind it and was back behind cover before Jones could spray a burst from the mini-Uzi.

Next, the last of Philip Carlisle's armed guards in the room. Crouched inside the great fireplace, he had to expose his head and shoulders to get a shot at the balcony. Big Thunder shredded the guy into red gore before he could even fire.

Third, the two surviving IRA men. From behind a leather chair and the couch they observed the power of Bolan's gun, the uselessness of their positions for fighting back, and took the only way—they ran out the far door and disappeared.

Last, Philip Carlisle. In the cover of a recessed bay window above the lake he was safe but couldn't attack. He raged at the escaping IRA men, "You fucking cowards! Come back! Get Bolan, you yellow assholes!"

Bolan was crouched on the balcony. The IRA men were gone. Jones waited behind the stone angle to get a shot. Carlisle huddled in his safe window, screaming, "Jones! Go up and blast the son of a bitch out of there! What am I paying you for? Fight, you hear me?"

Bolan rose to try a shot at Carlisle. Jones leaned quickly and got off a burst from his mini-Uzi. Bolan ducked back and blasted Big Thunder at the angle, shattering stone but not hurting Jones.

"Go and get him!" Philip yelled. "You're the fucking soldier, Jones! Do your goddamned job!"

Jones said quietly from his cover, "Shut up, Philip."

"Don't you tell me to shut up! You're a hired hand, Jones. Earn your money. Go and get Bolan!"

"You want him, boss? Okay, we'll get him together. Step out with me. He can't hit us both at once. You always wanted to be a real soldier. Here's your chance."

Carlisle laughed, high-pitched and shaking. "You're a coward, Jones, a coward! You're fired, you hear?"

"Don't be too much of a jerk, Philip," Jones said wearily, then shouted, "Bolan, can we make a deal?"

Bolan yelled back, "Sure. Tell me everything about H. Boll, who killed the American agents and why, and I'll only turn you both over to Interpol."

Jones laughed. "You're a comedian, Bolan."

Bolan heard a sound and whirled to see one more of Philip Carlisle's armed men in the room behind him, assault rifle up and ready but not yet seeing Bolan on the balcony. Then the guy saw him, but too late. Bolan's big AutoMag blasted him back through the door into the carpeted hall, the assault rifle and the dead man's bloody head shattered by the single round.

"Boss! Now!"

The shout came from the room below. Bursts of rifle fire kicked pieces from the balcony.

Bolan whirled back again and saw the last two armed men back in the room in front of the bay window. They were sidestepping toward the door, firing their assault rifles wildly up at the balcony, Carlisle shaking, hidden, behind them.

The warrior squeezed off two hammering rounds to pin Jones behind his angle and blasted each of the frightened guards with a well-placed single shot. Their dead bodies were flung backward, pinning Carlisle under them.

Philip crawled out, covered with blood and brains, and fell to his knees, staring up at the balcony. "Don't shoot, Bolan! Don't shoot! I'll make you rich! I'll give you anything you want. I'll—"

Bolan stood and looked down at the cowering man.

"Fuck," Jones swore from below. He leaned out and fired a burst at Bolan. Bolan blasted back.

"Stop it, Jones!" Carlisle screamed as he groveled. "I'll have him killed, Bolan! You can be my top man! I'll make you rich. Name your price!"

"Start talking, Carlisle," Bolan snapped from the balcony, his weapon trained on the coward. "What is H. Boll? Who's behind it? What's going on?"

"Of course! Just don't shoot. I—"

Michael Jones stepped out from the cover of the stone angle, his mini-Uzi in one hand, muzzle down. He looked up at Bolan. "You want him, Bolan? You can have him," the ex-soldier said, disgust in his voice.

Bolan lowered the .44. "You want to talk to me, Jones?"

"Talk?" Jones said. He walked across the room toward the kneeling Carlisle. "No, I don't want to talk."

Carlisle looked up at where Bolan stood with his AutoMag lowered. His cruel, cunning eyes shone. "Kill him, Jones! Kill him! Look, his gun—"

Jones raised his mini-Uzi with one hand and fired at Carlisle, three slow shots through the head. The magnate fell backward, dead before he hit the floor.

Bolan froze on the balcony. Jones whirled and fired a burst up at the Executioner. Bolan went down under the balustrade, then got to his feet, Big Thunder ready.

By then Jones was balanced on the parapet of the bay window above the lake. The ex-soldier laughed, flung his mini-Uzi at Bolan and shouted, "See you later, soldier!" And he dived through the night into the lake below.

Bolan leaped from the balcony to the floor below and ran to the window. He could barely make out Jones swimming across the dark water toward the far shore, a silvery wake behind him in the moonlight. For a moment he thought Jones waved back at him, but he couldn't be sure.

He had to admire the style of the guy. A tough, skilled soldier who did what he had to, just like Bolan. Too bad he was on the wrong side.

Bolan bent down over Carlisle. Damn! He couldn't get any answers out of a dead man.

Was this the end of the chase? Maybe not. Maybe Philip Carlisle carried some clue, some answer to it all, on him. Bolan searched the dead man with the three perfectly placed holes at the center of his forehead.

There was a wallet containing ten thousand American dollars, a single credit card in the name of Carlisle Mining Corporation, Johannesburg; drivers' licenses from ten countries; and membership cards in private clubs all over the world.

Nothing about H. Boll. Or Trans-World Arms.

And the dead man's pockets were completely empty. The small belt holster he wore was empty now, whatever tiny gun Philip Carlisle had carried lying somewhere in the room. He'd probably never used a gun, except to shoot animals after someone else had cornered them for him. Just a fantasy tough guy with too much money and power.

Bolan stood up, and the insect bit his neck. He raised his hand to brush it away, and felt the dart.

A tiny glass and metal dart was embedded in his neck. He whirled.

They stood across the room. A big man in a gray suit who resembled the dead Philip Carlisle; the IRA commandant, Charlie O'Neill, who had vanished the instant he knew Bolan was alive; and two dark Hispanics, one with a dart gun.

Bolan tried to raise his gun. He ground his teeth, forced his dead arm up, then fell backward to the floor.

He heard a pleasant laugh, and a quiet voice. "You'll be all right, Mr. Bolan. After all, you're a very lucky man. I wasn't at all sure you'd escape this little trap of Philip's, but Charlie was certain you'd survived, and I'm glad to see he was right. I owe you a great deal for eliminating Philip so efficiently. I wouldn't want to harm you, now would I?''

Bolan struggled to raise the AutoMag. Then he fell into a black pit.

CHAPTER TWENTY

Bulba and Sam Walsh stared at their boss, who stood pale in the living room doorway at the lodge deep in the Blue Ridge Mountains.

"Mr. Carlisle?" the ninja said.

"David?" Walsh said.

David Carlisle, Sr., replied, "Philip's dead. Bolan has killed him."

Bulba turned and left the room. Walsh went to a window and stared out into the night. On the couch Arnold Capp paled and swallowed hard. "Your son? Bolan? That can't be!"

Carlisle looked at him coldly. "Why not, General?"

"Because . . . I mean . . . because you asked me to get Brognola to send Bolan out to investigate H. Boll. You said Boll was a threat to the free world who worked with anyone, even the ComBloc, and Bolan was the best man to find and expose them."

"I was sure he was," Carlisle said, and suddenly sat down. He shook his head. "Everyone said he was the man. His record of patriotic service was perfect. All those reports about his killings and thefts and terrorist operations were supposed to be false." Rage flashed in his strong eyes. "How was I to know those reports were true! He *is* an outlaw, a cold-blooded killer, an international mercenary and renegade."

"But…but…" Capp stammered from the couch. "I mean, rumor has it that he's Brognola's most trusted man."

"Yes." Carlisle nodded. "Is Brognola a traitor, too? A spy? No, that couldn't be. Brognola's been duped like everyone else by this terrorist Bolan."

"It's all that makes sense, General," Walsh said. "It's impossible to think that Hal Brognola is a tool of the Marxists."

Arnold Capp went on shaking his head. "I…I've had doubts about Bolan, I admit. But with Bolan's record fighting against terrorism, how can he be a kind of terrorist himself?"

"There are some men you want to believe in," Carlisle said. "But something happened to him, Arnie, and he's changed. We didn't know about it until we got the reports of the investigation we had done on Bolan."

"It was a shock, let me tell you, General," Walsh said.

"An unbelievable shock," Carlisle admitted. "Perhaps none of his heroic efforts ever happened, perhaps it was a propaganda campaign to fool us. The truth is something else. Since Brognola turned him loose on H. Boll, he's murdered one man in Paris, been in an ambush of freedom fighters in Angola and worked with drug smugglers in Ireland." Carlisle shook his silver-haired head. "We have the truth now. Too late for Philip."

The fact of Philip Carlisle's death hung like a fog in the room.

"You're sure, sir?" Capp said, his voice as pale as his face. "About Bolan?"

"Sure?" Carlisle turned and called out. "Bulba!"

The man in black appeared in the room. Carlisle pointed to Capp. "The general wants proof about Mack Bolan. Bring the report file."

Bulba nodded and disappeared. The senior Carlisle continued to pace the room as they all waited.

"What exactly did happen in Ireland, David?" Walsh asked.

"It began when Bolan broke into a bank in Anguilla, British West Indies, apparently to make contact with some well-known New York drug smugglers who also ran guns for the IRA. Supposedly he was tracking H. Boll's connection with the McMurrays and the IRA."

Carlisle shook his head. "There was an ambush. The McMurrays were killed, the arms lost and Bolan escaped. Philip has been supplying the IRA with arms and other aid, and the survivors of the ambush went to report to Philip at his Irish country estate. Bolan must have followed them. He had probably arranged the entire ambush for that purpose."

Carlisle's eyes blazed with fury as he paced and gestured. "Bolan broke into Philip's estate, and then went kill crazy, murdering Philip's staff, IRA patriots and Philip himself. Only Michael Jones seems to have escaped, and it's possible he was working with Bolan all along."

"Why? What reason could Bolan have?" Capp asked.

"Perhaps to protect H. Boll. We've all been trying to identify H. Boll, and maybe Philip had learned something vital."

"Who found them?" Walsh asked.

"Robert. He'd come to visit Philip, discuss our IRA aid, and he found them all dead, Jones and Bolan gone. Jones is a Vietnam veteran, too. Seems to have known a lot about Bolan. Now he's disappeared, and Bolan is still on the loose to kill again."

"No one knows where Bolan is?" Walsh asked.

Carlisle shook his head as Bulba reappeared in the large room, a file folder in his hand.

The tall, hawk-faced business leader grabbed the file, opened it and began tossing papers at Capp. "You need proof of Bolan's crimes? Here, read this report from Mossad. From the CIA. Here's MI5. Here...here... here..."

Capp read each of the terse reports with an increasingly sinking heart. It was all there: the killings, kidnappings, thefts, attacks on friendly countries, interference in negotiations with ComBloc nations, overthrow of neutral governments, everything. Capp nodded, becoming angrier and angrier as he read. He looked up at Carlisle finally and said, "I feel in some way responsible. I got Brognola to send him after H. Boll."

"We all make mistakes," Carlisle said. "Laying blame is a waste of time. What counts is correcting the mistakes. It's too late for Philip, poor boy, but we can still stop Bolan. The first thing to do is isolate him from his U.S. government connections. He's a lone wolf, but through Hal Brognola he's penetrated Justice *and* State. We've got to neutralize that by closing down Brognola."

"But, I can't—" Capp protested.

"I can," Carlisle said. "I'll have the CIA interdict Brognola, cut him off from any contact with Bolan. The FBI and State, too. No problem. Carlisle International will put all its influence, resources and manpower into finding and terminating Mack Bolan!"

Capp nodded. "What do you want me to do?"

Carlisle came and stood over Capp, his hand on the general's shoulder. "Go on with your work. Serve the President and the cause of freedom. You're doing what no government agency can under the present restrictions."

"With your help, sir."

"That's what Carlisle International is for, Arnie. And we'll go after Mack Bolan. You continue all your projects, but be alert for Bolan and his schemes, and tell no one in the government about all this."

"I understand." Capp stood up. "I hope you get Bolan, sir. We have to go ahead with our work."

Carlisle smiled. "We'll get him, Arnie. Carlisle International has been around for almost three centuries, and we intend to be around for many more, eh?"

Capp shook hands fervently with his benefactor, then hurried out to his car. He had a long drive and a tiring flight ahead of him and a lot to do back in Texas.

As the sound of Capp's automobile engine faded away down the dirt road, the two older men sat in silence.

"Capp's in a hurry to do battle for the free world," Walsh finally said.

Carlisle smiled. "A simple man, our general. Give a man like him his big truth early, and he'll run with it forever without any more questions."

"You helped a little." Walsh smiled back. "To make him realize just what his truth was, I mean."

"One must sometimes point the direction for simple men," Carlisle agreed.

The two businessmen thought about that for a while. The silent Bulba appeared with brandy and glasses on a tray and poured each a glass. The older men sipped appreciatively.

"Are we really going to send everyone after Bolan?" Walsh asked after a time.

"No reason," Carlisle replied. "I know where Mack Bolan is—or, at least, where he's being taken."

"South America? You think Robert has him?"

"Of course," Carlisle said cheerfully. "The crap I gave the general is mostly what Robert told me, and is just that—crap." The slim older man shook his head in admiration. "I expect Robert rearranged Philip's action against Bolan to eliminate Philip, or had a lot to do with it, and he would have made sure he got his hands on Bolan, too. I assume Bolan is on his way to the main base of Cordoba Construcciones in South America."

"Enterprising," Walsh said. "And audacious."

Carlisle nodded. "Robert is showing promise. Let's see how he handles Bolan and the rest of it." The austere leader of Carlisle International sighed. "We know about Philip now."

"Yes," Walsh agreed.

"Now Robert and David, Junior, eh?"

Both men sipped their brandy.

"Aren't you forgetting someone?" Walsh said after a while.

"Forgetting?"

"Janet."

"An interesting thought," Carlisle said.

THE HEADLIGHTS SWEPT the night as General Capp drove at a steady eighty-five miles per hour toward the outskirts of Washington. He always felt fired up after a meeting with David Carlisle. The man was a giant, a brilliant thinker and, with others like him, the last real hope against the forces of darkness.

Tonight the man's strength in the face of his tragic loss had been amazing. Anger was what he had shown, not sadness. David Carlisle would mourn in private; in public he would fight. Capp wondered if he himself would have shown such strength if his son had been killed by an animal like Mack Bolan.

The telephone in his car rang. The sudden sound made Capp jump, jerk the wheel and almost slide off the deserted highway. He took a deep breath, righted the vehicle and drove on as he picked up the receiver. "Capp here."

"Are you alone, darling?" Janet's voice seemed to fill the car like a soft, sensuous perfume.

Capp had to steady the speeding vehicle again. "Janet? Where are you?"

"In Washington, darling. Did you think I'd let you fly all this way alone? I'm in my apartment, dear. I'll be waiting."

And she was gone before Arnie Capp could protest. Not that he would have protested much or long. He would have wanted to, for he had work to do in Texas and Martha would start being suspicious again if he were delayed, but he knew he wouldn't have protested.

The sound of Janet's voice was all he needed, to know that he had to have her tonight.

He passed the Alexandria exit and went straight on into downtown Washington and parked in front of the elegant building where Janet had her secret apartment. He had never known for certain if Senator Lovelace knew about this apartment, and he didn't give a damn. In the apartment Janet was his. He didn't ask questions about what her husband might or might not know.

"My tired darling!"

She was in his arms before he had the door closed, and clung to him all the way into the living room, her legs hanging free as she buried her face in his neck.

It was a lush room, all brocade and authentic antiques and thick Oriental rugs that would have cost a year of Arnold Capp's pay. A living room she seemed to stare at in surprise when she raised her head from his neck. A flash of anger seemed to cross her face.

Capp didn't realize that by not taking her into the bedroom as she had expected, he had annoyed her. He told himself it hadn't been anger he'd seen, after all—it was concern. She knew him too well.

"Arnie? Something's wrong," she said.

He gently loosened her fingers from his neck, solemnly sat her down on one of her antique brocade chairs and made his voice as tender as possible. "Janet, have you spoken to your father or brother Robert tonight?"

"Father? Robert? No, why should— Arnie, what is it?"

"Then I'm sorry I have to be the one to bring you the terrible news."

"What news?" she asked, her voice suddenly impatient.

Capp took a deep breath. "Janet, your brother Philip is dead. He was murdered in Ireland by that insane mercenary terrorist, Mack Bolan."

"Philip?" She stared up at Capp. "Dead?" She covered her face with her hands. Her shoulders seemed to shake. "No, I can't believe it."

She sat like that for what seemed like an eternity to Capp. Then she looked up at him, dry-eyed. "No, you must be mistaken. How could you know so soon?"

Capp told her how he knew. He told her everything her father had said about Robert's call and what had happened on Philip's Irish estate.

Janet stood and walked to a window, which looked out on the busy nation's capital, her back to Capp for some minutes, to hide her emotions, he was sure. Then she seemed to take a deep, shuddering breath, and spoke without turning around. "How did my father take it?"

"Very well, of course. Outwardly, that is. Inside, I don't know. He's not a man who would show emotion."

"No," Janet said. "What did he show?"

"Anger mostly. And determination to go on, to stop this Bolan and all the others who serve the darkness."

She nodded and turned to smile wanly at Capp. "Yes, that would be my father."

"He's determined to get to the bottom of this H. Boll business, and to stop Mack Bolan," Capp said seriously. "I admit I'm a little confused, baby. I thought

Bolan was after Boll, not working for them the way
your father says."

Janet sat down again, took a long, silver-tipped cigarette from a silver box on the coffee table and lit it. She
blew a stream of smoke and looked up at Capp. "My
father could be wrong, Arnie. I think there's something he doesn't know."

"Something he doesn't know about what?" Capp
said.

"About H. Boll, Arnie."

Something in her eyes, in the way she smoked, made
Capp slowly sit down. He watched her.

"H. Boll is part of Carlisle International, Arnie," she
said. "Bolan could have found that out."

Capp sat frozen. He didn't look shocked, or angry,
or disgusted, or even confused. He just sat as if the
words had no meaning, as if he had heard, but had no
way of understanding.

"Part of Carlisle?"

She nodded. "I only received the information a few
days ago. I knew you were coming to the ranch, so I was
waiting to tell you then." She blew smoke into the room
as she paused, as if reviewing in her mind what she had
found out. "H. Boll seems to be one or all of my
brothers. A venture either to break away from my father and the board and go on their own, or to make
some move to take over Carlisle."

She was up again, smoking and pacing the room.
"They've been getting restless lately under my father,
saying he's losing his grip. Of course, they have to take
over at least the family side someday, maybe even the
whole cartel, but they could be losing the old ways that

made Carlisle what it is. They could be going bad. If that happened, it could be a disaster for the whole world.''

Capp blinked at her. ''Well, I mean, Carlisle is a big company, but I don't think—''

She went on pacing. ''You don't understand, Arnie! Carlisle isn't just a company. It's an international network of companies more than three hundred years old! We have branches and associates in every country, every part of the world, even in the ComBloc. The biggest arms producers everywhere have been part of Carlisle for centuries, and most still are. Krupp, Skoda, Bofors. Men like Khashoggi are street corner pushers to Carlisle. No one knows this—we're very discreet and unknown—but no guns are sold in the whole world we don't have a share in.''

Capp stared at her. ''Even if that's true, I don't see what your brothers could be after through H. Boll, with its killings and double-dealings.''

''Neither do I, but there has to be some good reason, and my brothers are behind it. This Mack Bolan could be part of it, and maybe Brognola, too. I wouldn't be surprised if Robert or David sent Bolan to kill Philip! They'd do anything to get more power, and perhaps Dad *is* losing his grip, getting old and weak.''

''He didn't look old and weak tonight,'' Capp said.

''I hope you're right, Arnie.''

In silence he watched her continue to pace the room. A faint dawn was beginning to lighten the sky to the east.

''What do you want me to do, Janet?'' he said at last.

She stood still and looked at him. "I'm going to find out what my brothers are doing. I can't tell my father yet, or get his help—it would kill him—but I've got to try to find out and stop it. I may need all our Falcon International people. Soldiers, planes, weapons, intel, everything. You'll stand behind me, Arnie?"

"Of course."

"I don't know where we might have to fight in the end, but I know Venezuela is where we'll have to start. That's where Robert is based, and we know he was in Ireland when Philip was killed."

Capp felt a thrill deep inside him. Janet's strength and daring and courage and power excited him the way no woman had ever excited him. The power of a man in the body of a beautiful woman. Fighting back even with her brother dead, just like her father. He stood and took her in his arms.

"I'm with you all the way, sweetheart. Anywhere you want me to go."

"Oh, Arnie," she said softly. "I knew, but I had to be sure."

"Be sure," he said, and picked her up.

They kissed passionately. He carried her into the bedroom as the first light of the morning sun seemed to glow in the lush apartment.

THE AFTERNOON SUN shone through the windows of Janet Lovelace's bedroom when Arnold Capp woke up. Panic shot through him for a moment. He'd lost almost a whole day, and that always made him feel guilty, as if he'd abandoned his post in the face of the enemy. The training of a lifetime was hard to shake.

But he was the general; he had delegated all necessary duties at the White House and in Texas. There was no need for him to be personally on duty at all times. He could take a day off and lie in bed with the beautiful woman still asleep beside him.

Then he remembered Martha, and panicked again. If he was away one day longer than he had told her, she would start looking for him. He jumped out of bed and began to dress. Sleepily Janet opened her eyes and watched him.

"You have to leave?"

"Afraid so. A lot to do, sweetheart."

"And Martha will begin to wonder."

"Until you let me tell her, tell the world about us."

She smiled lazily. "Soon, darling. As soon as this H. Boll thing is over. When I know my father and Carlisle are safe."

"I understand."

He finished dressing in his rumpled business suit, making a mental note to have it pressed, and take a shower and shave, before appearing where anyone knew him. He kissed her and held her close. "You can count on me for anything," he promised.

"I know," she said with a tender smile. "Thank you, dear Arnie."

He left her there in the bed and hurried down to his car, so busy thinking about getting his suit pressed, shaving and bathing that he didn't see the taxi parked just up the street, or the tall skinny man who got out of it and entered Janet's building.

Upstairs Janet listened to the doorbell ring. She didn't get up, but lay quietly and waited until her bedroom door opened again.

"He's dead," said the IRA commandant, Charlie O'Neill.

"I know," she said. "You got here fast, Charlie."

"The miracle of supersonic travel."

"Robert has Bolan?"

"At his base."

"He doesn't suspect you really work for me?"

"He hasn't a clue, love."

"Marvelous. Then we'll make plans later."

"What do we do now?"

She laughed. "Charlie O'Neill, even an Irishman should be able to think of something." And she held her arms open as the renegade IRA man walked to the bed.

CHAPTER TWENTY-ONE

The sounds were tropical bird calls, the chatter of monkeys, the slow ripple of a deep river under thick, rustling trees. An overpowering odor was a blend of heat and steaming moisture and fleshy vegetation.

Mack Bolan shook his head and tried to clear away the sounds and smells of the jungle, the heavy fog that seemed to lie thick in his brain. Open your eyes.

He opened his eyes and saw a gray concrete wall. No, a gray concrete ceiling. He was lying on his back.

Philip Carlisle's dead body appeared on the gray ceiling before his eyes. He saw his hands searching the man's pockets, and—the dart!

He felt his neck. The tiny wound was still sore. Then it must be less than a day later. He saw in his mind the face of the man who looked like Philip Carlisle, and that of the skinny IRA commandant, Charlie O'Neill. And that was all.

He sat up. He wasn't tied. He was still wearing his blacksuit, but his weapons were gone.

The room seemed to sway and float and shimmer, but he braced himself with his arms and looked around. A concrete floor. Concrete walls. No windows, no chairs or tables. Just a concrete box with a metal door.

Bolan lay down again with a sigh.

Okay, soldier, you're in a concrete box in some jungle a day or so from Ireland. The dart knocked you six ways from Sunday, because for one moment you let your guard down like a raw recruit. A double trap, the IRA commandant working triple. Neat, but beatable. The eternal lesson—be alert, always alert, take no one and nothing for granted, trust no one but yourself.

The sudden glare of light almost blinded him.

A shadow stood in the open doorway, a lean shadow wearing a straw bowler, the muzzle of an AK-47 jutting above its shoulder. It spoke Spanish. "*¡Vámonos!* Let's go, *yanqui.*"

Bolan didn't move.

"You need help, Señor Bolan? If you do not, what is the point, eh? You want to know what is going to happen as much as Señor Carlisle wants to interrogate you, *sí*?"

Bolan got to his feet. His legs felt weak, but he didn't sway. "Where are we?"

The man's smile was thin. "He will answer your questions."

Bolan went out with the lean, craggy man behind him. No one seemed worried about him escaping: one man with his rifle slung, no cuffs or leg chains. When his eyes finally adjusted to the brilliant sunlight, Bolan looked around and had a pretty good hunch why they weren't worried.

They were walking through a mammoth installation of large, windowless concrete buildings that extended as far as he could see, all half buried in earth and with grass covering the roofs. Bolan knew an arms and ammo dump when he saw one, and from the size of this one it could supply all the armies in South America, and probably did. In the distance a twenty-foot-high steel mesh fence surrounded the whole complex, obviously electrified. Beyond the fence the jungle towered thick on all sides and, just outside, a deep river flowed.

There would be guards to watch the fence, piranhas and caimans in the river, and the jungle was probably impenetrable for a thousand miles in all directions. An isolated base in the middle of nowhere.

Bolan was somewhere in the heart of South America.

"Enter," the lean, dark-skinned man said.

It was the only building Bolan had seen so far with windows. No more than another concrete block at the base, but its upper floors were timbered in dark mahogany and roofed with jungle thatch, and glassed all around between the dark wood and the thatching.

"Up."

The inside stairs rose to a long air-conditioned room with a sweeping view through the windows of the entire installation. Bolan could see that from the air the huge base would be damn near invisible.

"Bolan! Come and sit down."

It was the man Bolan had last seen in Philip Carlisle's Irish castle through the haze of whatever drug had been in the dart. He was lounging now on a deep purple futon, on a raised platform in the Spartan room. The entire room looked like the reception hall of a Japanese daimyo, from the low, sparse, lacquered furniture to the silk wall hangings and floor mats.

Against a window at the side of the room, leaned the slender IRA commandant, Charlie O'Neill.

A single red cushion had been placed on the floor directly in front of the low platform for Bolan to sit on. He ignored it and stood with his thick arms folded.

"As you like," the man on the platform said. "You know Charlie there, I think."

"How do you fire that bloody cannon of yours?" the IRA man asked. "It fair knocked me on my arse."

"Practice," Bolan told him.

"The man who just brought you here is my assistant, Emilio Harter," the man on the futon went on. "And do you know who I am, Bolan?"

"If your name's Carlisle, like the man said—" he nodded to where the slender Hispanic in the straw bowler leaned on a silk-covered wall "—and this is South America, then you've got to be Robert, or Roberto, Carlisle."

"You know Carlisle International then?"

"Everyone knows Carlisle. But maybe we don't know enough."

"What do you know?"

"That it's one of the biggest multinational corporations, started in banking and arms and munitions. That it is, I guess, the oldest arms manufacturer and dealer in the free world."

"In the whole world, Bolan. You'd be surprised how much we sell and advise in the ComBloc," Carlisle said. "Do you know why we're so big? How we got that way?"

"You tell me."

"I will." Carlisle took out a thin cigar. The lean Hispanic produced a lighter and lit it for him. "*Gracias,* Harter." He blew a perfect smoke ring. "We're the biggest and best because one branch or the other of us sells to anyone and everyone, and we don't care who wins or who loses."

"I'm sorry for you."

Carlisle's face tightened and his eyes grew dark as he stared at Bolan, who still stood with his arms folded, looking directly back at the lounging business tycoon. Then Carlisle's face relaxed and he shrugged. "Yes, I suppose you really are. A patriot. I've never been able to see the point."

"How about loyalty?"

"To what? To an idea? Perhaps. To a leader? Okay. To a family? Yes, I'd accept that. But to millions of people you don't know and probably wouldn't like if you did?"

"To life, Carlisle. A free life for the ordinary guy who just wants to live and have some fun. A free, honorable life, which is what America stands for. Everyone doing what he wants the best way he can, with no one else telling him what to do. No soulless idea, no leader, no big Daddy family. Just a plain, individual man doing what he's got to do."

"Loyalty is your honor, eh?" Carlisle said.

"You got it."

"I can use a man like that. Want to work for me?"

"Doing what?"

"What you do best—fighting." Carlisle drew on the cigar and looked at Bolan steadily. "You know you're in South America, but you don't know quite where. So let me enlighten you. We're in Suriname. Why? Simple—it's relatively unpopulated, and then only on the narrow coastal strip, with not even many Indians in the interior: it's weak and needs money. It has a narrow, militaristic, Marxist government, and there is a significant ethnic minority that feels oppressed. In short, this is a land of great opportunity for the right person.''

"Meaning you."

"Meaning me." Carlisle sat up cross-legged on the futon and leaned toward Bolan. "First, I paid for and supplied a military coup by the present strongman, Colonel Desire Bouterse. Then I built this base astride the Suriname-Brazil border. It holds the entire arms inventory for my Central and South American operations. It's so remote it will never be spotted, much less interfered with."

He puffed on the cigar. "Second, through our Dutch branch I pay and equip the entire three thousand-man army of Suriname. Third, I whipped up the maroons—descendants of black slaves who escaped into the bush centuries ago—against Paramaribo, and gave them a leader, Ronny Brunswijk, a maroon who used to work for Colonel Bouterse until I showed him how to work for himself. It's building into a nice little civil war."

"And you sell guns and ammo to both sides."

"Sure do, Bolan, but it's small potatoes compared to the big company's operations."

"Then what's the big opportunity here?"

"Land, Bolan, interior land. Thousands of square miles with no one on them except some primitive Indians already dying out. There's gold and gemstones on that land, and I get it no matter which side wins. Before I'm finished, I'll have half the country, and then half of Brazil, too. Land and power, Bolan. A power base that's going to give me the clout to take over the whole of Carlisle International someday, and maybe soon."

Bolan watched the young tycoon smile behind the cigar smoke at his vision of power. "You keep saying 'I,' not 'we.' What happened to the company?" he asked.

"To hell with the company," Carlisle snapped. "That's for the old fogies like my father, the biblical patriarchs, the goddamn Moses types. It's time for change in Carlisle International, and I'm going to bring it when I take over."

"So you decided to help yourself out by getting me to go after H. Boll and your brother?"

"Me? God, no, but I'm glad you did. Philip was a stupid idiot who would have ruined us all." Carlisle stopped and blinked at Bolan. "You think someone got you to go after H. Boll? On purpose?"

"That's what I think," Bolan said. "Is H. Boll one of Carlisle International's companies?"

Carlisle looked thoughtful. "I guess I better find out." Then he smiled at Bolan. "I could use a man like you to help me. Good pay, some real rank, the best professional soldiers you can hire. What do you say, Bolan?"

"If I say 'shove it'?" Bolan asked. His eyes met Carlisle's. Neither man flinched.

"You know what I'd have to do," Carlisle said.

Bolan nodded. "I'll think about it."

"Good." Carlisle stood up. "You've got a day. Don't even think about escaping. If you got out of the base, we're so remote you'd never make it. Even the river flows south into Amazon tributaries, hostile Indians all the way on the river, and no way of moving a thousand miles through the jungle.''

''I get the point.''

''Good. Emilio will bring you food and fresh clothes. Any problems with that dart wound or any other injuries? In this climate, a small cut can turn bad in days.''

''I'm fine.''

''Then we'll talk again, maybe tomorrow.''

''After that?''

Carlisle shrugged.

The craggy Emilio Harter tapped Bolan, and they walked out and down into the wall of heat of the jungle, with Charlie O'Neill, the IRA renegade, grinning behind them.

IN HIS WINDOWLESS CELL, Bolan thought about Carlisle International. The multinational corporation had started out a long time ago in banking and arms manufacturing, and now had subsidiaries in a lot of businesses. But Roberto Carlisle made it sound as if weapons were still its main business, with a finger in every conflict, selling to anyone who could pay. Just like H. Boll. Was Carlisle behind H. Boll? And if it was, why the hell didn't Roberto Carlisle know it? Or did he? Was he just conning Bolan?

It looked like a civil war was going on among the sons inside Carlisle, but Bolan still couldn't figure why he'd been dragged in? Was there really something Roberto didn't know? Something maybe Philip hadn't known? Something else going on inside Carlisle International?

In the dark blockhouse cell Bolan figured his chances. They weren't good in the river or the jungle.

But because the river and the jungle were bad news, the camp itself should be a walkover. He hadn't seen any real guards, and if there were any they'd be as relaxed as a stateside MP on weekend maneuvers. The fence was more to keep wanderers out than to keep anyone in.

The camp was no problem, but that still left a river that flowed nowhere and a thousand miles of jungle.

It could be better to play along with Roberto Carlisle.

Except that Roberto Carlisle had no intention of playing. Sure, he'd talk and smile and treat his captive well, and try to get anything out of him he could. But Bolan wouldn't leave this camp alive. It was only in second-rate movies that the villain really wanted the hero to work for him. In real life the dark side only wanted the good side dead. No deals, no games, no tomorrow.

The only way an enemy could help you was by being dead.

It would have to be the jungle, the sooner the—

He sensed the approach outside before he heard the footsteps. Steps and the door being unlocked. This time the light that came in was the more gentle glow of late afternoon in the tropics.

"Hello, Mike. Or can I say Mack now?" Malva Gomez, in tailored jungle fatigues, stood in the open door of the blockhouse.

"You said Mack before," Bolan said.

She came in and sat down on the only chair. "I thought maybe you'd made me in New York. Was it just that I slipped and called you Mack?"

"It was all too easy from the start, Malva, too neat."

She nodded. "Yes, I told Roberto it would be, but he wouldn't listen. He can be damned pigheaded."

"That seems to be a Carlisle trademark."

"Probably. I wouldn't know. I just work for Roberto."

"Is that what you're doing now? Working on me for Roberto?"

"Yes, I am," she acknowledged, pointing with her right hand to the ventilation grille at the top of the wall and touching her ear with her left hand. "But not the way you think. I want to help persuade you to join Roberto."

"Did he send you, Malva?" Bolan nodded to show he understood the blockhouse was bugged.

"Yes, he sent me. But I came on my own, too. To talk sense to you." She carefully took a piece of paper from inside her bra under the fatigues and held it out to Bolan. "You know he has to eliminate you if you don't join us. He has no choice, Mack."

Bolan took the paper. "There's always a choice."

He read: *My real name is Micaela Infante. I am an agent of DIG, Cuban counterintelligence. Your friend Brognola can check me out. We are still enemies, but in this job on the same side.*

"Don't be stupid," she said aloud. "Roberto has you neutralized right now. You know there's no escape from this place." She shook her head to show that wasn't true. There was escape.

"I'll have to think it over." He raised his eyebrows to ask how he could escape.

She pointed to herself. "Don't take too long, Mack. I'll talk to him, but he's going far, and he's a man in a hurry."

"It's not an easy thing to do, Malva." He extended both hands palms up, to say he didn't understand how she could help.

"Nothing's easy, but everything can be done," she said, and nodded. She added, "I'll be back, Mack. Think hard."

Then she was gone, the door slamming and locking behind her. Bolan sat on the cot and looked at the door. He rubbed slowly at his jaw and thought, among other things, that he needed a shave.

IT WAS DARK when the guard brought Bolan his food—a single guard, his rifle slung, plates in both hands, smiling. "*Hola, hombre*, the food is good tonight."

Bolan lay on his cot, unmoving.

The guard, still smiling, looked at Bolan, who lay facedown on the narrow cot. He looked at Bolan's arms hanging limp on each side, and saw the small metal capsule on the concrete floor under Bolan's right hand. He watched the man on the cot carefully to see him breathe. He didn't see him breathe.

"*¿Hombre?*" The guard put the food on the small table and walked to the silent man on the cot. Hitching his rifle up on his shoulder, he bent down to feel the body.

Bolan rolled and drove a straight right into the guard's chin in the same instant. He felt the head snap back, and the guard dropped silently to the floor.

Bolan had the guard's AK-74, the latest 5.45 mm Kalashnikov. After closing the door, he came back to the fallen guard and tore off the man's shirt. Ripping it into strips, he tied him hand and foot, gagged him, and just as the guard began to stir and groan, laid him out on the cot facedown so that the bound hands didn't show.

"Sorry, *amigo*, but I need help. I hope to hell you understand English. I'm going to be over there next to the door and I don't want you to move or make a sound. Got that, *hombre*? Just lie on the cot and do nothing. I'll be right here watching, and if anyone spots me, you'll die first, I promise. *¿Comprende?*"

He turned the guard's head toward him to look him in the face. The guard's groggy eyes rolled, but he nodded his head. As the eyes cleared, Bolan saw enough fear in them to satisfy him. "Good." He turned the man facedown once more.

In the shadows behind the door he waited. Malva Gomez, or Micaela Infante, or whatever her real name was, had said with her signs and nods that she would return to help him escape, and it would be that night.

As he waited, Bolan studied the short Kalashnikov. It had been made in China—or rather, was marked as having been made in China. How many Chinese weapons were really made by Carlisle International in one of its subsidiary companies? How many Soviet weapons? Swedish? How many American weapons—made and sold to anyone who would pay?

He heard the soft footsteps, the key in the door.

The door opened, and a small figure in camouflage fatigues and carrying a pistol crossed the blockhouse without a sound, hardly visible, and bent to the man on the cot.

Bolan came out of the shadows, locked one massive forearm across Malva's throat and clamped his left hand on her wrist. The pistol fell from her hand as he bent her neck back. He dropped her paralyzed wrist and patted her down, but found no other weapons. "How many waiting out there?"

She bent back with his pressure, unresisting, her voice strangled and choked by his grip. "No one."

"We'll find out."

Her voice was a whisper. "Careful... there are other guards... smarter than this one."

Bolan walked her slowly to the open door.

"I am what... I said...."

No one seemed to move in the night.

"I... can get us out...."

He waited. "I'm already out."

"Not from the camp."

"I can beat the camp," Bolan said, and continued to watch the night, the dark bulks of the concrete block-houses.

"Not the jungle."

"And you can?"

"Yes."

"How?"

"I have contacts."

The only sounds were some distant laughter from what had to be the barracks at the far end of the compound. He released his forearm, helped her to the single chair. She sat for a time in the dark, rubbing her throat.

"Inside the door," she said at last, her voice still a hoarse whisper. "A canvas bag. For you."

The AK-74 on her, he backed to the door, looked and saw the bag on the floor against the wall. He picked it up. Inside were Big Thunder, his Beretta, two grenades, his combat knife and all the holsters.

"I took them from Harter's office."

The Executioner was glad to have them back, feel the heft of them as he strapped on the leather, the solid weight against his leg and under his arm. But they proved nothing. She'd know that, no matter whose agent she was, or whom she worked for.

"You've got a way out of here?" he asked.

"I said I did." She rubbed her throat, but her voice was clearer now. "But that doesn't prove anything, either."

"Not a thing," he said.

"The easier we get out, the more suspicious you'll be." She bent over in the dark room, her head almost between her legs. She shook her head as if to clear it.

"You got it."

"If I have a way to get us through the jungle, does that prove I can be trusted?" she asked, still bent over.

"It's better," he said.

"And this?" She straightened up. The tiny two-shot pistol was almost invisible in her small hand. It was aimed at his heart.

Bolan watched her. "You had it all along?"

"You're not used to searching a woman."

There was no way he could unsling the AK-74, or unleather his own guns, before she shot him, and he was too far from her now to use his hands or feet.

"Okay, it says for now you want me around," Bolan acknowledged.

"Maybe that's enough. Do we go?"

"We go."

Bolan checked the guard, who rolled his eyes to show he would do nothing, and they slipped out of the blockhouse. The night was dark and silent, except for distant voices from the barracks, and the sound of music from Robert Carlisle's headquarters.

She led Bolan swiftly among the dark grass-covered mounds of the buildings to a distant corner of the high fence almost on the riverbank. Any sound they made was drowned by the ponderous flow of deep black water.

"I hope," she whispered in the night, "you're not too big."

She pulled away bushes, lifted a manhole cover and dropped through. Bolan squeezed after her. They were in a small underground room with two pumps and pipes going toward the river—the base's water supply. The pipes were inside a larger metal-lined tunnel so that they could be serviced.

"At the end we're outside the fence and not three feet underground," Malva said. "There's a shovel over there."

Bolan got the shovel and crawled after her through the service tunnel to where it ended, the pipes going on into the river. He dug at the top of the tunnel. Ten minutes later they stood in the night on the bank of the river outside the high fence.

"Now?" Bolan asked.

"Now we walk."

And she started off into the jungle. First south along the great black river. Then sharply west into the heart of the jungle itself on some kind of trail only she could see.

Bolan could only follow her, alert and wary, listening to the night and the distant screams of a prowling jaguar.

IT WAS NEAR DAWN when Malva Gomez, or Micaela Infante, stopped at the edge of an almost hidden Indian village in a slash-and-burn clearing so small the canopy of the jungle showed barely a break up high.

"This is it," she said.

"What?" Bolan said.

"Our way out of the jungle."

Bolan looked around.

"I don't even see any Indians."

"The village is abandoned. Bad medicine."

"Then . . . ?"

"We wait."

They crouched at the edge of the village as the sun rose and the sky, visible through the small break in the jungle canopy, grew bright and blue. Then Bolan heard the approaching column. Men were moving quickly through the jungle toward the abandoned village.

Malva slipped through the tiny cluster of thatched huts and stepped onto the hard-packed dirt in the center where the communal cooking fire was located. The approaching men suddenly fanned out and ran through the jungle, encircling the huts.

Malva froze.

Bolan saw uniforms.

"Government troops! Run, Mack!"

But there was nowhere to run.

Uniformed troops marched out of the jungle all around the tiny village.

CHAPTER TWENTY-TWO

The Surinamese troops at one end of the village, AK-47s trained on Bolan and Malva, parted like a wave, and the commander, a Caucasian Creole with a thin mustache, pale skin and arrogant eyes, stepped through. His pistol drawn, he walked slowly toward the pair in the center of the village.

His eyes were excited. He was clearly going to enjoy what he was about to do.

Malva stepped forward and spoke to him in Spanish too rapid for Bolan to understand. The commander answered curtly in the same language, turned to Bolan and said something in Dutch.

"Sorry," Bolan said. "You know English?"

"I speak English. You are an American mercenary."

"No," Bolan said.

"Yes," the commander said, and raised his pistol.

And he fell bloody to the hard-baked dirt, his head exploding in a shower of blood and brains. All around the small clearing the Surinamese soldiers were dropping.

The thunder of incoming fire shattered the jungle and sent monkeys and birds screaming and shaking the canopy overhead.

Bolan was down, his AutoMag out and blasting. Malva lay at the corner of a hut, the AK-74 she had brought from Roberto Carlisle's base hammering at the rear of the Surinamese soldiers trying to fight back against an unseen enemy.

A frantic squad of some ten Surinamese tried to escape past Bolan and Malva Gomez. Bolan hurled a grenade, which blew five of the men into the air. He shredded two with his AutoMag, and Malva shot down the other three.

Then silence, except for the groans of the dying. The stink of high explosive was everywhere.

They came slowly, warily out of the jungle around the clearing. Caucasians, mostly tall, young, in American camouflage fatigues, carrying M-16s and wearing the patch of a swooping hawk on their shoulders. It was a patch Bolan had never seen before.

One of the men, with the stripes of a sergeant, looked at Malva as she stood up. "You the Infante woman?" He spoke English. American English.

"Yes," Malva said.

"Sorry we were late. We spotted the Surinamese and lay low to suck 'em in."

"You got here in time," she said. "That's Mack Bolan. He's going to join us."

The sergeant looked at Bolan. "Glad to have you aboard. That was pretty good fighting out in the open like that."

"Who are you guys?" Bolan asked. "What patch is that?"

"I think I can answer those questions," a voice sounded from behind the sergeant.

She came through the ranks of soldiers in a sleek, custom-tailored, green silk jumpsuit that seemed to melt into the lush vegetation of the jungle as if she were some exotic jungle plant herself. A pair of small pearl-handled Walther PPKs hung in holsters from a narrow, darker green belt. She wore no rank, but she was the leader.

She stopped in front of Bolan and looked him slowly up and down without a glance at Malva Gomez. "These men are all private volunteers in the fight against Marxism, brave Americans like yourself. They fight in an organization called Falcon International. That's what the patch they wear so proudly represents."

"And who are you?"

She smiled, her brown hair catching the stray sunlight that came through the canopy of trees and vines high above. "Another volunteer with Brigadier General Arnold Capp, who works closely with the President of the United States and heads Falcon. Captain Jennifer Crowe, U.S. Army, retired."

She held out her tiny hand, and Bolan took it, smiling down at her. "What's the job down here, Captain?" he asked.

"The same as everywhere, fighting against the forces of evil. We're here now on a special mission so important even the Cubans are with us, eh, Micaela?" She looked now at the Cuban agent. "I'm sorry those Marxists blundered onto us, but we had no choice. They wouldn't even have believed you."

"It couldn't be helped. The mission is too important."

"What mission?" Bolan said.

"To destroy Roberto Carlisle," the captain said simply. "You've seen his base. Without his weapons the wars down here couldn't go on. He supplies all sides. He subverts governments and creates rebels so that he can make his dirty money. He lives on death and destruction. He believes in nothing but money and doesn't care who wins or who loses."

"The dictators won't stop him," Malva put in. "They need his arms too much."

"The Marxist rebels won't. They need his guns," the captain said. "When our government tries to stop Carlisle legally, the courts always let him go. Congress won't act or let the President act."

"What about the big corporation, Carlisle International?" Bolan asked. "Is it behind him?"

"We don't think so. It looks like a power play on Roberto Carlisle's part alone."

Then was it Carlisle International that had pulled the strings and sent Bolan after Roberto and Philip Carlisle? Set up H. Boll for him to chase? Killed the agents? Were they that ruthless?

"It's up to us, Bolan," Captain Jennifer Crowe said. "Will you sign up? Fight with us through this?"

"Even with a Cuban," Malva said.

Bolan looked at the Falcon mercenaries and nodded.

The leader of the Falcon International troops extended her small hand, shook Bolan's hand and waved to her people. The sergeant began to bark orders, and the column formed up and moved out up the trail Mack Bolan and Malva Gomez had followed from Roberto Carlisle's secret base.

To OFFICERS AND GENTLEMEN educated in prep schools, military schools and Ivy League universities, Martha Webster Capp was a good-looking woman even now, an attractive and desirable woman, a woman of class.

When she appeared in their offices in the Pentagon, or at the State Department, or in the White House, they hurried out to usher her past their guardian secretaries and sit her down and ask her how Arnie was and the kids, and how she was.

"I'm fine," she told George or Frank or Percy or Sam. "I came to find out how Arnie is. Tell me what he's doing."

"Now, Martha, you know we can't reveal details about the National Security Council, not even to you. Arnie's doing fine. A good man, your Arnie."

"Just what is Arnie doing for NSC? Tell me about Falcon International. About that big ranch installation in Texas."

"Falcon International is top-secret, Martha," Sam at State told her.

"Never heard of Falcon International," Frank at NSC said.

"Just some weapons-testing stuff, Martha," old General Percy at the Pentagon said. "You and Arnie should get away more."

The soft, smooth, polite runaround. No one wanted to talk to her about Arnold Capp. And after a time she realized that none of them knew anything about Falcon International except that it was an NSC project, and they wanted no part of knowing about it. As far as they were all concerned, Arnold Capp was working for the President, and they didn't want to know doing what.

Congress might be interested, especially after the Iran-Contra deal, but Martha had grown up with generals, and Congress had always represented the enemy, forever tying the military's hands. So she went around again on a different level, where everyone was even politer, knew even less and cared even less, and where Arnie finally found her and insisted she accompany him home.

"They don't know what you're doing, Arnie, do they?" she said when they were seated in the beautifully furnished living room he was so proud of, the room she had spent two years of her life making perfect for him, for the home of a brigadier general and member of the National Security Council, close associate of confidants of the President himself. "None of them know. Not at State, not at the Pentagon, and I think not even at NSC."

"They know at NSC," Capp said. "What started this, Martha? What's gotten into you? I've always had my confidential work, detached service. You've never questioned it before. What made you do it? The whole project could have been damaged."

"They don't know at NSC. Not what you're *really* doing, not where you got the money for the ranch. I can see it in their eyes. They all think you're working for someone else, someone secret. They think Falcon is some top-secret project, and they don't want to ask any questions that might get the FBI or CIA down on them."

"It *is* top-secret, Martha, and I am working for someone else. It's for the President himself. I'll have to ask you to forget it and go back to Texas."

"Does the President know you're working for him, Arnie?"

Arnold Capp stood up, paced and drank whiskey from his tall glass. "You're overtired, Martha. Worn out. Maybe it's being out there away from your friends, our old friends. You need a rest, a long vacation, and then I think you should live here. I think Texas is too lonely for you."

"But it's just right for you?" Martha asked, watching him pace. "Is that it? Falcon International is going to make you big, important, a leader. Another Douglas MacArthur?"

He turned to look at her. "It's not for me, Martha. It's for our country. Perhaps for the whole free world."

"And for Janet Lovelace?"

Capp stood there for some time in the silent room. "So?"

"So?" Martha returned.

He stood like a man trying to make up his mind if the time was right. Was it the time to take the step, to let go, to damn the torpedoes, to go for broke? But he had already decided when he had said "So?" He nodded. "How long have you known?"

"Known?" she repeated. "I suppose not until now. Suspected, sensed, been pretty damn sure? A long time. She's very smart and very rich, Arnie."

"She's very wonderful."

"I know," Martha said. "Is she working closely with you?"

"Yes."

"On Falcon?"

"She's part of the staff."

Martha raised an eyebrow. "An office romance?"

"Don't make it sound cheap!"

She shook her head. "Cheap wasn't at all what I had in mind. The NSC is rather a high level for office romance, don't you think?"

"We believe in the same ideals, see the need for the same actions, recognize the same enemies that would stop us, know what has to be done."

"Policy? She helps you with policy?"

"She and her father. David Carlisle is my principal private backer—a great patriot."

"The munitions multibillionaire?"

"Who knows better the horrors of aggression, of violent Marxist takeovers?"

"And who makes more money from both?"

Capp finished his whiskey. "You'll never understand, Martha. You belong to the past, the days of polite wars with honor and purpose. There is no honor among the forces of darkness that want to devour the world, no purpose except to grab naked power over the people."

Martha watched her husband as he went to the liquor cabinet and poured himself another whiskey. It was a long time since she had seen him so excited, so determined. Sadness touched the strong lines of her face.

"Does David Carlisle know about you and his daughter?"

Capp waved his free hand angrily. "She won't let me tell anyone—to protect that weak, sick husband of hers."

"Of course. Where is she now? Your Janet?"

"It isn't necessary to sneer, Martha."

Her voice was quiet. "I'm not sneering, Arnie. I'm trying to find out what's happened to you."

"Nothing's happened except that I've understood what has to be done in this world, and that I'm one of those who must do it." He took a sip of whiskey. "As for Janet, at this moment she's down in the jungles of Suriname, leading my Falcon International volunteers in a dangerous operation to put an end to an international outlaw named H. Boll, Ltd., and to her own brother, who is behind that menace to peace and freedom."

Capp drank again. "I think that's all I need to say about her or about us. Janet and I waited a long time, but we found each other as destiny intended. The same destiny that finally showed me the work I must do."

He went on pacing the floor of the living room of the fine house, but said no more. His wife sat and watched him. The silence was so deep that they could both have heard the far-off traffic of the nation's capital had they not both been wrapped up in their thoughts. It was Martha who finally spoke.

"Something *has* happened to you, Arnie. You were always so practical, so realistic, ready to face facts and the limitations of human beings."

"Nothing has happened to me!" Capp raged. He turned on her. "It's you, them, everyone! I've seen the only way to save the free world from destruction. Our nation is weak, Martha. The old ways have made us weak, and we'll be destroyed if men like David Carlisle and myself don't act.''

"No matter how many people disagree with you, oppose you? No matter what the people say?"

"The people are easily duped," he said, draining his glass. "Everyone else is blind."

DAWN BROKE RED over the Suriname jungle.

A thin mist rose from the black river that flowed under the great green roof. Inside the high steel cyclone fence a few guards yawned.

The sun had not yet penetrated the jungle canopy as the volunteer freedom fighters of Falcon International, using the heavy vegetation of the riverbank for cover, moved into position along the entire eastern fence.

Bolan lay on the bank in the center of the assault line with Captain Crowe and the sergeant.

"Then we agree," the captain said. "We use the MM-1s loaded with HE, the grenades and the rocket launchers to blast holes in the fence and short-circuit it. After that we use only small arms so we don't set off the dump and blow the whole thing to hell and us with it."

"Sounds like a good idea," the sergeant said.

"Those bunkers are too thick for grenades to penetrate anyway," Bolan said. "Later we'll have to blast them open to set charges to blow them after we're far enough away."

"We will," the captain said. "Now the order of battle is set. I'll take the center and head for Carlisle's headquarters. Bolan, you take the right and neutralize the barracks. Sergeant, the left, and keep anyone out of the rows of bunkers. Our Cuban friend can bring up the rear. I don't feel all that safe with her."

The two men nodded, and each crawled back through the heavy brush of the riverbank to their positions.

The sun was up over the sprawling grass-covered concrete bunkers of the remote jungle base, the heat already heavy, as the first grenades, high-explosive projectiles and shoulder-fired rockets slammed into the cyclone fence.

Cyclone mesh, steel posts, earth and concrete ripped apart and blew into the air amid showers of sparks and smoke as the fence short-circuited. Inside the shattered fence confused voices shouted, and men began to run in the distance.

"Go!" Bolan shouted.

The Falcon International mercenaries poured up and over the bank and straight for the shattered fence. They were mostly Americans, veterans of Vietnam and El Salvador, Lebanon and Grenada, and even some old hard types from Korea. They knew what war was all about, and they knew how to fight, and they knew why they were fighting. They were men Bolan was proud to lead anywhere.

The soldiers hurtled toward the fence with a great roaring shout, the cry of war they had all heard many times before. Experienced in battle, they were through the debris of the fence without breaking stride, hoping the electricity had shorted out, but plunging ahead anyway because it was what they had to do. Since time began wars had been won by the brave who seized the initiative, who ran across open ground, exposed and vulnerable, never knowing when the withering wall of fire in their faces would begin.

And this time, because they charged fast, because their attack was unexpected, there was no deadly hail of fire, no resistance, no battle.

Bolan ringed the three barracks at the north end of the vast base with his Falcon soldiers, and the white flag fluttered at a window almost immediately.

"Come out single file, hands clasped behind your necks." Bolan shouted through a bullhorn. "Leave all weapons inside the barracks."

Out they came, the hired guns of Cordoba Construcciones S.A., shaking and with no stomach for the kind of fight they would have had to put up to resist Bolan and the Falcon soldiers.

Bolan left a squad to guard them, then sent a second squad to sweep the barracks, gather the weapons and flush out anyone trying to hide. He double-timed the rest toward the center of the camp, where the story was different.

Heavy firing from the second floor of Roberto Carlisle's headquarters building had Captain Crowe and the Falcon soldiers pinned down. The windowless concrete ground floor was impregnable to grenades and MM-1 projectiles. Only the antitank charges of the shoulder-fired rocket launchers had a chance to breach the wall with any speed, and they had only two.

"We'll have the Surinamese government troops and maroon rebels down on us faster than a lawyer sends his bill," the sergeant said, having crawled up with some of his men. "We've got to blast them out."

"With what?" Bolan asked. "We don't have enough rockets. We'll have to go in."

"No," Captain Crowe said. "We won't have to blast *or* go in."

"How—" the sergeant began.

Shots erupted inside the building on the ground floor. Then there was silence. The firing from the upper floor stopped. Nothing seemed to move inside the headquarters. Then the heavy front door opened.

"Hold your fire!" Captain Crowe ordered.

Bolan watched the door.

Roberto Carlisle came out, grim-faced, his hands empty. He walked stiffly. The former IRA commandant, Charlie O'Neill, walked behind him with an Uzi trained on Carlisle's back and a smile on his face.

"They're coming out," O'Neill shouted. "All of 'em except Harter bought the deal we offered. Harter's dead. I figured you'd want to handle this weasel yourselves."

He continued to march Roberto Carlisle toward the attackers' position. Behind him, Carlisle's employees filed out of the building, laid their weapons on the ground and stood against the concrete wall with their hands in the air. Two Falcon soldiers began to collect the weapons.

Captain Crowe addressed the Falcon sergeant. "Talk one at a time to those who have surrendered, to find out how we can use them. They're part of our team now." She nodded to Bolan. "You stay with me, Mack. I think you'll enjoy this."

The captain stepped forward toward Charlie O'Neill and Roberto Carlisle. She stopped as the IRA man brought Carlisle to stand in front of her. Smiling, she said, "Hello, Robert."

"I'll nail your hide for this one, Janet," Carlisle said, shaking with rage.

Janet Carlisle Lovelace laughed, the red highlights of her dark brown hair catching the tropical sunshine. "The way you did with Philip?" she asked.

"That was business! He was going to get us all in big trouble with his stupidity, his failure to stop Bolan. I had to let Bolan kill him. He asked for it."

"What makes you think *this* isn't business, Robert?" she said.

Her brother paled. "Does Dad know what you're doing?"

"Not yet, but he will. Everyone will before I'm finished. You see, I'm going to do everything Philip and you and David planned to do, only I'm going to succeed, and then father will know who is best suited to take over the family business."

"You? Don't be crazy, Janet. You can't—"

Her face darkened. "I can! I already have. I have troops, I have Washington under control, I have Dad's money behind me, even if he doesn't know it." She grinned. "I even have Mack Bolan. Neither you nor Philip could stop Bolan, but now he's joined me. Bolan, where are you?"

The Executioner stepped from the ranks of the Falcon International volunteers and nodded to Roberto Carlisle. The tycoon stared at him and then at his sister. He suddenly licked his lips. "Janet—" he began.

She ignored him. "I even had Philip in my pocket, didn't I, Tripper?"

Bolan saw Michael Jones, Philip Carlisle's right-hand man—and killer—appear from somewhere in the rear of the Falcon mercenaries. He nodded to Janet and Roberto, and he grinned at Bolan. The Executioner nodded to the ex-soldier, then he eased back into the ranks of Falcon soldiers.

"Janet—" Carlisle tried again to speak, but his sister cut him off once more.

No longer smiling, her gaze cold on her brother, she said, "I had you under control, dear Robert, thanks to Charlie O'Neill there."

The renegade IRA man shrugged. "The money was too nice, old man. She made me a much better offer than Philip or you. Hard lines, but that's the way she's wrote."

Janet looked at the IRA man. "You mean you didn't do it all for my sake, Charlie? Only for money? Not for my gorgeous body, my tender loving in the bedroom?"

Charlie O'Neill grinned. "That, too, me darlin', but a man can't live on love alone, eh?"

Bolan slipped slowly back through the ranks to where Malva Gomez, aka Micaela Infante, Cuban agent, stood watching Janet and the IRA man.

"I think," Janet Carlisle said to the renegade, "that makes you unreliable, Charlie. Too bad. Tripper?"

Jones raised his M-16 and shot the IRA man down with a short burst.

Janet Carlisle gazed at the dead man sprawled in the jungle sunlight, then looked around to make sure she had the attention of the Falcon volunteers and Roberto Carlisle's men. "We couldn't trust him. He'd played too many sides," she told them. "I'm not fighting for small stakes. Any man I can trust will be well rewarded, but if I can't trust you . . ." She let them imagine what else she might have said, then shrugged and faced her brother.

"Janet—" he began once more, his voice now just a croak.

"I'm sorry, Robert, I really am. But there's no way I could trust you." She took out her pearl-handled PPKs. "Dad taught us all—never let an enemy out of your hands to hurt you later."

At the rear of the ranks of Falcon soldiers, Bolan whispered to Malva Gomez. "She wants us to check out Roberto's helicopters while no one's watching, in case we have to leave fast."

Malva nodded. "Over behind the barracks. That last building is a hangar."

"Come on," Bolan said.

They heard the shots, looked back and saw Roberto Carlisle fall to the ground, then hurried on. As they approached the barracks, they could still hear Janet Carlisle's voice behind them, loud and commanding.

"He was my brother, but he was weak and small. Carlisle International is big. It has room for everyone. Carlisle will make us all rich. Robert wanted too much for himself. I won't make that mistake. This is a dog-eat-dog world, but for the top dogs there's enough for everyone.

"War, conflict, will always be with us, and it makes no difference who wins—the Marxists or the fascists or the capitalists, Russia or America, ComBloc or so-called free world, industrial countries or third world nations. Conflict will go on and on and men will always need weapons. For three hundred years Carlisle has supplied weapons to all sides in all wars. Let the fools and patriots fight. We'll do the winning. Everyone who's with me, step forward now!''

Mack Bolan and Malva Gomez opened the hangar doors. Behind them, in the distance, where Janet Carlisle harangued the troops, they heard the shuffling of many feet, then silence, then some shots. Some men hadn't volunteered.

"Nice girl," Bolan said. "Let's get this chopper out of here."

They pushed the helicopter out onto the landing pad.

"You're not going to join her, Mack?"

"No. I don't suppose a Cuban agent will, either, eh?"

"Of course not," Malva said. "You're going to fly out in the chopper?"

"That's the idea." The warrior turned to the helicopter door—and instantly turned back to face the Hispanic woman, his Beretta in his hand.

Gomez had her pistol half out of its holster. She froze for an endless second. "You know?" she said, her voice trembling.

"That you work for Janet Carlisle? It had to be, Malva. A Cuban agent wouldn't deal with me, wouldn't let those Surinamese Marxists get shot up. Janet had people planted everywhere. You were just another one. I figured she had you watching me to see which side I would come down on in the end, to eliminate me if I came down wrong. Only you'd have to be sure about me, so you'd go along with anything I did until you were sure."

"You used me to get to the helicopter. You're a lot smarter than I thought. Now what?"

"Toss me the gun," Bolan growled.

The woman hesitated, staring into Bolan's diamond-hard gaze. She did not like what she saw there. She threw the weapon toward Bolan, who deftly caught it. Then he turned and climbed into the chopper.

Moments later it rose into the air and swung steeply west and north. On the ground Janet Carlisle ran toward the helipad with her troops behind her.

Bolan looked back and saw the tiny woman standing alone, staring up after him.

CHAPTER TWENTY-THREE

The massive edifice of the Pentagon was ablaze with light. Mack Bolan took no chances. It was a night recon like any other, city or jungle. You picked your terrain and your cover and your vantage point, and then you watched and waited. The only difference was the traffic, and that only gave him cover.

The Starlite scope swept back and forth in a slow traverse. Bolan was looking for any sign of special precautions, a stakeout of civilians, unusual guards—that small change in routine that always gave away a special operation.

At the guard post inside the night door they checked credentials, briefcases, packages. The armed guards watched, alert since the recent attempt by an armed intruder to crash past. It had cost the intruder his life.

It all seemed routine—until the janitor sweeping inside the entrance disappeared briefly, and when he returned he was a different janitor.

Bolan left for his next stop.

THE HOUSE in the Washington Suburb was dark, except for a single light in an upstairs bedroom.

Mistake number one before they'd even started, Bolan thought. It was barely 9:00 p.m. Hal Brognola never went to bed that early—if he was even home from the office that early. There would be no light on in an upstairs bedroom in Hal Brognola's house at this hour unless someone had turned it on to try to fool an outside observer.

They would be all around the house. It was just a matter of spotting them. The sound came from his left—a button had struck against metal.

Bolan moved in. The guy was sitting in a car in the next driveway. He had probably shifted his gun on his lap to keep his hand from stiffening. Before he could shift the gun again, all of him stiffened, as Bolan slipped an arm around his neck and shut down the carotid artery. He used the man's own belt and shirt, and a length of heavy cord he'd brought with him, to tie and gag the unconscious man and lock him in the car.

The next shadow was under the trees at the rear, picked out against the paler sky between two houses on the next street.

Bolan went on his belly.

The man under the tree didn't see the dark shape rise up out of the grass to put his light out with a single blow behind the ear. Bolan dragged him unconscious into the bushes and tied him securely with his own belt and another length of the thick cord carried for the purpose.

Silently Bolan continued in a slow circle until he had neutralized all those he found watching outside the house. There were five. Their papers said two were CIA and three were NSCI—National Security Council Intelligence, the secret boys from the White House basement.

The Executioner left them all tied and gagged and hidden in the night. He had at least a few hours before anyone came to look for them.

Bolan settled down to wait, with that nerveless patience that had made him so deadly in Nam, one of the few Americans with the iron to sit in the night and the jungle and outwait the infinitely patient VC.

Tonight the wait wasn't as long. A car pulled into the driveway, and Hal Brognola got out. Bolan didn't move.

Brognola wasn't alone. A woman got out of the passenger side of the car. The two walked up the front steps of the house, Brognola looking up at the light in his bedroom.

"Damn, I must have left that light on," he said to his companion. "Getting old, I guess."

Brognola unlocked the door and they went inside. Bolan slipped into the house with them, standing flat against the wall as Brognola turned to close the door.

"They've got you blocked and watched, Hal," Bolan said.

Brognola saw him. Then he closed the door and double-locked it.

"Martha, sit down over there. Don't do anything unless one of us tells you." Brognola walked casually around the room, lowering the shades, not looking at Bolan but talking to him. "How do you know, Mack, and what's been happening with H. Boll?"

Bolan reported his tries to get through to Brognola, with every way he could think of blocked, the screen around the Fed's office, and the five men outside his home.

"Who, Striker?"

"Carlisle International, I think."

"Impossible! Carlisle is one of the biggest—"

After Brognola assured him he could speak openly in the woman's presence, Bolan told him everything that had happened since their talk in a taxi in New York before Bolan went to Ireland. Brognola listened in silence, pacing the room in growing agitation.

"Someone in Carlisle is behind H. Boll," Bolan said, "and it's got to be Carlisle blocking you off. What I still don't know yet is who sent me after Boll."

Brognola shook his head. "I didn't even know I was being interdicted. They're doing it smooth and slick as greased pigs. What about the ones outside? Who are they?"

"CIA and NSCI," Bolan said.

The woman across the room said, "Arnie."

Bolan looked at her questioningly.

"This is Martha Capp," Brognola explained, "wife of Brigadier General Arnold Capp of the NSC. She's worried about Capp. Says he's been acting strange the past year or so. They've been together a long time, and he always discussed his work with her. Lately he's busy all the time, travels a lot and tells her very little about where he goes and what he does."

"There's a woman, of course," Martha Capp said. "But there's more than that, too, Mr. Bolan. The woman is Janet Lovelace—Janet Carlisle Lovelace."

Brognola continued. "All Mrs. Capp knows is that the general talks a lot about saving the free world, and has this big ranch installation in Texas where he tests weapons and trains volunteers into combat units. The units go out when they're ready, but Mrs. Capp never knows where they go. Capp has private backing from various sources, but she says she thinks most of it comes from David Carlisle."

"Does your brigadier general call his operation Falcon International?" Bolan asked.

"Yes," Martha Capp said, "he does."

"There it is, Hal," Bolan said grimly. "Capp and Carlisle International put the order out on you to keep me away from you. I don't know what shit they told State, NSC, Justice and the CIA, but it looks like Carlisle's got the clout to close you down."

"If they do, it's all illegal, Mack."

"I doubt that worries Carlisle." The warrior turned to Martha Capp. "But I figure it might worry General Capp. Do you know where your husband is now, Mrs. Capp?"

She looked at Bolan and nodded. "In a lodge in the Blue Ridge Mountains." There was fear in her eyes. "I think he's meeting David Carlisle."

Bolan turned to Brognola. "Can you get us there, Hal? Fast?"

"Are those five outside inoperative?"

"Until their relief looks for them."

"Then let's go. We'll call in some standby sources of mine they couldn't be onto, then do an end run."

They hurried out to Brognola's car and drove away through the quiet, suburban Washington night.

OUTSIDE THE MOUNTAIN LODGE a horned owl hooted and a small rodent squealed its last as a bobcat pounced. The neutral and timeless laws of a savage nature were being played out once again.

Inside the lodge the less neutral laws of a species that could be nearing the end of its time were being played out far more savagely. Brigadier General Arnold Capp faced David Carlisle, Sr., the old billionaire's younger namesake and Sam Walsh.

"You've used me," Capp said. "You gave me money, set me up with that training and testing ranch in Texas, and all the time I was testing weapons and training troops to fight not for freedom but for you! For Carlisle International in its private wars."

David Senior's voice was harsh. "Sit down, Arnie, and tell us what the devil you're talking about."

The younger Carlisle glanced at his watch. "We don't have a lot of time if we want to reach the island tomorrow."

"Why go to all the trouble to back me in the first place?" Capp demanded, ignoring the suggestion that he be seated like the others.

"We back efforts like yours in many countries, General," David Junior said. "Everyone has ideas, hopes, ambitions they want to fight for."

"Everyone?" Arnold Capp said incredulously. "*Everyone* has ideas and ambitions?" He stared at the Carlisles. "How can you be so neutral, so uninvolved except for making money, observers, except when it comes to earning a profit?"

"Really, Arnold—" David Senior began.

"Just any ideas? Just any ambitions?" Capp asked, as if he didn't believe his ears. "You don't care what the ideas, hopes and ambitions are? Are they all equal? All relative? Is there no right or wrong?''

David Senior looked at Capp coldly. "We aren't responsible for the stupidity of people, or for their morals or lack of them. Everyone has his great idea that he is sure is best for everybody else."

Capp watched them. "You didn't support me to train men to fight for freedom. You gave me money just to train men to fight. You don't care what men fight for, only that they fight!"

David Senior abruptly sat down, took out a cigar and lit it. "You're a fool, Capp. You and your *truth* that's going to save the world from darkness. You idiot, darkness always wins because it's inside all of us!"

"Dad—" David Junior began.

David Senior waved his cigar. "No, dammit, I'm sick of this Boy Scout." The older man glared up at Capp, his austere face a mask of disgust. "You're a complete fool, Capp, you and everyone like you. You know nothing about how the world really works, or how a great company like Carlisle works. Work for peace? Democracy? Love? Justice? They're all just words, Capp, empty words! Illusions. Stupidities. I work for Carlisle International, period. You hear? For the company, our company, nothing else."

"I think we should—" David Junior began.

"Don't think. It's not your time yet," his father snapped. "The general is of no further value. We'll have to find some other gullible patriot to use." He continued to glare at Capp, who stood white and silent. "Carlisle International, under many names but always under the control of only one family, has survived for three centuries because we're loyal only to ourselves. We owe allegiance only to the company.''

The cigar glowed in his thin mouth. ''What do we care about nations, causes, ideals, empires? We've supplied all nations, all causes, for three hundred years, and we'll go on supplying anyone who wants to kill someone else for any reason.

''We supplied the colonists *and* England in our revolution. Napoleon *and* Wellington, the czar *and* the Prussians. The Union forces *and* the Confederacy. The Kaiser and the French. Hitler and Stalin and Tojo and Churchill and Roosevelt. Today we work for China and Moscow, Washington and Havana. You want to fight a war, a revolution, a crusade? Carlisle will supply you. That's what we do, and all we do, and *all we will ever do*!''

In the heavy silence of the lodge they were frozen in a tableau: David Senior glaring up at Capp; the general pale; the younger Carlisle uneasy; Walsh, quiet and relaxed in his chair.

General Capp was the first to break the hush, speaking haltingly, as if he feared the answer. ''Janet, too? Is she . . . part of your using me?''

David Senior shrugged. ''That was her own idea. I never understood what she saw in you, Capp.''

''Then . . . ?'' Capp shook his head.

''It's time we leave if we're going to make the island on time,'' David Junior prompted.

''Yes,'' David Senior agreed. He got to his feet.

Walsh didn't move. The adviser was watching Capp. ''I think General Capp has something special on his mind, David. Perhaps it's what brought him here. I've been wondering what made him so suddenly doubt our purposes."

The two Davids both stopped. All three men looked at Capp. The general didn't speak right away; he seemed to be thinking things through.

"I've been wondering, too," Capp said at last. "You had me doing everything you wanted. Why did you blow it all by sending Janet to lead my Falcon people against her brother?"

"Janet?" David Junior questioned. He turned to his father. "Dad?"

"No," David Senior stated emphatically. "I didn't send Janet anywhere to do anything, certainly not to lead troops. I know nothing about it." He turned to Walsh, who had got up slowly from his chair. "All my reports said Robert was attacked by Surinamese troops and maroon rebels. All the reports I got from Sam. Isn't that right, Sam?"

"They were the reports I got, David," Walsh assured him.

"Bolan?" David Junior wondered out loud.

"He was down there," Walsh said. "He may have killed Janet, too."

"Or joined her," David Junior said. "What does it mean, Dad? Is *she* after your job, too?"

David Senior said nothing, but studied Walsh, who stood shaking his head. When he spoke, it was to his son.

"It means this isn't over. We've got to get to the island immediately. Bulba!"

The cobralike man appeared as silently as ever, a MAC-10 in his gloved hand.

"We're leaving now," David Carlisle, Sr. said. "Kill them."

THE HELICOPTER SWEPT LOW over the trees in the Blue Ridge Mountain dawn.

"That's Shenandoah Lodge," the pilot yelled over the rotor noise, "but like I told you, sir, our contact said it's been empty for years."

There was no smoke from the double chimneys, no light, no sign of movement, no cars in the parking area.

Hal Brognola turned to Martha Capp. "You're sure Shenandoah Lodge is what your husband said?"

"I'm sure."

Slipstream wind scoured through the open door.

"Someone's been down there, all right!" Bolan shouted above the rush of wind and noise. "Look at the parking area in back."

In the morning light just coming over the rolling, blue-tinted mountains to the east, the fresh tire marks of more than one vehicle were clear in the dirt-and-gravel parking space below.

"Take it down!" Brognola yelled. He drew his pistol.

Bolan unleathered his Beretta.

The pilot swung in a slow circle examining the terrain, then hovered and descended gently onto the large barbecue area behind the lodge. Bolan and Brognola watched the woods and the building, but there was no sign of opposition or even of life. Both men kept their weapons ready, just in case.

Bolan didn't wait for the rotors to stop, but was out and running toward the lodge before the chopper had really settled. Brognola covered him, watched the windows of the silent lodge. But no one appeared inside or outside.

Bolan reached the lodge and flattened against the wall. He listened, then kicked the door in and jumped inside, the Beretta steady in both hands.

In the helicopter they waited. Bolan's shout came back across the parking area as the helicopter rotors shuddered to a halt and the noise stopped. "Hal! Mrs. Capp! Fast!"

Brognola helped Martha Capp out of the chopper, and they ran across the dirt and gravel. Bolan stood in the open doorway, the Beretta hanging down in his hand. "In the living room," he said.

Brognola looked at the pain in the big man's eyes, and took Martha Capp's arm as they walked inside. The morning light hadn't yet penetrated the gloom, and they had to wait until their eyes adjusted.

"Oh, my God!"

They lay in the living room: Sam Walsh huddled near the fireplace, blood caking his silver-white hair, his banker's-gray pinstripe suit ripped to shreds by the Ingram bullets; Brigadier General Arnold Capp sprawled behind the long leather couch, facedown, arms and legs moving slowly as if he were trying to creep toward some illusory goal.

Martha Capp stumbled to him and dropped on her knees. "Arnie...Arnie..."

Crawling through his blood, Capp heard the familiar voice and raised his head like a blind turtle to look for the woman it belonged to. She took him in her arms, rocking him, speaking softly, as if no one else were in the room.

"Oh, Arnie, I'm sorry. I should never have let you come here alone. I should have stopped you, made you go to the President, anyone, to tell them what you were doing. I shouldn't have doubted you. Why did I ask all those questions? I should have stood by you, not doubted you. Oh, Arnie..."

She held him close, blood smeared across her dress.

Bolan had checked Walsh for a pulse, and shaken his head at Brognola. Now they both stood helpless as the woman rocked the dying man. Capp suddenly shuddered and opened his eyes. He seemed to stare up at his wife, and at something far away at the same time, his eyes distant. His voice came as a whisper, but it was clear and unexpectedly strong.

"I was a fool just as Carlisle said, Martha. A damn fool, but not for the reason he said. No, I was a fool because I let him use me, dupe me. They manipulated me into involving Bolan. I know that now, too. I was a damn fool all the time, Martha. It's so hard sometimes to see the truth even when it stares at you. Evil can smile, Martha, and I was wrong, very wrong. But I only wanted what was right. They just fooled me."

She rocked her mortally wounded husband. "Hush, don't try to speak. We all make mistakes, don't we, Mr. Bolan?"

Capp's eyes widened. "Bolan? Here?"

"Right here, General," the Executioner said. He moved closer. "Can you tell us who—"

Capp moved his head slowly and looked toward Mack Bolan. "Get them, Bolan. It's too late for me, but you have to stop them. There's no time to waste."

"I'll do my best," Bolan said quietly.

"Where did they go, General?" Hal Brognola leaned down toward the dying man.

The general's eyes grew weaker, his voice almost inaudible. "I don't.... No, wait, they said they had to go to the island."

"What island?" Bolan urged.

Capp's eyes closed. "He shot us. That Bulba. In cold blood. No warning."

Mack Bolan leaned down close to the dying man. "General, why did they shoot the other man? Who was he?"

"Sam Walsh. David Carlisle's adviser. I think he was spying for Janet." His voice was below a whisper as he breathed hard. "She used me, too. I should have known."

"The island, General," Brognola prompted. "Where is it?"

"Janet ... all lies ... Martha ..."

His bloody head fell back against his wife's breast, a shudder ran through his body, and he was gone.

Martha Capp held him close, cried and went on rocking him.

Bolan stood up. "You know of an island that belongs to Carlisle International, Hal? Or to David Carlisle?"

"They probably own a thousand islands."

"We just need one," the warrior said.

They made a quick search of the lodge. They found nothing useful. It was Bolan who finally made the discovery. He rolled over Walsh's curled-up body. The words were scrawled underneath him in blood: The Dying Place.

"What the hell does it mean, Striker?" Brognola wondered.

"He thought it was important," Bolan said. "If I was dying, shot by the people I worked with, trusted, I'd want to leave a message that would help get them. My guess is he was trying to tell us where we can find them."

"Then let's find this dying place," Brognola said.

Bolan and Brognola knew it would cause time-wasting complications if the police found them in the lodge with the dead men, and there was nothing Martha Capp could do for her man now. An anonymous tip would bring the police in a few hours. They persuaded Martha to go back with them in the chopper and wait for the police to notify her of her husband's apparent murder.

"I'm so sorry about the general," Brognola said to her. "But the work goes on. He'd want it that way. We didn't always agree, but we wanted the same things."

"Of course," she agreed.

The helicopter lifted off in the now-bright morning and swung north and east, the lodge with its grim contents silent below.

THREE DAYS LATER, Mack Bolan and Hal Brognola sat in the War Room of Stony Man Farm, only a few miles from Shenandoah Lodge, where Brigadier General Arnold Capp had died.

"It's in Fiji, Mack," Hal reported. "Our research man dug it out this morning. A large, isolated, volcanic island in the Lau chain southeast of the big island of Vanua Levu and farther from Suva than from Tonga. It's mountainous, covered with jungle and no one had lived on it for a hundred years before old David Carlisle bought it."

"No one?"

Hal shook his head. "That's how it got its name in Fijian—the Dying Place. One of Fiji's most ferocious chiefs wiped out everyone on it for defying him, then used it to maroon enemies. When he felt like some sport, he went there and hunted down the marooned prisoners like animals."

"Nice guy."

"Yeah. There are rumors David Carlisle and his boys have been using it for the same purpose. The stories say they test new weapons on live people. A lot of their enemies have vanished without trace or explanation over the years."

Bolan was on his feet. "When can you get me there?"

Brognola chewed his lip. "We've got no excuse to go in, Mack. What have they done that we can prove? Selling armaments to all sides may be immoral, but like a lot of immorality it's not illegal. We can't prove they killed anyone. If we reveal what's happened, you come off looking like the killer. The best we can do is send you in with Able Team."

"With no one," Bolan said. "This is something I have to do alone. If we tried any size force, they'd just do nothing, act innocent, lie low. I have to make them try to take me out—hunt me down the way that old chief did."

"What if it's a trap, Striker? The message in blood. Letting Capp hear about the island."

Bolan smiled. "All the better. That way I won't have to waste any time smoking them out."

"You'll be totally alone until you can call out."

Bolan nodded. "That's okay. It's the only way to get David Carlisle."

"How do you want to go in?"

The Executioner told him.

Brognola nodded slowly, admiration in his eyes for the big soldier in front of him.

CHAPTER TWENTY-FOUR

High in the dark sky, northeast of the long chain of the Fiji Islands, the slender black shape soared silently on long wings. It dropped steadily through the crystal-clear night above the vast Pacific Ocean, the only sound the soft rush of wind over the slim wing surfaces.

Mack Bolan piloted the glider down in the long arc begun twenty minutes ago when Jack Grimaldi had dropped the tow cable, waggled his wings in dim farewell and disappeared back toward the remote airfield outside Apia, Western Samoa.

Grimaldi had done his job and delivered Bolan once more to his target, but this time there would be no pickup. This time Bolan would get off the Dying Place on his own, or not get off at all.

Like a ghost in the oceanic night, darker than a soaring and solitary wandering albatross, the glider hissed softly down and down until Bolan saw the outline of the isolated island dead ahead in the rising moon.

He guided the soundless craft down to a thousand feet, checked his watch by the tiny instrument light, sighted the landmarks below that he had memorized from the innocent flyover two days ago and kicked the first chute out into the moonlight. Ten seconds later he locked the stick, opened the canopy, climbed out and dropped into emptiness.

The glider would soar on to finally plunge into the sea hundreds of miles to the north.

Bolan dropped clear, pulled the rip cord and floated down toward the black mass of the ancient volcano slopes that formed the center of the remote island. The dark chute arched in the windless night, and Bolan picked out the shoulder of the jungle-covered mountain through his PVS-5 night-vision goggles. In his black combat suit, his hands and face darkened with cosmetic, he was a shadow descending through the night.

He checked his equipment as he dropped. The Beretta was leathered under his left arm, the Fairbairn-Sykes dagger rigged beside it. Two ammo bandoliers crossed his chest, and a half dozen frag grenades hung from his D-rings. His M-16 was slung and tied down, his map case and compass on his belt.

He humped the shrouds, sliding sideways in the moonlight to pinpoint the treeless slope he'd selected for his drop zone, just under the ancient volcano's shoulder. Then he was under the shadow of the peak, aware of the trees tall below the lava slope, the craggy, razor-sharp ridge above it. Centering on the bare slope. Dropping...

He hit and rolled, and was up and pulling on the shroud lines to collapse the black chute in the moonlight. Trees and ridges were all around to conceal him, alone in the exact center of the slope covered only with low, thick brush.

The Executioner scraped thin volcanic dirt over the chute, hid it under brush and turned quickly to float into the shadows of the trees on his way down the slope. The soil over the lava rock was too thin for him to be able to bury the chute. It made no real difference if it was found, anyway. By morning they would know he was there.

Checking his compass and detailed map of the island, Bolan trotted through the night as silent as any other predator in his long, easy, ground-covering stride.

The island, abandoned for centuries except for the poor wretches marooned there to live off the land as best they could, had no roads, no villages, no buildings beyond the one small complex on the south coast where the Carlisles lived.

Bolan circled the central peak of the dead volcano to reach the south slopes. A tiny electronic instrument on his belt emitted low, steady beeps that came closer and closer together until he stopped in a clearing on the line between the central peak and the buildings on the south coast.

He studied the dark clearing and the trees around it through his night goggles. The chute and its cargo hung high in a tall tree just beyond the clearing. He quickly swarmed up the tree, cut the heavy bundle loose and lowered it to the jungle floor.

Back on the ground, Bolan cut the bundle open and took out two bulging backpacks. He shouldered one and covered the other in jungle growth. Then he stood and listened.

Far off he heard the faint sounds of music. It was coming from the private resort of David Carlisle, Sr.

The Executioner turned and trotted into the jungle, toward the sound of the distant music, the weight of the new pack light on his back.

IN THE BLUE LIGHT of the TV monitor, David Carlisle, Sr., leaned over the man who watched the screen. "Anything?" the older Carlisle asked.

"No, sir, the sensors aren't picking up anything near the compound." The man glanced toward the sweeping beam of the radar screen to his left. "There's been nothing for hours, not since that blip disappeared from the radar."

"You picked up no engine noise, no machinery on the blip?"

"Nothing, sir." The man shrugged. "It could have been just a large bird, a wandering albatross maybe. The radar sometimes picks up a bogey that small."

"I doubt it was a bird, Johnson," David Carlisle, Sr., said quietly.

"It didn't stop here. It just went on north until it was off the screen."

"In a straight line?" the weapons tycoon asked. "How many birds do you know that fly a hundred miles in a straight line?"

"Well, an albatross could, sir."

"No, Johnson," David Carlisle said. "He's here. He parachuted on the far side of the volcano so there'd be no chance radar could pick him up. Now he's out there somewhere getting ready to attack." The older man smiled. "Alone."

The chairman of the great octopus of Carlisle International left the small room and walked along the dim night corridors of his resort on his private island. He entered a large comfortable room with a sweeping view of the tropical sea, which sparkled in the moonlight to an unbroken horizon.

"Anything?" David Carlisle, Jr., asked.

"No, he's too smart for that." The older man sat down in a soft tan leather chair. "But he's out there, getting ready. He'll probably come in at dawn."

"Alone?"

"He has to. We've done nothing he can prove that would justify any force coming after us. If he came with troops or police, we'd simply deny everything and not resist. Brognola and his associates might like to assassinate us, but the fools don't operate that way, and we're too valuable to everyone else, from the CIA to the KGB. They all need us, so if Bolan wants to stop us, he'll have to do it alone."

The younger Carlisle was pale. "It should be good sport."

"The best," his father said, "but don't underestimate the danger. He'll be well armed. He's clever and experienced. We'll have him outnumbered twenty to one, but it's still a dangerous hunt. There's no animal more dangerous than a battle-skilled human being, and that's the thrill."

The younger man licked his lips nervously. "Anyway, Bulba should be a match for him, even man to man."

David Carlisle, Sr., studied his son with a frown.

As if his name had been a signal, the cobralike man in the black ninja costume appeared soundlessly in the room. He stood in front of the elder Carlisle. "Any sign?" the silver-haired weapons merchant asked.

"No," Bulba said. "It will be at dawn, a moment before."

"Are we ready?"

"Everything. Five men watch, the others rest."

David Carlisle, Sr., nodded and stood up. "Then I suggest we all get our rest. Tomorrow should be interesting, eh, Bulba?"

The cobra man said nothing.

The two Carlisle men left the room and went up wide stairs to the second floor of the plush complex, David Senior still talking to his son about the excitement of the hunt they would have in the morning.

THE SUN WAS STILL below the eastern horizon as Bolan, the second backpack now empty, humped over the last volcanic ridge and moved down through the jungle. Ahead was the sprawling complex of two-story white buildings, behind a high fence at the edge of the turquoise ocean, which became a deep blue beyond the reef.

He saw the electronic sensor along the trail and belly-crawled under the beams. The perimeter outposts were dug in just inside the jungle. Bolan squatted in the shadows and listened. He heard a cough, a click of teeth, a faint sound of scratching.

Like a wraith, Bolan slipped up to where the coughing sentry lay in a shallow depression in the jungle duff, his weapon resting on a narrow log.

The warrior's foot jammed the weapon into the ground and snapped the man's trigger finger. In the same instant he shoved his commando dagger between the man's ribs and into his heart.

Next, the teeth clicker, who put his weapon down for a moment to stretch and died with his arms still wide open, the Executioner's knife penetrating his heart.

The scratcher sat against a tree in full view, dozing in the dawn, sure no enemy was within a thousand miles. He died with his windpipe crushed against the tree and Bolan's knife under his rib cage.

Bolan listened again.

There were two more. They died the same way.

He moved on to the edge of the jungle. The fence and buildings were across an open area burned and cleared all around the complex to afford protection from any attack on the jungle side.

Behind the fence fifteen Fijians in khaki shorts, safari hats, high socks and boots stood with submachine guns aimed at the jungle. The guns were unfamiliar to Bolan, modified versions of the Colt Commando, with folding butts extended and no flash hider.

On a balcony of the building behind the Fijians, Bolan saw a tall but slender man with silver-gray hair and a lean face like some giant eagle. He wore khaki and a battered brown slouch hat that shaded his eyes, and held a custom-made, engraved, semiautomatic Mannlicher big-game rifle with a telescopic sight.

Beside him was a younger man who might have been a copy of the first, but in softer clay, less hard-edged, with a careful, calculating face and black-rimmed glasses pushed up on the thin bridge of his nose. His safari clothes were newer, as if just out of the box, and his weapon was a powerful Heckler & Koch MP-5 submachine gun.

On the other side was a slim cobralike man dressed all in black. His snake face was expressionless. He held an Uzi submachine gun and had a short *wakizashi* samurai sword thrust into his black sash.

The older man looked at his watch, and then to the east where the sun was just rising over the edge of the sea. He paced, spoke to the cobra man, looked at his watch again, then stopped to check it against the watch of the younger man.

The ninja suddenly spoke to the older man, who turned sharply and looked toward the jungle wall. The cobra pointed straight to where Bolan crouched just inside the shadows.

"Mr. Bolan," the older man called out, "you can step out. We've been expecting you. Don't be afraid. We plan to have a little sport before we eliminate you. If you don't know, I'm David Carlisle, chairman of Carlisle International and, of course, H. Boll, Ltd. This is my son, David Junior, and the man on my right is my aide, Bulba."

Bulba said something else.

"Lower your weapons, men," David Carlisle, Sr., called out.

The fifteen armed Fijians behind the fence uneasily lowered their submachine guns. They didn't like not being ready to face whatever came out of the jungle.

Mack Bolan stepped out into the open.

"So," David Carlisle said as he stared from the balcony at the big soldier in the black combat suit. "Mack Bolan. You came to kill me, I presume, as you caused my sons to be killed?"

"Did I cause your sons to get killed, Carlisle?" Bolan questioned across the distance as he watched the three men on the balcony and the fifteen Fijians.

"So you've thought it out, Mr. Bolan?"

"It was a snipe hunt," Bolan said. "You set me up, used me the way you used General Capp, the way you use everyone. All for profit. You don't care what you do to innocent people. You don't care how much you hurt the world. You're an elite, white-collar Mafia, you and your partners in every country."

David Carlisle's gaze was steady. "The Mafia, Bolan, are street thugs, pickpockets. We are quite different."

"A lot more dangerous, and a lot richer."

"True," allowed David Carlisle, Sr.

"Why set me up to go after H. Boll? What did you want from me?"

"Let's say I had a dilemma, and you helped me solve it."

"A test for your sons. Did it work?"

"It worked perfectly, I no longer have a problem."

"And only one son."

"We all die, Bolan. The good of the company required it. I had to know. That's how we've survived so long, held our power so well."

"So what now?"

"Now some sport. You know how this island got its name?"

"Yes."

"Then you know what we're going to do. You'll be a fine hunt, a worthy quarry. We'll give you a five-minute start. It's not fair that we outnumber you twenty-three to one, but what hunt is ever fair? When is life fair, for that matter?"

"Eighteen to one," Bolan said.

"What?"

Bulba stared down at Bolan then spoke to the older man.

"The sentries?" David Carlisle questioned. "All of them?"

"All of them," Bolan said, nodding. "You won't like my way of fighting, Carlisle." The warrior saw Bulba move his hand in, a short, quick motion that was almost imperceptible. He fell instantly back into the cover of the jungle, rolled and came up behind a thick tree.

The fusillade of fire ripped all around him. All fifteen Fijians fired their modified Commandos into the jungle.

"Get him!" Bulba ordered, leaping down from the balcony.

The Fijians ran to the gate in the fence and swung it open. Bolan pulled a grenade off its D-ring and lobbed it in a high arc to land directly in front of the gate. The Fijians saw it, scrambled and scattered, but it was too late for three of them. They flew into the air in showers of crimson gore.

Mack Bolan turned and melted back into the jungle.

THE FIRST TRIP WIRE was across the trail less than a hundred yards into the jungle. Three Fijians, running in the lead to show David Carlisle how brave and tough they were, became shredded meat and bloody bone in the explosion of the mine. A fusillade from ahead sent the remaining nine running back to huddle under cover.

"By Christ, he came with mines, trip wire, the works," David Carlisle, Sr., said with a kind of admiration. "He must have planted them last night."

"The target's not supposed to hunt us," David Junior said. "Maybe we should forget him, Dad. He can't prove anything against us."

"He's not going to beat me. He killed your brothers and he'll pay for that."

The younger Carlisle stared at his father. "But—"

"Come on, dammit!" David Senior swore. "Get after him, men! Go on!"

Bulba ordered the nine remaining Fijians to move on and to watch for the wires across the trail. They found two more within another hundred yards, disarmed them and continued following the broken but clear trail left by the fleeing Bolan as he slipped on through the jungle where even the birds had stopped singing now.

The hunters moved carefully, with the Carlisles and the cobralike Bulba in the rear, the monkeys chattering overhead, and small animals fleeing in the undergrowth. Bulba ordered them to spread out and stay alert.

"He leads us on to where he wants," Bulba warned the Carlisles. "I do not like that. It is dangerous to pursue a tiger into its own territory."

"What the hell else can he do?" David Senior asked. "He's a tiger, but can't stand up to us. All he can do is keep on running until we corner him. Just watch for him. I don't want him going to ground and evading us."

The hunt moved on, the Fijians spreading through the jungle in a thin advancing line.

The third wire was at the edge of a narrow clearing. Two Fijians found it and followed it to the mine. As they bent to disarm the mine, a burst of fire across the clearing cut them both down.

Bolan appeared for an instant beyond the clearing. The Fijians returned a hail of fire. There was no answering burst, no cry from across the clearing, only the sound of feet running on farther up the volcanic slope.

The hunters went after the vanishing Bolan.

"Dammit, he's making us fight his fight," David Senior raged. "We've got to hunt him, not just chase him. Spread out, keep in sight of one another, but flush him out."

The ten hunters spread through the jungle and moved on up the slope toward the distant peak, seven Fijians in front, the two Carlisles and Bulba behind.

From time to time they heard Bolan's booted feet running lightly ahead of them, or somewhere beside them, once even behind them. Through the thick vegetation and dim light among the tall trees they caught brief glimpses of the big soldier. Always just too far away to get a clear shot. Taunting them with his silence and immobility until they came almost within rifle shot, and then slipping away. Always moving too much for a clean shot. There, and then in an instant gone, behind some tree, vanishing into some gully.

"Get ahead of him!" David Senior barked. "Force him back to us. Box him in!"

The hunters moved on through the jungle and up and down the volcanic slopes, and still they got no more than glimpses of the elusive quarry.

"Corner him, damn you!" David Carlisle fumed.

The third Fijian in line stepped through the camouflage into the hole with the net and grenade. He died in a shower of blood with the men on each side of him.

From a rise, Bolan appeared to look silently down at the bloody dead, and at the living hunters. He watched them without expression, and then vanished again among the trees and volcanic slopes.

There were now seven hunters.

"Dad?"

"We'll get him!"

They moved on across the island. Up and down the volcanic slopes, through the thick vegetation, across the small river that flowed down to the waterfall and the coast. Across the river again, and again.

Through the whole morning, as it grew warmer and into the hot, stifling afternoon, the hunt went on, and still all they saw of their victim were sudden glimpses, fleeting visions—and the unexpected bullets that sent them down onto their bellies in the fetid jungle growth.

A punji bear trap crippled another Fijian as he ran toward the silent Bolan, and two more died high on the slope of the mountain in a narrow gully between ridges when a grenade rolled suddenly down on them from above. The last turned and ran down through the thick vegetation toward the distant ocean. Bulba went after him.

"Bulba!" David Junior cried, nervous.

"He'll stop that coward," David Senior said.

"Dad!" the younger Carlisle croaked.

Mack Bolan stepped out from behind a bare ridge.

Alone, the two David Carlisles faced the Executioner. The father jumped behind the cover of a stump and got off two quick shots from his Mannlicher.

Bolan stood unmoving, the wild shots missing him by a foot or more.

David Carlisle, Jr., froze. In the thinner jungle of these higher slopes he shook with fear as he faced the silent Bolan, tears of terror running down his soft face. The heavy Heckler & Koch submachine gun in his hand fired wildly into the ground as his finger convulsed on the trigger.

Bolan shot once.

The last Carlisle son fell sprawled on the volcanic rock, a hole in his forehead, tears still welling from his dead eyes.

Mack Bolan moved toward the older Carlisle.

"That's far enough, Bolan."

Her voice came from above.

Bolan was surrounded. Above on the bare slope, and on all sides.

Bulba came up from below, his *wakizashi* red with the blood of the last Fijian.

Janet Carlisle stood on the hill in her battle fatigues. "Hello, Father. You seem to have gotten yourself into one hell of a mess."

David Carlisle watched his daughter come down the slope toward him.

CHAPTER TWENTY-FIVE

They moved in warily, fifteen well-armed men with the bird-of-prey patch of Falcon International, and encircled Bolan. Michael Jones came down the slope behind Janet Carlisle, and behind him, Malva Gomez, nervous, remained on the ridge.

"The game's over, Father," Janet said. "I never really thought very much of your cowboys and Indians imitation."

David Carlisle, Sr., put his hunting rifle aside and strode to his fallen son. He bent over him and stared down at the small hole in his forehead, the gaping wound in the back where the tumbling M-16 round had come out. He stood and looked at Bolan. "He didn't even really know how to use a gun, Bolan."

"He should have thought of that before he picked one up," Bolan said.

"You killed him in cold blood!"

"No," Bolan said, "in hot blood. I despise everything that you and your company stand for."

The silver-haired man whirled to his daughter. "Kill him, Janet! Kill him now!"

She shook her head. "In good time, Father. I haven't decided yet just what I want to do with Bolan."

"*You* haven't—"

"I've won, Father," she said simply. "They're all dead. They all failed. You'd be dead now if I hadn't arrived. I've beaten you all, used your own people against you: Capp, Walsh, Jones and Gomez there."

David Carlisle looked around at the armed men, at Jones with his arms folded behind Janet, and at Bolan standing alone in the center of the ring of men. Finally he looked at his daughter. "Am I next? Is that what you want, Janet? Are you going to try to take over my job now, with no more waiting? It won't work, you know. Carlisle International is far more than one man, even me. You would have to defeat them all, or win them all over, and I don't think you can do that, with or without your Joneses or your Bolans."

She shook her head. "I know that, Father. You're head of the company, and head of the family. I've still got a lot to learn from you. I only want what you would have done for any of the boys. I won your test, so do I get your backing when the time comes? Will you let me run the companies the boys had, stand beside you, get rid of that weak fool I married and come home where I belong?"

The silver-haired man seemed to study his daughter as they stood in the tropical noon on the remote Fijian island. To study her and to think. Then he nodded. "It won't be easy. The board is made up of old men. They won't want to accept a woman, not even my daughter. We'll have to fight."

"I don't mind a fight," she said.

"No, I don't think you do. Maybe old Sam was right after all."

"Did you have to kill him?"

"He was disloyal, Janet."

She nodded. "I suppose you had no choice."

"No," David Carlisle said. "If you're going to lead in the company, you'll have to remember that."

"I'll remember," she said.

"I think you will. I think you're my best, after all. The test did work out, didn't it?" David Carlisle shook his head. "If not exactly the way I'd expected."

"I appreciate that, Father."

David Carlisle looked again toward Mack Bolan. "One condition, Janet."

"What?"

"That I kill Bolan."

Janet looked behind her to Michael Jones and Malva Gomez. "What do you two say?"

Jones eyed Bolan and scratched at his jaw. "I kind of had my heart set on doing the honors myself."

"Do...do you have to kill him, Janet?" Malva asked. "I mean, you've gotten all you wanted."

Janet smiled. "He is a hunk, I admit, but I think my father's going to insist."

"We can't let him walk away," David Carlisle said. "He's a time bomb, a one-man army. He'd never leave us in peace now."

"No," Janet agreed. "You're right. Too bad."

Jones came down the slope to Janet. "Going to put Bolan's head up on your den wall with the other trophies, Mr. Carlisle?"

Malva turned and walked away over the ridge and disappeared. Janet Carlisle watched her go and shook her head.

"She's been a big help for a lot of years, but she's not really tough enough."

Jones looked up at where Malva Gomez had vanished. "Does that mean she's got to go, too, boss?"

"We can't use weak people, Michael."

"No," Jones said, and moved so fast no one saw him draw the big .357 Magnum until he held Janet Carlisle in front of him, the muzzle of the big blaster pressed into her temple. "Bolan! Get the hell out of here! No one move or the boss gets it."

The armed men all around the clearing raised their assault M-16s. Then they hesitated. Jones's desperate move had put Janet Carlisle in his hands. It looked like a standoff. They had Bolan, but Jones had Janet.

Then Bolan pulled one of his grenades from its D-ring, the pin dangling from the ring, only his big fingers holding the handle down.

"Your boss likes tough troops," Bolan shouted. "Let's see how tough you are. Shoot me and the grenade goes off before some of you can jump far enough. Shoot Jones and the boss loses her pretty head."

"Jones...let me go!" Janet Carlisle sputtered. "Dad, make him...Michael..."

Bolan held his grenade, which would explode seconds after it was dropped. Jones held Janet Carlisle, the Magnum against her head. David Carlisle stood frozen, his hunting rifle ten yards away. The fifteen armed men waited. Bulba took a step toward Jones, his hand on his short *wakizashi*.

"Watch the ninja, Jones," Bolan warned.

Bulba stopped.

"Michael," Janet said, her voice choked. "We—"

"It was fun, boss," Jones said. "But someday you might decide I wasn't tough enough. I don't think I really like you, or how you play the big game." He raised his voice. "I can see none of you is tough enough to want to get fragged, and the lady here isn't tough enough to take a .357 in the skull by telling you to shoot Bolan and me. So what are we going to do, eh?"

"What Jones and I are going to do is take a walk out of here, right?" Bolan said. "Jones, the lady's going to walk with us. Hold your piece right under her chin and back up to the trees over here. Remember, all of you, one little wrong move and this grenade blows some of you to hell along with your leader."

Bolan backed toward the trees, the grenade still in his right hand, his M-16 in his left. Jones followed, carrying Janet Carlisle, her feet off the ground, the Magnum still at her head. When they all reached the trees, Jones looked back at the frozen troops in the clearing and spoke quietly over his shoulder.

"Okay, big guy, what the fuck do we do now?"

"Kill her, and they blast us," Bolan said low. "So I'll count to three, you shove her out as far as you can, and I'll roll the grenade toward the troops. That should keep them all busy long enough for us to high-gear it down the slope. Okay, one...two...three!"

Jones shoved Janet Carlisle five feet out into the clearing on her belly.

Bolan rolled the grenade.

Janet screamed, scrambled on hands and knees away from the grenade and dived for cover.

The armed men, David Carlisle and Bulba fell flat behind anything they could find and covered their heads with their arms.

Bolan and Jones tore into the trees, running as fast as they could.

The grenade exploded in the clearing behind them.

Jones headed down the slope.

"No!" Bolan breathed. "Up."

The two soldiers ran up the steep slope through the thick jungle vegetation until they could run no more and then began to climb the volcanic ridges toward the summit.

THE TWO SOLDIERS LAY in the volcanic depression just below the bare summit of the Dying Place. For now their work was done, but their eyes automatically watched the open slope below as they talked.

"You think it'll work?" Jones asked.

"It'll work. Something I learned in Nam—the VC always set up a camp and made an attack the same way. So did we. By the book. Comes from too much training and discipline."

"All I learned in Nam was how to kill and survive a hundred different ways, all of them bad."

"You didn't ask the right question."

"What question?"

Bolan didn't answer right away. Instead he added, "Where did you hump in Nam?"

"Hue and north. Out in the boonies. Fifth Marines."

"Why did you end up working for someone like Philip Carlisle? Crawling ass for a hollow woman like Janet Carlisle?"

The ex-Marine shrugged. "After Nam what the hell else? Who gave a shit about this rotten world? The Commies didn't beat us. The blind and the stupid and the soulless back home did. They threw us into hell and let the devil eat us alive. So when I got out, I decided to join the devil and be an eater, not one of the stupid suckers who get eaten."

"Wrong answer," Bolan said. "The question is— when does the war against the darkness end? Nam was only one battle. We've got a whole war. The answer is— you do what has to be done. Not the devil and not the sucker. A hard man with your head high and doing the job."

Jones looked away down the slope. "Maybe I should have known you back then."

"It's never too late to sign up, Jones," Bolan said. "And that's what you just did."

Jones nodded slowly. "I guess I did."

The two old boonie rats grinned at each other.

Then the war began again. Screams of agony suddenly came from below among the jungle trees.

"What in hell?" Jones rasped.

"Tiger trap," Bolan explained. "Ground's too hard to dig a hole, so I found a deep gully last night, set the stakes in the bottom, covered it all with vines and branches and made a trail over it."

"God." Even the hard ex-Marine went white at the thought of lying impaled in a pit of sharpened stakes.

"An advantage of retreating," Bolan said. "You lead them where you want. The VC taught me that, too."

The two soldiers lay at the edge of the shallow depression, their weapons on the berm.

The screaming had stopped. Now they could hear movement in the thick vegetation.

"They're coming on," Jones said.

Bolan nodded.

Below there was the faint sound of glass breaking.

"Now!" Bolan snapped.

The Executioner's M-16 opened up on full automatic, his hand holding it down to fire into the vegetation. Jones fired the M-16 he'd grabbed on the way out. Both men lobbed grenades, then went on firing flat out.

Yells, screams, cries of pain echoed from below as the hail of bullets tore into the advancing Carlisle men pinpointed by the broken bottle signal Bolan had rigged. Then silence.

"They've pulled back," Jones said.

"They'll circle left. The slopes are too exposed. They'll have to come through the cut over there on the right. You stay here. When you see them, open up."

Bolan snaked out of the depression, crawled to where a low ridge hid him, then stood and trotted toward the narrow cut in the mountain to the right of the depression where Jones waited. Above the passage, Bolan lay flat on the volcanic rock, a grenade in each hand.

In the depression, Jones waited. He saw the first Falcon International mercenary appear in the cut and opened fire. The attackers went to ground, returned a hail of fire.

Bolan let the two grenades roll down into the cut. They exploded in the center of the narrow passage, fragments ricocheting from wall to wall and chewing the attackers into bloody meat and bone chips.

Bolan ran back behind the ridge to dive into the depression again. "Five left. No sign of the Carlisles or Bulba."

"There wouldn't be," Jones said. "They let the others die for them."

Again the two ex-grunts waited.

"Here they come," Bolan said.

The last five Falcon soldiers came slowly and warily out of the cut. Bolan and Jones opened fire, pinning them down.

"Go," Bolan said.

Jones jumped up and out of the depression with Bolan right behind him. They raced across the open in full view.

Shouts came behind them.

"There they go!" The renegade mercenaries had seen them, and they leaped up in pursuit.

Jones and Bolan raced on to a row of boulders Bolan had set up earlier. They fell behind them and opened up on the pursuers. The five mercenaries dived into the same shallow depression Bolan and Jones had just left. Bolan smiled and pulled the thin, almost invisible wire behind the boulders.

An eruption of rock, dirt, blood, flesh and bone hurtled into the air from the depression in a geyser of destruction. Debris of rocks and pieces of what had been men showered down over the slope and the two ex-boonie rats behind the boulders. The echoes of the explosions and the screams died away across the mountain and the silent island.

Bolan stood slowly, wiping the blood and torn flesh from his black combat suit. Jones stood beside him.

"Okay," the Executioner said, "now it's our turn to do the hunting."

CHAPTER TWENTY-SIX

The two former soldiers came down the mountain and through the thick jungle of the Dying Place in a long circle.

"They won't come after us now," Jones said. "They send their poor hired slobs to do that, then move in safe behind to make the kill. Without anyone in front of them, they'll beat it out of here."

"How did Janet get you in?"

"Submarine. It's lying off the coast near the complex. Only the crew aboard, Chileans. They owe Carlisle favors. They won't fight, but they'll take them off."

"Then that's where we find them," Bolan said.

They paced through the jungle toward the Carlisle buildings, using the ground-covering lope they'd both learned back in Vietnam. The sun filtering through the green canopy was low and to the west now. The only sounds were the cries of tropical birds and the chatter of small monkeys. Animals stirred in the vegetation as the men trotted past, but nothing else did.

They stayed away from the trails, skirted the unsprung traps Bolan had set the night before and followed the small river that flowed swiftly toward the steep coastal bluff. They saw no one, met no defensive fire.

"You think they're gone?" Jones wondered.

"Maybe."

"You'll never get them if they are."

"I'll get them," Bolan said. "Sooner or later I'll get all the destroyers."

Jones looked at the big guy as they jogged along beside the fast river. "I believe you, Mack. I hope I can help."

"You already have."

They stopped long enough to drink from the pure, crystal-clear water of the stream, and then moved on down toward the white buildings behind their high fence.

The waterfall where the river met the sea thundered in their ears when Bolan saw the shadow move behind a thick tree festooned with moss. In that split second when he saw the tiny movement of a jungle shadow, he reacted, swerved hard right, his rifle ready.

Jones didn't see the shadow move. The ex-Marine had been out of action too long. The skills once so swift and sharp were now rusted and a second too slow.

The cobra man, Bulba, came out of the shadows of the jungle with his *wakizashi*. Bolan couldn't fire without hitting Jones. The samurai sword plunged into Jones, and Bulba vanished back into the shadows.

"Shoot!" Jones cried, holding tight to his belly where the blood spurted between his fingers.

Bolan shook his head. He would still hit Jones if he fired. He leaped past the bleeding man and plunged into the shadows after the ninja, stopping abruptly at the brink of the thundering waterfall.

"Bolan!" Bulba was behind him, an Uzi in his thin hand now.

The Executioner threw himself sideways as the long burst from the Uzi missed. He rolled in the jungle vegetation and came up ready to shoot.

The Uzi didn't fire again.

Jones staggered out of the thick greenery above the waterfall behind Bulba and clamped his hands around the man's thin throat.

Bulba twisted in the iron grip, dropped the Uzi, frantically pulled the short *wakizashi* from his sash and slashed it into the ex-Marine, again and again. Jones grunted, and his knees buckled. With a mighty push, the last effort of a dying man, he shoved Bulba backward over the brink of the waterfall. The momentum of the push sent Jones, too, plunging over the edge after the cobra man, the trace of a smile on his ravaged face. Together they fell the long three hundred feet. Neither made a sound as they smashed on the jagged rocks below, crimson staining the white water, Jones's hands still locked on Bulba's throat.

Bolan looked down. There was no movement. The river ran red for twenty yards. The big soldier muttered a silent prayer for the ex-Marine who'd lost his way but had regained it at the end. He turned toward the cluster of white buildings.

Alone now. Again. Always.

THE HOLE STILL GAPED in the fence where Bolan's grenade had exploded that morning. The bodies of the Fijians lay rotting in the afternoon sun, the giant tropical flies growing fat and bloated.

Bolan made a slow visual recon, but saw no movement. Out on the deep blue ocean, however, beyond the reef, he saw the submarine. The Carlisles were still on the island; this was where they would be.

Only two now.

Waiting for him.

He wondered which one would try for him first. But he knew. There would be no honor here, no love, no protection of the younger and weaker. The daughter would defend the father.

The warrior slung the M-16, unleathered his specially silenced Beretta 93-R and moved out across the open space. He double-timed through the fence past the stinking bodies of the Fijians, and into the first two-story building.

The buildings were of concrete, the interiors paid for with a king's ransom. But when it came to war, they weren't much different from the huts of the Vietnamese or the slums of the Mafia victims.

The first building was a conference center, with an assembly hall, library and file rooms, offices. The soldier padded silently from room to room, but found nothing and no one.

He returned to the main conference hall.

The burst of automatic fire ripped through the floor and ran up the walls as Bolan hit the deck and snaked across the floor behind the cover of a pillar.

He couldn't see where the burst had come from.

"Bolan?" Janet Carlisle's voice was directionless, seemed to roll around the large room. "If you leave now, we won't stop you. There's a small boat down at the dock. You can make Lakeba safely in a couple of days."

Bolan searched for the source of the voice, but it came from all sides at once.

"Don't try to find us, Bolan. If you're afraid to leave, stay here. Toss all your weapons out where we can pick them up, and we'll go out to the sub. You have our word."

She was talking over hidden loudspeakers, that was the only answer. A public address system.

Which meant there had to be a control room.

"Bolan? Don't try to think it out. You're not a thinker. You're a man of action. Like poor Michael. When he started to think, it killed him. Call it a draw. We've sent for help. If you don't give up now, let us leave, we'll have to kill you in the end."

The control room should be high up, probably on the second floor. Bolan left his cover and sprinted up the wide stairs. The machine gun fire bit at his heels, chewing wood splinters and plaster dust until he sprawled through an open door.

He lay flat inside the small storeroom. The firing had stopped.

It was more than a public address system they had. Their gunfire showed they could see him when he was in the main room, on the stairs and probably in the hallways and corridors.

He put his black knit jungle cap on the end of his M-16 and stuck it out into the second-floor hall. A withering fire erupted. They could see him in the halls.

The building had to be rigged with fixed machine guns that covered the public rooms, stairs, hallways.

They were in a control room somewhere among the buildings where they could watch him on a TV monitor and operate fixed machine guns. Luckily for him, the fixed guns weren't that accurate, especially when fired by remote. They lost the quick response and adjustment of the human finger on the trigger, the human eye directly on the target.

It was the only edge he had. They'd have done better to stalk him in person, but that meant risk, and the Carlisles took no risks they didn't have to. They fought with money, not courage.

But how was he to locate them somewhere in the four buildings, and before reinforcements arrived?

Since no TV cameras surveyed individual rooms, the system must have been designed to watch for intruders, not anyone inside. The outside walls wouldn't be under surveillance, only the grounds and the fence.

The storeroom he was in had a single narrow window. The Executioner climbed up on the windowsill, crouched and looked out. There was a narrow ledge, and the roof rim was no more than three feet above the window. He went out onto the ledge, grabbed the roof lip and swung himself easily up and over and onto the flat roof.

The nearest TV camera moved like a one-eyed monster and fixed on him. His silenced Beretta closed down that camera, and its mate at the other end.

He trotted quickly to the far edge of the roof. There were cameras on all four roofs, but no fixed machine guns there. They would have been too obvious. He unslung the M-16 again and squeezed off six careful shots.

The roofs were now blind. They knew he was up here somewhere, but they couldn't know exactly where—unless one of them came up to find him.

On this roof he didn't locate what he was searching for, though he knew it had to be somewhere. You could always find a hidden position if you knew what to look for.

The roofs were all connected by metal walkways, hot in the fading afternoon sunlight. He found what he sought on the third roof, on the building closest to the ocean and to the silent submarine that waited to take the Carlisles back to their position of wealth, power and primacy among the forces of darkness.

Mack Bolan silently promised the dead federal agents and André Villela and Arnold Capp and Mike Jones that the Carlisles would never make that trip.

He looked over the edge of the roof at the large metal box and thick cables that went through the wall into a room on the second floor below. Electronics need power, closed-circuit TV needs cables.

The room had a shade-covered window. Mack Bolan lowered himself over the roof and braced his feet against the side wall. He unleathered his Beretta, hung on to the lip of the roof with his other hand, swung out away from wall and swung in toward the window.

SEATED AT THE TV MONITOR, the trigger of the fixed guns under her finger, Janet Carlisle swore at the empty screen as she spoke into the microphone. "Shit! He's still on the roofs."

"Unless he shot out some other cameras, too." The voice of David Carlisle came to Janet over the speaker from his position somewhere among the buildings. "We should make a run for the boat."

"With him up on the roofs? We'd be sitting ducks, for God's sake! And all the other cameras are working. You've got to get up there and blow him off the roofs!"

"Not if you can't tell me where he is."

"Christ, the great and powerful David Carlisle!"

"You want him, daughter, you get him. I'm going to make a run for that sub."

"You stupid—"

The smashing of glass and ripping of metal drowned out whatever else she was going to say, as the large figure of Mack Bolan crashed through the window into the banks of electronic hardware, sending chairs, cabinets and equipment flying everywhere.

"Father! He's here! Hurry!"

She drew one of her pearl-handled PPKs and fired at the man sprawled on the floor. Bolan blasted with the Beretta, but her pill took him in the left arm and jerked his aim left. The 9 mm parabellum round grazed her shoulder, knocked her to the floor and smashed the monitor.

"You bastard!" she hissed, pumping three shots from the little PPK. "Father!"

"He won't hear you," Bolan said grimly. The big soldier lay behind a fallen bank of electronic equipment.

"Stay here then," she said. She pulled a switch on the wall, while firing to keep Bolan down.

Bolan shot low through the banks of fallen equipment, and Janet Carlisle crashed to the floor, screaming in pain, her left knee shattered. The warrior was up and over her. He kicked the little PPK away, but Janet Carlisle wasn't thinking of a weapon now.

"Out! Get me out! It's going to blow!" she yelled.

The Executioner looked at the switch she'd thrown. It was a self-destruct. The time clock over it read thirty seconds.

"Help me!" Janet Carlisle cried. "The whole room's going to explode!"

The terror in her voice was naked, chilling. It was one thing to fight in a shoot-out she expected to win; it was another to lie helpless waiting to be blown into pieces.

"You won't make it," Bolan said. "If you know any prayers, you better say them." He turned on his heel and walked out the door of the control room.

"No!" she screamed in horror. "Don't leave me! For God's sake, Bolan!"

The Executioner walked on down the long corridor. He was looking for David Carlisle.

Her screams followed him. "No! Come back! I don't want to die! I'm rich. I've won. I'm going to have all the power! Come back, you pig! Help me! I'm rich, rich rich!"

Bolan reached the stairs down, looked at his watch, dropped flat to the floor and covered his head.

"No! I want to live! Bolan! I'm—"

The explosion shook the whole building, which rocked as if in an earthquake. Dust and debris rolled out of the second-floor hall. Plaster showered down on Bolan.

A final scream of hate echoed in his ears. Then silence.

Bolan ran downstairs, walked through the shattered living room and found a bathroom. He used pressure to control the bleeding from his wounded left arm, then dabbed on some antiseptic and applied a bandage.

He went out into the evening sun again.

Now there was one.

THE BOATHOUSE WAS on the turquoise shallows inside the reef of the remote island. Outside the reef the submarine still waited to take David Carlisle back to safety and his billions. The small boat bobbed at the boathouse dock.

Mack Bolan lay flat on the downslope of the peaked boathouse roof.

"Bolan?" David Carlisle called from inside the boathouse.

Bolan lay silent.

"Bolan? I know you're out there. They're all gone now, Bolan. All my sons. My daughter. All dead. I don't blame you. I blame myself. I must have been insane, power mad. I made you come after them. I killed them. I was crazy. I know that. I've suffered enough, Bolan. I know now I've been wrong all my life. Let me go out to that submarine and I promise you Carlisle International will be different from now on. Bolan?"

Bolan cradled the M-16 in his left arm.

He almost felt sorry for the older man. He had lost his whole family. His arrogance had cost the lives of all his children, and he would have to live with that knowledge for the rest of his life. For an instant Bolan wondered if that was punishment enough? Were Carlisle's promises to reform sincere? Should Bolan walk away now, let the older man go free.

No! David Carlisle wasn't like other people. He was a cold-blooded killer. A devourer. Power and wealth and domination and death were all he cared about. He had proved that over and over. He lived only for his faceless company, Carlisle International. And ultimately for himself.

"Bolan? Janet was a fool. They were all fools. I know you're the best. I can use a man like you. I've got a lot of openings in Carlisle now. You could go far, maybe take over for me the way I planned for one of my sons. You won the test. You get the job if you want it. I'll make you rich, Bolan."

Bolan's eyes flashed his rage at Carlisle. And at himself, too, for almost believing for a moment that David Carlisle was human.

"I'll toss out my gun, Bolan. I can't fight you. I know that. I'm not as stupid as my children. I was right to test them. They failed, and the company can't have failures leading it into the future. I'm coming out unarmed. You do what you want. But remember, I can make you an important man, Bolan."

Bolan uncradled the M-16, raised the sight to his eye and aimed the gun at the small boat below.

The big Mannlicher hunting rifle rattled out through the boathouse door and hit the dock. An Uzi came out and slid off into the crystal-clear water.

"That's it, Bolan. I'm coming out."

Bolan sighted down the M-16 and clicked it on semiautomatic.

David Carlisle came slowly out the boathouse door. The silver-haired man looked right and left, behind him and out to sea. He moved toward the bobbing boat. In his right hand, close to his body and almost out of sight, he held an Ingram submachine gun, not much bigger than a Colt .45.

He began to hurry faster toward the boat, his eyes searching eagerly for Bolan. Right. Left. Behind him. Up...

Mack Bolan squeezed off two slow shots.

The first drilled David Carlisle, Sr., through the heart, blasting blood and flesh out a gaping hole in his back. The second punched a hole between his eyes before his body hit the dock and bounced off into the sea, to float spread-eagled and motionless, the red river of blood spreading around him into the clean blue water.

On the roof Bolan stood up.

It was almost over.

Bolan stepped in the doorway of the boathouse. "I know you're here. You might as well come out," he said.

There was silence in the dim, thatched building. Then Malva Gomez came slowly down from the sail loft, beautiful in shorts and a silk top.

"Are you going to kill me, too?" she asked him.

"Should I?"

"Why not? You like to kill, don't you, Mack?"

The warrior turned away.

"Mack?" she said behind him. "I liked you from the first time we talked. I liked you more in New York. I was a fool like the rest. I thought I wanted the money and power Roberto and then Janet promised me. I know now I don't want it."

Bolan turned. She was standing naked. Through the door shone the low evening sun of the tropics, its rays bathing the curves and shadows of her body in a golden glow.

"What do you want, Malva?"

"You, most of all. I want your strength, Mack, the excitement you carry with you."

"Why?"

"Just for me! For us! To enjoy!"

"No. That's wrong. Whatever I am, it's not for you or for me. There's a war going on, Malva, and you don't even know who the enemy is or what the war is all about."

She moved toward him, her body eager and warm, the soft brown skin almost touching him.

"Mack," she said, her voice low, coaxing, "we could be so good."

Bolan shook his head. "Go home, wherever that is. Or go to New York and find your fun as long as it lasts. There are forces out there working every day to destroy you, but you'll never know that. You'll be too busy having fun."

He picked up her clothes, tossed them to her and walked out the door. He climbed the hill back to the main building, on into the jungle and up the slopes toward his cache of equipment. There was a radio there. It was time to call Hal Brognola.

Bolan heard the splash as Malva Gomez dived into the sea to swim out to the submarine. He didn't look